ZANE PRESENTS

YOU
MIGHT
JUST
GET
Burned

Dear Reader:

Some men have the ability to disguise their true identity and lure women to fall in love with a person who doesn't exist. Such is the case with Avery Woodson, a personality magician who disguises himself as three different egos: Marcel, Camden and Julian.

Shamara Ray has created an intriguing novel where these women are fooled and captured by his charm. It's a merry-go-round where Avery constantly fakes his persona, depending on his love interest at the moment. He switches up roles effortlessly. It isn't until he meets Indiya that he's stopped in his tracks. He finally meets his match and his game is threatened.

Readers will surely enjoy the cast of characters led by the perpetrator who wears various masks and manages to keep his game in action.

Readers were first introduced to Shamara, a culinary artist, with her novel *Recipe for Love* in which she shared her own delicious recipes.

As always, thanks for supporting the authors of Strebor Books. We always try to bring you groundbreaking, innovative stories that will entertain and enlighten. For a list of complete titles, please visit www.zanestore.com and I can be located at www.facebook.com/AuthorZane or reached via email at Zane@eroticanoir.com.

Blessings,

Zane

Zane
Publisher
Strebor Books
www.simonandschuster.com

ZANE PRESENTS

YOU MIGHT JUST GET Burned

A NOVEL

SHAMARA RAY

SBI

STREBOR BOOKS

NEW YORK LONDON TORONTO SYDNEY

Strebor Books
P.O. Box 6505
Largo, MD 20792
http://www.streborbooks.com

ISBN 978-1-59309-441-6
ISBN 978-1-4516-7909-0 (ebook)
LCCN 2013933640

First Strebor Books trade paperback edition August 2013

Cover design: www.mariondesigns.com
Cover photograph: © Keith Saunders/Marion Designs

10 9 8 7 6 5 4 3 2 1

Manufactured in the United States of America

For information regarding special discounts for bulk purchases, please contact Simon & Schuster Special Sales at 1-866-506-1949 or business@simonandschuster.com

The Simon & Schuster Speakers Bureau can bring authors to your live event. For more information or to book an event, contact the Simon & Schuster Speakers Bureau at 1-866-248-3049 or visit our website at www.simonspeakers.com.

For My Mom

CHAPTER 1

Julian

I leaned against the wall in the back, motionless, intuition whispering that I was the inspiration for the piece. Incense wafted through the air, the fragrant haze massaging the room, stimulating receptors and heightening senses. Notes of jasmine and vanilla mingled with the melodic cadence coming from the stage. I was concealed in the shadows, but the words shined on me, radiating a message that I was meant to hear. A smirk settled on my lips and I clapped along with the rest of the crowd as the final words were spoken.

Miko waded through the tables, smiling and touching the hands of her followers. She joined her friends, peering over her shoulder as she sat, eyes scanning the room.

The emcee stepped to the microphone and introduced me. The applause commenced before he finished saying my name. I pushed away from the wall and headed toward the front of the club. I took to the stage, the glare from the lights blinding me. I signaled to the engineer to switch it up. The white lights dimmed and a red glow enveloped me. Some of the ladies started to whoop it up. I stood at the mic, head bowed, hands clasped in front of me, until the calls subsided and the room went silent.

"Your ebony skin reminds me of home.
Sacred. Abundant. Lush.

Land waiting to be explored.
Sun in the sky golden like honey waiting to be poured.
Niles that overflow with the waters of life waiting to be tasted.
Exotic and rare species waiting to be wild.
Breezeless deserts as hot as fire waiting to be quenched.
Your ebony skin I'm ready to explore,
with warm honey I'm going to pour,
your flowing waters I'm willing to taste,
rare and exotic I want to see you wild,
your hot fire I promise to quench.
Wait no more.
Take me home to lush lands, golden sun, overflowing Niles,
exotic species and breezeless deserts and I'll take your sacred ebony
to abundant paradise."

The audience was held captive, chained to the verses, their experiences linked to mine. I took a step back from the microphone. The crowd erupted in cheers.

I cracked a smile and moved back to the mic. "At the last minute, I decided to freestyle a little something tonight. I guess you liked it. Thanks for the love."

I turned and walked from the stage. I returned to my spot in the shadows while the next spoken word artist performed.

"I loved it," Miko said, sidling over to me.

I looked down at her. "My muse..."

Her ebony skin glowed in the darkness. Natural curls framed her face in a disheveled mass. A tiny stud glistened in her left nostril.

"I was hoping you were talking about me."

"Who else would I be talking about?"

"Any woman in here."

I brushed a lock of hair from her eyes. "No one but a Nubian queen could move me to create on the spot."

"Did you catch my performance?"

"Yeah. I didn't know you had such a weakness for jewels."

"I wasn't talking about j-e-w-e-l-s. I was talking about J-u-l-e-s...as in Julian."

"So I'm the chocolate diamond that glitters in your mind?"

"You knew it was for you, Julian."

"I did and I was flattered. So I responded with an impromptu ode to you."

"Which made all of my girls jealous, especially Romel. She can't stop looking back here now."

I looked toward her friends' table. Romel was indeed staring. I leaned over and whispered into Miko's ear. "Let's go."

"Where are we going?"

"Weren't you paying attention? I want you to take me home, so I can explore every inch of your body." I grabbed her hand and began leading her to the exit.

"Wait." She pulled back on my arm. "Let me tell my friends that I'm leaving."

"Romel will let them know. Look. She's watching our every move."

Miko waved to her friend as I led her out of the club.

CHAPTER 2

Marcel

I sprinkled more cinnamon on my latte while keeping my eye on the line. She had caught my attention from the minute she entered the coffee house. The way she smiled at me—like she was filled with sunshine—made me linger longer than necessary. When she went over to the counter near the window, I followed and sat on the stool next to her. I stared out of the window. From the corner of my eye, I saw her peeking at me as she sipped her beverage. A minute passed and she started to shift in her seat.

I turned to her and smiled, more with my eyes than my mouth. "You're beautiful."

"He speaks…"

"Words can sometimes fall short. I try to make sure what I say counts. I'm Marcel," I said, extending my hand.

"Quinn."

She had a firm handshake considering her petite stature.

"Quinn… There was something in your smile that wouldn't let me carry on with my day without knowing your name."

"And now that you know it?"

"I don't want to carry on with my day without getting to know you."

Quinn tinkered with the lid on her cup. "That was direct."

"I believe in being direct. Does that make you nervous?"

"Not really."

"Are you sure? You seem to be destroying that lid."

She giggled and placed her cup on the counter. "Well, maybe a little bit."

"Why? I know I'm not the first man to tell you how beautiful you are."

"No, but I get the sense that I'm one of many women that you've bestowed with such generous compliments."

"You're right. I compliment women all the time. That doesn't diminish the veracity of the compliment. I appreciate women who are beautiful, inside and out, and I have no qualms about letting them know."

She reached for her cup. "It was nice meeting you, Marcel."

"You can't leave yet."

"And why not?"

"Because you haven't accepted my invitation."

She tilted her head and narrowed her eyes at me. "I must have missed something because I don't recall receiving an invite."

I returned my gaze to the people passing by outside and let silence settle between us. I could tell Quinn wasn't sure what to think of me. I wanted to give her a moment to decide if she would walk away or stay and find out.

She cleared her throat.

"I guess I wasn't direct enough when I said that I didn't want to carry on with my day without getting to know you." I rested my arm on the back of her chair. "I'm going to the jazz festival at Marcus Garvey Park this afternoon. Will you join me?"

"I don't even know you."

"I'm inviting you to get to know me. We'll be with lots of other people in the middle of the day and listening to great music."

Quinn nodded. "I accept your invitation."

I pulled out my phone and asked her to input her number.

She handed it back to me. "I live on 127th Street between St. Nicholas and Convent."

"I'll see you in two hours." I grabbed my latte and stood up to leave. "Enjoy the rest of your coffee."

I smiled at Quinn as I walked by the window. She was where I left her, still fiddling with her lid, probably trying to decipher what she had just gotten herself into.

CHAPTER 3

Camden

My dinner guest was already seated when I entered the private room at the back of my favorite restaurant. The sommelier followed closely behind me. He knew the routine and waited as I leaned over and greeted her with a kiss on the cheek.

"My meeting ran over." I unbuttoned my suit jacket and sat down. "But I'm all yours now."

"Is that supposed to resemble an apology, Camden?"

"I flew in from London this morning, had a board meeting, two lunch meetings, a conference call and a briefing with my staff that literally ended fifteen minutes ago. I rushed here to wine and dine you because there's no other woman in New York City that I want to be sitting across from right now. So, no, Natalia, I am not apologizing."

She nodded. "Perhaps a call next time to say you're going to be late?"

"Perhaps," I said with a smile. "What are you in the mood for this evening? Red or white?"

"I'll defer to your taste."

"Gervaise, what red do you suggest?"

The sommelier cleared his throat and approached the table. "I have something new that you may enjoy, Mr. Tennyson. It's a medium-bodied cabernet with strong notes of cherry that pairs very well with steak or lamb chops."

"That sounds good. We'll have a bottle."

"Very well, sir. I'll send your waiter right in with your selection." Gervaise swiftly exited through the black curtains that separated our private room from the main dining area.

I assessed Natalia—what she was wearing, her jewelry, and hair. She had on a black dress that revealed a hint of cleavage, diamond teardrop earrings, a wide diamond bangle around her left wrist, and a thin diamond band on her middle finger. A large, loose bun adorned the top of her head and matte red lipstick accentuated a pair of luscious lips. She was understatedly sexy, yet patently classy.

"You look picture-perfect," I said.

"I spent the day getting pampered to hear you say that. By the way, thank you for my sparkly gifts," she said, touching her earrings, then bracelet. "Your assistant has great taste."

"Now, I'd say you owe me an apology. I know you, and I know what looks good on you. I picked out everything you have on, from head to toe. Even the La Perla that's underneath that dress."

"Really, Camden?" she asked with a gleam in her eyes and a grin to match.

"Is that so unbelievable?"

"I wouldn't think that you would have time to shop for me in the midst of all of your deal-making."

"I make time for what's important."

The waiter came in with the wine. He poured a taste for me to sample. I nodded that it was to my satisfaction and he filled our glasses. He took our dinner order and left us to enjoy our privacy.

Natalia held her glass up to the light. "Dare I propose a toast?"

"If you're inspired to do so; I'm not stopping you."

"What do you think about a toast to reconciliation?"

"Who's reconciling?" I asked, my face sporting a mask of puzzlement.

"Maybe that was a poor word choice. I should have said to reconnecting, since I haven't laid eyes on you in two months."

"We both know that isn't true. I attended your charity event in the Hamptons three weeks ago and made a sizeable donation."

"You stayed twenty whole minutes."

I clearly had a bit of damage control to do. I hadn't been giving Natalia enough face time. Whoever said expensive gifts can get you out of hot water didn't know what the hell they were talking about. I worked hard juggling many things, and, when I had the time, I played hard. She had been along for the ride for about eight months. She shouldn't have been complaining. I had made sure that she attended the best parties, received the finest gifts, and had taken her on more than a few weekend getaways.

"But tonight, it's you and me. We'll have dinner and then go back to my place to make up for lost time. I almost want to take that dress off of you now."

"We can always skip dinner…"

I stood and pulled out her chair. "Let's go reconnect."

CHAPTER 4

Julian

My cell phone rang for the third time. I sent the first two callers to voicemail, but answered the last incoming call. Miko was on her way over to my place in Brooklyn. I had promised her an intimate candlelight dinner for two and had pulled out all the stops to make it an evening she wouldn't forget.

I fluffed the pillows on my bed and placed a single rose along with a few rose petals in the middle of the comforter. I scattered additional petals around the bed on the hardwood floor. I went into the living room and pulled Nikki Giovanni's *Love Poems* from the bookshelf, then placed it on the coffee table. In the corners of the living room were mahogany floor candle holders. I lit the scented pillar candles and dimmed the lights. I put on smooth jazz, and then went to check on dinner.

I had hired Chef Mark Bailey to prepare dinner for the evening. Chef Bailey was a personal chef and had created an entire menu from hors d'oeuvres to dessert. He was in the kitchen packing up his supplies when I entered. Pots and pans, filled with the nouvelle Jamaican cuisine I had asked him to prepare, were on the stovetop. He had laid out the dishes, glasses, and utensils I'd need on the counter. He gave me reheating instructions, then departed.

I headed into the living room to wait for Miko. I must have

dozed off because I was startled when I heard hard knocking on the door. I went to let her in. She sauntered into my apartment with rhythm and flow. She went straight to the living room sofa and kicked off her sandals.

I sat next to her and softly kissed her neck. "You smell good."

"Thank you. So do you."

We stared at each other for a moment. I grabbed her hand and raised it to my lips. "My Nubian queen."

She demurely looked down at her lap. "You have a way of making me blush."

"Even after all this time?"

"It's only been three months, Julian."

"Feels longer."

"I hope that's a good thing."

I ran my fingers through her natural hair and massaged her scalp with my fingertips. Her head lolled back and she moaned.

"I think you know the answer to that," I whispered into her ear. "But I plan to show you how good it is."

"The candlelight and the music is a great start."

"That's nothing. I also cooked you dinner."

"You cooked for me?"

"I certainly did. That should erase any doubt. I don't cook for just anyone."

A smile played upon the corners of her mouth. "You are too good to me."

"Is there such a thing?"

She leaned back and looked into my face. "I can honestly say I don't know."

"Isn't that what women want—a man who treats them right?"

"I'm learning that maybe I've been wanting the wrong things. You're making me realize that I'm not accustomed to this level of attentiveness."

I grabbed the book of poems from the coffee table, paged through until I found my favorite selection and began to read to her. Miko leaned into the crook of my arm and melted into me. I paused to kiss the side of her face. We sat huddled together for half an hour, taking turns reading passages to each other. I read my last verse, then ended the intimate session with a deep kiss. When she looked up at me, her eyes were filled with abundant stars and infinite galaxies. She blinked a couple of times and then shook her head. It was as if she was trying to clear the cosmos from her mind, searching for clarity in a nebulous moment.

I took her by the hand and led her into the dining room. "I hope you're hungry because I have prepared something very special for you."

She simply smiled at me while I poured her a glass of wine. I left her with her thoughts, and the smooth jazz to fill in any blank space, while I went to reheat the feast Chef Bailey had prepared. When I returned with our dinner, she had made herself extremely comfortable.

"I don't know how I'll be able to concentrate on dinner with you looking so scrumptious."

Her legs were crossed and thrown over the arm of the dining room chair. Back arched and head thrown back, all I could see was skin and a hint of color from her string bikini panties. Miko's bra dangled from her fingertip.

"You won't be upset if we have dessert first, would you?"

I placed our plates on the table, silently glided over to her, and scooped her from the chair. I carried her to the bedroom and laid her on my bed. I handed her the rose. She smelled it, then toyed with the petals as I undressed.

I climbed on the bed and lured her to me. "Dessert is my favorite part of the meal and, right now, I'm in the mood for a taste of your luscious dark chocolate."

CHAPTER 5
Marcel

I checked my watch again. Quinn was fine, but I didn't have the patience to wait on her for twenty minutes. I cleared my throat loud enough for her to hear, and know, I was trying to get her attention. She dashed out of the fitting room in a pair of tight black pants and a shiny silver tank top with a plunging neckline and an open back, connected by a thin strip of fabric.

"It's perfect; let's go. We're going to be late."

"You don't think it's too much?" she asked.

"I thought you looked fine in what you were originally wearing. Could you please slip your heels on and let's get going? I'll give you all the compliments you need once we get in the cab."

She ran back into the fitting room and collected her belongings. I hurried her over to the cashier and she paid for her new outfit. She shoved her jeans and T-shirt into a shopping bag the cashier handed her, then we jetted out of the boutique.

I hailed a cab and we sped off to an exclusive album release party for a hot new R&B diva on the scene.

"I'm sorry, Marcel, but when I saw you, I felt underdressed. I guess I didn't realize it was that type of event."

"I told you that you looked fine. You'll see when we arrive that people will have on any and everything."

"Yeah, but I'm walking in with you, looking like you stepped off the cover of *GQ* magazine. I should have asked about the attire when you called me this afternoon."

"That's my fault. I decided to attend this event at the last minute and I wanted you on my arm tonight. Honestly, though, you did look great in your faded jeans and fitted tee. You were definitely giving off a casual, sexy vibe."

"And now?"

I looked her over. "Now you're giving me pure fire. You will definitely be the hottest attraction tonight."

"I'm glad you offered to meet me at my office. If I had met you at the party like I wanted to, I wouldn't have had the chance to run into the boutique for a different outfit."

I reached over and straightened the twisted strap on her shoulder. "I don't know why you're making such a big deal over this. I told you the first time I met you that you're beautiful. What you're wearing doesn't change that."

She pulled out a makeup bag and reapplied her lipstick. "You sure know how to charm a lady. I have to be careful around you because I could really get caught up in your gratuitous musings."

"You shouldn't look at it as getting caught up. You should take it for what it's worth—the truth. I'm not going to stop speaking the truth, so I guess you will have to get used to hearing it."

Quinn laughed and radiance permeated through her. Everything about her was bright and sunny. She wore her hair in a short, cropped style, dyed platinum blonde. Her lipstick was a bright pink that glowed brilliantly against her sandy complexion. She told me she hit the gym at least five times a week and it showed in her sculptured arms and toned back.

I stroked her shoulder and she shivered. "Stop," she whispered.

I shook my head and continued to trace a finger along the lines of her collar bone down to her bicep. "Maybe tonight, after the party, you'll invite me up to your place," I said, letting the bass in my voice fill up the back of the cab.

"I have an early morning tomorrow, so I don't know about that."

I nodded and stopped touching her. The cab pulled up to the curb in front of the lounge. I paid, then offered my hand to help Quinn from the car. We stepped inside the dimly lit establishment where cuts from the soon to be released album were playing. People were huddled in small groups throughout the room, talking, drinking, and some purely listening. I escorted Quinn to an available sofa, then went to get us a couple of drinks.

As soon as I positioned myself at the bar, the single ladies had me in their sights. I waited for the bartender to finish dealing with the onslaught of colorful and sweet drinks he had to make for the female patrons before giving him my order.

I felt a brush against my leg and turned to see the R&B diva squeezed in next to me. She called out a drink to the bartender, skipping over everyone that was already waiting.

"So you're simply going to ignore the rest of us and put your order in like we're not waiting?"

She gave me a sideways glance, barely looking at me. "It is my party. I should get some perks, don't you think?"

"Not really."

She gave me her full attention then. "I'm about to take the stage and perform, to entertain you all, and I can't get a drink without having to wait all night for it?"

"I get it. You're important. But remember it's a two-way street. You need someone here to entertain, right? We're all here to support you. So I think that makes us equally important."

The bartender handed her a drink and she rolled unkind eyes at me. "Enjoy the show," she said before strolling off to mingle with the crowd.

I grabbed my drinks and headed back over to Quinn. She was waiting with a question in her eyes. "Was that the artist you were chatting with?"

"Yeah, that was her."

"You two seemed pretty chummy."

"I wouldn't say that."

"What were you talking about?"

I smiled and stroked her cheek. "Nothing that would interest you, I'm sure."

I didn't cater to the green-eyed monster, but I have been known to use him to my benefit on occasion.

Quinn sipped her drink. "I was thinking," she said, fiddling with her stirrer, "if we don't get back too late, maybe you can come upstairs for a minute."

"I like the sound of that," I said, with a nod. "As a matter of fact, we can leave as soon as we finish these drinks. I'm not impressed by anything I've heard from this artist and would rather we spend our time making our own music."

"You know just what to say, don't you?"

"The truth is like that—the things you say are always right."

CHAPTER 6

Camden

The wind picked up and a cooling breeze swept underneath the umbrella. I lowered my hat over my face to keep the sand particles at bay. I had promised Natalia a half-day of relaxation on the beach with no cell phone, discussions about business or anything that wasn't centered on her. I was creeping up on hour number four on Fire Island, lying on a double chaise in the sand—Natalia next me—with a huge umbrella providing shade for both of us. I was doing my absolute best to live in the moment, but the idle time was starting to wear on me.

"Want to take a dip?"

I shook my head. Natalia removed her sarong and headed toward the water. She played at the edge for a while, dipping her feet in and then retreating when the waves rolled in. She'd take a few steps closer when the water receded, only to run back when the surf returned.

I took off my hat and laid it on the chaise. I ran up next to Natalia and grabbed her hand, coaxing her into the ocean with me. She resisted slightly, but I lifted her in my arms and waded deeper into the Atlantic Ocean. When I was waist deep, I lowered her to her feet and steadied her by the waist.

"This is how you take a dip. I don't know what you were doing."

She laughed. "I was dipping my toes in."

"Your toes and a whole lot more of you is in now." A large wave was rolling in. "Here comes a big one," I warned. I lifted her and turned my back before it hit us.

Natalia tightened her arms around my neck. "The surf is a little rough for me. You can take me back to the beach, so I can continue to dip my toes."

I marched through the water and deposited her where I had found her. I returned to our chaise, toweled off, then tilted the umbrella so the sun would hit me as I reclined on the chair.

I was going to take her for a lobster dinner before we made our way back to Manhattan. I'd probably invite her to stay with me for the evening, take her to brunch at Norma's in the morning, and have a car take her home thereafter. I took note when she said we hadn't spent any time together in two months. I couldn't devote every waking hour to her, but I could give her a day or two from time to time.

My hat lifted off my face. I squinted up into the sunlight. Natalia leaned over and kissed me on the lips. "I'm proud of you, Camden."

"I can't afford to be off the grid all the time, but every once in a while is fine. I only hope you're enjoying yourself."

She leaned over and kissed me again. "I don't want the day to end."

I took my hat from her hands and repositioned it over my eyes. "Don't worry about the end when we're in the midst of our day. We have a lot more to do and you should be focusing on what's going on here and now. Maybe you wouldn't fixate so much on the time we're not together if you concentrated on the times when we are together. I know my time is scarce, but right now you've got me. Let's enjoy it."

Natalia returned to her spot next to me on the chaise. I shifted the hat so I could see her. She took out her tanning oil and sprayed her body. She lay back and the sun glistened off her skin. She untied the strings on her bikini top and tucked them inside the cups. My eyes lingered on her full-bodied curves. She was in great shape, but she wasn't muscular—stomach flat, but no cuts. She was soft in all the right spots.

"You know it goes both ways," she said, her eyes closed as she sunbathed.

"What does?"

"That you've got me too. I'm not accessible to merely anyone. It's a privilege for you to be with me as much as it is for me to be with you."

I smiled. "I've always known that, Natalia. It sounds like you're presently figuring it out."

She didn't respond. I knew she had some thoughts brewing, but I hoped that she would take my advice and live in the moment.

When I invited her to spend the day on Fire Island, she insisted that she had to check her schedule and would get back to me. Ten minutes passed before she confirmed that she wanted to go. I knew it was a ruse, but I played along. Out of all the time we'd been seeing each other, Natalia had never told me no to anything that I had requested. That was the one thing I could rely on. If I contacted her at the last minute to attend an event or gala, she was there. If I invited her for a weekend jaunt, she was there. If I wanted a dinner partner, she was there.

It certainly came at a cost, though. On many occasions, I had funded her wardrobe for the evening and even presented her with gifts to match the engagement. She didn't need me to do either of those things because she had her own money, but she liked gifts and I would indulge her.

"What do you think about meeting a few of my friends and family next month?" she asked. "I'm in a wedding and I would love for you to join me as my date."

A thick silence settled between us. "Let me know the specific date. I'll have to check my schedule."

"It's not a no, so I should probably be happy about that."

That time I didn't respond. Maybe I'd think about attending the wedding, but I wasn't up for meeting any family or friends. I had basically delayed my response. Ultimately, I knew what my decision would be. I would definitely say that I could not attend. Of course, I would let her down easily and use some sort of business-related rationale.

"If I had my phone handy, I could have told you my availability. Since I don't, I'll have to wait until later to let you know for certain." I covered my face from the sun rays and closed my eyes, returning to the here and now. "Let's sit out a little while longer and then I'll show you precisely how much I've got you too."

CHAPTER 7

Avery

I pulled the stack of letters and bills from my post office box and slipped them into the messenger bag slung over my shoulder. I locked the box and headed out of the building. It had been a long while since I stopped to pick up mail from the post office, and each time I went, I swore that I wouldn't wait so long between visits.

The rain was coming down in a steady stream. I rushed inside my car, turned on the AC and the windshield wipers, then jetted out of the parking lot. The humidity was stifling and all I wanted to do was to get back to the house and chill in the central air with a beer and a good movie. I wasn't taking any calls and didn't plan on going back out until Monday morning.

I drove down Route 107 through Jericho, headed to Brookville. A line of cars were backed up at the intersection to Brookville Road. I hit my left turn signal and joined the procession. After missing three consecutive lights, I darted from behind the five vehicles in front of me and made the turn on the yellow. Horns blew and fingers flew, but I was done waiting and was cruising toward my destination while they waited for the next green light.

I entered the house and turned off the alarm. Everything was still; and though it may have been early afternoon, the house was dark. With the dreary sky outside and the blinds drawn inside, it almost felt like it was evening. I pulled off my loafers and set them inside the shoe rack in the foyer. I walked barefoot on the cool white tile of the hallway and through the white room. All of the rooms of the house were called by their specific color, not by the room it actually was. The white room was the living room. Everything in it was stark white—the carpet, the sofas, the lamps, the decorative accents, everything. The yellow room was the kitchen, the blue room the den. The red room was the master suite and the black room a private office. The black room was off limits to everyone except me. I kept the room under lock and key at all times.

I headed up the staircase that was located in the back of the yellow room. At the top of the landing, I followed the corridor to the end and unlocked the only door in the hallway. I didn't bother turning on the light. I tossed the messenger bag into the black room and proceeded to lock it up again. I'd worry about sifting through the contents of the bag later. At that moment, I was determined to make a sandwich and relax for the remainder of the day.

I lay in the middle of the floor in the blue room where midnight blended with shades of azure, royal, navy, and cornflower. It had been a busy week. A hectic week. Too many demands. Too little time. Too much left to do. It was during moments of solitude when I wondered what it was all for. I juggled too much and tried to accomplish too much for one person. I supposed I couldn't really complain. I was residing in Brookville with more house than I knew what to do with, more cars than I could drive, and more money than I could ever need. Well…maybe that was a stretch. You could never have too much money. In fact, instead of languishing the weekend away, alone with my thoughts—because that could make me crazy—I'd go spend some of that money on something to remind me what it's all for. Maybe I'd go on a shopping spree and get myself an entire new wardrobe, perhaps a new car; I'd been wanting a hybrid lately.

A pang of guilt hit me. Any time I thought about frivolously spending money, I felt like maybe I shouldn't. That I should be more responsible with my funds and remember that it could be here today and gone tomorrow. I never wanted to go without. Not again. It had taken a lot of work to get where I was and I was determined to stay there. No matter what the cost.

The ticking from the clock on the wall whispered to me that life's too short and I jumped up from the floor. Moments later, I was in my ride, heading to get a new wardrobe.

CHAPTER 8

A firm grip on my shoulder stopped me as I was about to exit the mall. My head turned, my eyes drawn first to the hand that grabbed me and then to whom it belonged. At first I thought I had dropped something, but when I realized that I hadn't, I didn't try to keep the surprise off my face.

"Yo, I thought that was you, Avery," he said, grabbing me in a brotherly hug. "What's up, man?"

I leaned in and patted him on the back. "Hey, Kev…good to see you." We stepped away from the doors.

"You are the last person I expected to run into. I'm in New York visiting with my wife's family. What are you doing up in these parts?"

"I live up here."

"Are you serious? Me and some of the boys were just talking about you a few weeks ago. We were saying how you had dropped off the face of the earth, and now here you are. I mean, what are the chances? How long has it been, about three years?"

I redistributed my shopping bags from one hand to the other. "That sounds about right. I left D.C. soon after Courtney and I…"

Kev briefly looked down at the floor, then back at me. "I was sorry to hear about that."

"It happens," I said, brushing it aside.

"Well, you look good. New York must be treating you well."

"I can't complain." I checked my watch. "Listen, Kev, I hate to rush off, but I have a function tonight and I'm already behind schedule, but it was great seeing you."

"Oh, I understand," he said, sounding a little disappointed. "I'm going to be in town until Wednesday. Maybe we can get together and catch up over a couple of drinks."

"That sounds cool," I said and was already making my way to the exit.

Kev reached in his pocket and fished out his cell phone. "How do I get in touch with you?"

"My number's the same," I called out over my shoulder. "Later, man."

I looked back and Kev was standing where I left him, staring out the glass doors at me. I kept up my pace and headed to my Range Rover in the parking lot. Yes, life had definitely been very good to me in New York.

When I had left Washington, D.C., I stole away like a thief in the night. I didn't tell a soul. I knew what I had to do and I didn't want anyone standing in my way. Kev was right—I dropped off the face of the earth. That was how I wanted it and that's how it's been ever since. I hadn't spoken to or seen anyone from D.C. since the day I left. I certainly hadn't heard mention of Courtney's name in the three years since I had been gone. Some things were meant to stay in the past and she was one of them.

I had told Kev the truth. I did have the same phone number from my days in D.C., but I also had a few new ones. My number from D.C. went directly to my call answering. I didn't carry the phone for it and I rarely checked the messages. I kept it just in case I needed it someday. If Kev called, he'd get my message, but he wouldn't get me. That's the way it had to be.

I shook it off as I drove through light traffic back to the house. Fate worked in mysterious ways. Had I not left the house—as I originally planned—I would have never run into Kev. He wouldn't have seen me and could have kept speculating about me with the boys. Now, he'd go back and let everyone know about our encounter. You never know what's intended for you when you set foot outside the door. No matter how much you try to do things your own way at all times, you can always be thrown for a loop.

CHAPTER 9
Julian

I sat at a table in the back, listening to a sister spit about unemployment, food stamps, and struggling to survive. I hadn't decided if I was going to take the stage. I was still trying to gauge the mood of the crowd. I liked to perform material that matched the tone of the audience. Tonight, it seemed that all the spoken word artists were on either a radical, angry, or negative vibe that I really wasn't feeling. I wasn't in that headspace. Everyone else seemed fine with it as they co-signed and cheered throughout her sobering piece.

I twirled the ice in my drink, half-listening, half-thinking about what I could perform to shift the energy of the crowd. I wouldn't take the stage unless I could take control of the crowd. That was one of the things I enjoyed most about spoken word—seizing the minds and the moods of the people.

Fingertips trailed across my shoulders. "You look deep in thought."

I looked up as Romel slipped into the seat beside me. I glanced around the club in search of Miko.

"She's not here," Romel said. "She's at home…not feeling well. But you probably know that."

I didn't know. I hadn't spoken to Miko all week. "Romel," I said checking her out, "you're looking good."

She was all smiles. "Thanks, Julian. You don't mind if I join you?"

"I don't need an entire table to myself."

"I guess that's as close to an invite as I'll get."

I ignored her comment and tasted my drink. Romel was a trip. I knew her type well. She was used to men fawning over her as if she were the only woman in the world.

"Where's your clique tonight?" I asked.

"We're not joined together at the hip. We have our own lives, do our own things."

"It was only a question."

"What about you?"

"What about me?" I said, gazing toward the stage.

"I never see you with anyone. Don't you have any boys that you roll with?"

I glanced at her and laughed. "Boys that I roll with?"

"You know what I mean, Julian. Don't you have friends? You're always by yourself." She paused, waiting for an answer. Met only with silence, she continued. "I even asked Miko if you had any attractive friends to introduce to her girls and she said she didn't know."

"We both know you aren't interested in any friends I may have." I gave her a knowing look.

"I'm not sure I know what you're talking about."

"Is that how you're going to play it?"

She bit her bottom lip, then met my gaze. "I was interested in you first and Miko knew it."

I nodded slowly. "It seems like you became interested after Miko started to share what transpired between us."

"That's not true. You had my attention way before Miko told me any details about the two of you."

I smiled. "So she does tell our business..."

"All women talk, Julian," she said with a smirk, "and nothing is off limits. I know how you kiss, what you're working with, how you work it and the things you say while you're working it."

"She told you all of that?"

"You seemed surprised."

"I am. I thought my Miko was a good girl."

"So you're into good girls. That's why you went for Miko instead of me?"

"I like bad girls like you, too."

"What makes me a bad girl?"

"Why don't you tell me," I replied with a grin.

She slid her chair closer to mine and lowered her voice. "I'm not a bad girl, I'm a grown woman and I do grown woman things."

"I stand corrected."

She reached over and placed her hand between my legs. "I want to know for myself what you're working with." Romel started to rub her hand along the length of my dick.

I put my hand on top of hers. "Like I said, you're a bad girl."

"I'll take that, but I also want this," she said, gently squeezing while she rubbed. "I want to know what Miko's raving about."

I grabbed her hand and moved it to the table. "Just like that?" I asked.

"Grown woman things..."

"All right. Go upstairs to the unisex restroom. Lock the door behind you. I'll be there in a minute."

She gave me a wicked little smile, then sauntered away from the table. I sat a couple of minutes, threw back my drink, and headed up to the second floor.

It was empty upstairs for the moment. After the performances, when the deejay started spinning, the crowd would be spread between both floors. I went over to the restroom and gave a quick rap on the door. I heard the lock release. I stepped inside the door and locked it behind me. We stood in the carpeted lounge area peering at one another. A large mirror covered one wall with a counter that ran the length of it.

I walked directly over to Romel and yanked her body against mine. I pressed against her and let her feel what she was grabbing downstairs at the table. "Is this what you wanted to feel?" I whispered in her ear.

She reached for my belt and unbuckled it. I grabbed her by the hips, spun her around, and guided her over to the counter. She bent over slightly, her already too short miniskirt rising even further. I reached underneath her skirt, pulled her panties over her round ass and down her legs. She lifted her heeled foot and kicked the skimpy satin to the side. I watched the rise and fall of her chest in the mirror as I unzipped my pants. She pushed her ass out in anticipation of what I had to offer.

"Don't you want to see what you've heard so much about?"

Romel turned around and looked down at my hard dick in my hand. She reached out and touched the head with the tip of her pointer finger. She wrapped her hand around it and massaged it with long, firm strokes. She dropped to her knees and rubbed her cheek against the smooth skin of my hard dick. She licked her lips and kissed it. My body went rigid. She kissed it again, full lips covering my tip like a skull cap. Then a flick of her tongue. My hand went to the back of her head. She sucked me into her warm mouth.

I leaned back against the counter, one hand bracing me, the other sliding through her hair. She worked me in and out of her mouth, sucking my dick like it was her favorite candy. I grabbed her head tighter and she slid her mouth back and forth faster. I moaned as I watched her try to take every inch into her mouth. Unless she could deep throat me, it wasn't going to happen. I put my hand over hers and eased her away from my dick.

I pulled Romel from her knees and leaned her over the counter, skirt pushed up exposing her ass, legs spread wide. I stroked a finger in her pussy and it came back glistening with her juices. I listened to the little man on my shoulder and rolled a condom on before I splashed in her pool.

I held my rock hardness in one hand and grabbed her hip with the other. I slid inside, then grabbed both of her hips and immediately started to pound into her. I grabbed handfuls of ass cheek as I slid in and out of the pussy. Her quiet moans were steadily building into loud cries. My reflection in the mirror signaled to her to keep it down. She put her hand over her mouth to stifle the sound.

I worked it deeper and harder and her pussy got wetter. The sound of skin slapping skin filled the room. She was whimpering that she was about to come, so I leaned her over further, placing my hand on her lower back. I hit the same spot over and over and she yelled in sync with each thrust. I looked at my dick coated with her wetness and let myself go. I thrust until each drop found its release and slowly withdrew myself. I went into one of the stalls to flush my sins, then cleaned up at the sink.

Romel came in on unsteady legs and did the same at the sink next to me. Her face was flushed and the front of her hair was sticking to her forehead. "I think you just turned me out," she said, "but I feel sort of cheated."

I dried my hands and then zipped up my pants. "How can you feel cheated when you got what you asked for?"

"Maybe because I know there's so much more when it comes to being with you."

"Sounds like a case of buyer's remorse to me."

"Definitely not. I simply want more."

I walked into the lounge and picked up her underwear. "Don't forget these."

She shoved her panties into her purse. "Come home with me, Julian."

Someone turned the doorknob, then started to knock on the door.

"I can't."

"Why not?"

"Because I'm going to check on my Nubian queen, Miko."

"Right now, and after what we've done?" Her expression was a mix of incredulity and embarrassment.

"Especially now. Like you said, women talk; and I may have some talking to do of my own."

"You're not going to tell her, are you?" she asked, fear flashing across her face.

The knocking on the door turned in to banging.

"If you don't want me to, I won't."

Romel looked relieved as I went to unlock the door. An angry short brother barged in and ran to one of the stalls.

"I think it's best if we keep this between you and me," she said.

I walked over to her and kissed her on the cheek. "Of course. If you think it's best. Enjoy the rest of your night."

I left Romel leaning against the counter in the restroom, looking completely confused. That was probably the last thing she expected to feel after our interlude.

CHAPTER 10
Marcel

Who needed chance encounters when you could orchestrate the meeting you wanted? I walked into the elevator immediately after the R&B diva, right before the door closed. She was headed up to the radio station for an on-air interview and I was going to my financial advisor's office located on the same floor of the building. The deejay had announced the day before that she'd be on the radio during her show and I conveniently had an appointment.

"Don't I know you?" she asked. "You were at my album release party. I'm Roxi...."

I tilted my head and temporarily feigned ignorance. "Roxi, hey. I didn't recognize you."

"It's a small world."

"That's what I hear."

"So what did you think of the album?"

"I thought it and you were great. I loved your performance," I lied. I hadn't even stuck around to hear her sing.

The elevator doors opened and we stepped out at the same time. "Are you going to the station too?"

"No, I have a meeting with my financial advisor."

"That's too bad. I was hoping we could continue our conversation while I wait to be interviewed. Would have loved to hear what you liked about my songs."

I looked at my watch. "I am a little early. I guess I can come and converse with you for a while."

I held the glass door to the station open for Roxi and followed her inside the suite. She went to the reception desk, then returned to me. We went to sit on the plush sofas in the waiting area.

"I don't know where my manager could be," she said with slight annoyance. "He was supposed to meet me an hour ago and never showed up. Every time I call him, it goes straight to his voicemail. I hope he's okay. Sorry, I'm rambling. I didn't even ask your name."

"Marcel."

"You look like a Marcel."

I laughed. "I didn't know the name Marcel had a look associated with it."

"It doesn't, I guess. I only mean that you wear the name well."

"Thanks."

"Don't mind me, Marcel. This is nervous energy. If my manager were here, I wouldn't be so all over the place. I'm excited about my album. The interview. This is all new to me."

"I'm surprised you remembered me from your event."

"I'm good with faces and I don't usually forget a name."

"So the next time you run into me, after you're a multi-platinum selling artist, you're going to remember that I'm Marcel?"

"I don't forget a face. At least I won't forget yours. Do you really think I'll go multi-platinum?"

She was right; she was all over the place, but she was fine. Flawless skin, not a hair out of place, and stacked. "After what I heard at your listening party, I know you'll go multi-platinum."

She beamed. "Really?"

"I wish I could stay and talk to you a while longer, but I have to get to my meeting."

"Do you have to go already?"

I stood up. "I do, but I should only be about an hour if you want to get together when I'm done."

"That would be nice. Why don't you meet me back here after your meeting? I should be finished by then as well."

"That'll work."

Four hours later, I was sitting on the floor in my living room with Roxi, drinking wine and listening to her CD. She was scrunching her toes in my thick, topaz-colored carpet. It could have been the wine, but the music was sounding much better than I had remembered at her album release party. She was singing along to one of her love songs.

"You have an amazing voice," I said after the song ended.

"Thank you. I've been singing since I was three. As far as I can remember, I have always wanted to do this."

"And you do it so well."

She took a sip from her glass. "Marcel, this is strange."

"What is?"

"I just met you and I'm in your home, relaxing with you as if we're old friends."

"New friends do the same things."

She sighed. "I know I was rude to you at my party. There's no excuse for my behavior. I'm a new artist and I can't go around getting a bad reputation for being a bitch."

"Don't worry about it. It's long forgotten."

"I feel like I've been dominating our conversation. Tell me something about you. What do you do for a living?"

"Do you watch sports?"

"Not really."

"Well, I'm a sports agent."

"You work with professional athletes?"

"Primarily hockey and soccer players, but yes."

"What do you do with them?"

"A lot of contract and public relations work."

"Do you enjoy it?"

"It's fulfilling, but it's a competitive business."

"Much like the music industry."

"I suppose it can be. I work long hours and don't have a lot of time for myself."

"Did I impose on your day?" she inquired, her brow wrinkling.

I moved closer to her and took her hand in mine. "You were a pleasant distraction." I placed a soft kiss across her knuckles. The setting sun streamed through the window, picking up the brown highlights in her hair. "Do you know that you have flecks of gold in your eyes?"

"They're hazel, so it depends on the light."

"I could stare into them all day."

She laughed and it was equally as raspy as when she spoke. It was sexy and cute at the same time.

The song changed on the CD and a tune with a reggae flow started to play. Roxi was bobbing her head, eyes closed, getting caught in the spell of her own music.

She opened her eyes and turned to me. "Dance with me," she said, holding her hand out.

She didn't need to ask twice. I got up, then pulled her up by the hand. I turned up the music and her melodious voice engulfed us. The deep reggae beat washed over us. She wined her body on mine like she was one with the music. She was in a trance, humming along to her lyrics. I stopped dancing and sat on the couch. Like a voyeur, I watched her twist her hips and move her ass like it was being pulled in different directions by invisible strings.

Roxi danced for me, peering at me with golden eyes. As the last few notes of the song played, she strolled over to the couch and sat next to me. I reached over, turned her face to mine, and kissed her lightly on the mouth. I pulled away and her eyes were closed. She licked her lips and smiled. I leaned in and kissed her again, applying more pressure. This time, when I pulled back, she was looking at me. She touched her fingertips to her lips as if she were willing them to be still. When I moved closer the next time, she met me halfway.

I pulled her legs across my lap and leaned in closer so that our upper bodies touched. I stroked my hand up and down her back until it arched toward me. I worked my way around to her waist, letting my thumb brush the side of her breast. She broke away from our kiss and gazed at me with those piercing eyes.

"Is something wrong?" I asked.

She moved her legs from my lap and scooted back a couple of feet. "Not at all," she said, dabbing her lipstick with the back of hand. "Everything is too right."

"I'm not sure what that means."

"I'll show you." She crawled slowly over to me and hovered above me. She leaned in and licked my neck. She kissed my chin, then my nose.

As she loomed over me, I kissed her neck, gently sucking and biting her. I felt a moan rumble in her throat and pulled her down on top of me. I kissed her deeply, letting my tongue drink her down. She started a slow wine on top of me. I palmed her ass and moved with her.

Roxi pulled away, breathless. "Do you see what I mean? This is too much, too soon. I'm not thinking straight. I feel like I'm barely thinking at all."

I placed my hand on the nape of her neck and drew her to me. I kissed her on one cheek, and then the other. I licked her neck and ended in a delicate kiss on her jawbone. I whispered in her ear how sexy she was and let her know that she was having an effect on me too. I pulled her down next to me so we lay facing each other. I touched my lips to every inch of her face—eyelids, the tip of her nose, forehead and lastly her mouth.

"Still too much?" I said, my voice husky.

She swallowed hard. "Not enough."

I touched my hand to her breast, bowed my head, and kissed her cleavage. "I want to take you into my bedroom, lay you across my bed, and do whatever you want me to do until you've had more than enough."

She nodded and I pulled her up from the couch. I started her CD over from the beginning and then led my favorite new artist into the bedroom.

CHAPTER 11

Camden

The fundraiser at the Metropolitan Museum of Art was in full swing. Natalia insisted that I attend even though she was working. I wandered through the different exhibitions, drinking champagne and wondering how much longer I needed to stay.

A unique clay sculpture caught my eye and I walked a circle around it. I was fixated on the detail, trying to determine how the artist had managed to capture the essence of flowing hair, when I sensed someone standing behind me. I turned to find that I indeed had company.

"Good evening," I said, stepping to the side. "I didn't realize you were waiting."

"You seemed so engrossed; I didn't want to disturb you."

I laughed. "I welcome the disturbance."

"Are you an artist?" she asked.

"Merely a patron."

"I see. I'm merely an admirer."

"I'm Camden Tennyson," I said, extending a hand.

"Hazelle Mason. Nice to meet you." She had a delicate handshake that matched her graceful demeanor.

Hazelle stepped closer to the sculpture.

"What do you think?" I inquired.

"I'm certainly no expert, but the realism is astonishing. The way the artist captured the pained expression is genius."

A server came over with a tray of champagne. We both exchanged our depleted glasses.

"I'm fascinated by the hair. Do you see the way the locks curl at the ends?" I asked.

"I always wished I had an artistic talent. Sadly, I do not. I'm too cerebral. I was blessed with all brains and no talent."

"And definitely beauty," I added.

Hazelle grinned. "Brains and beauty? I guess I have the full package."

We laughed together.

"Are you here alone, Hazelle?"

"Actually, no. I came with friends. A married couple. They support this event every year and insisted on bringing me along."

"Let me guess, perpetual matchmakers?"

She touched a finger to her nose. "Exactly. I agreed because they refused to take no for an answer. So here I am, wandering around, getting tipsy on champagne."

"I think I've had enough art for one evening. Would you care to join me for a nightcap? I know of a great establishment on West Fifty-Second Street that makes the finest cocktails."

"I'd love to join you. Let me tell my *chaperones* that I'm leaving. I'll be right back." She switched out of the room in search of her friends.

I continued to look at the sculptures as I waited for her to return. I hadn't seen Natalia in more than an hour. I knew I wouldn't see much of her and that was one of the reasons why I hadn't wanted to attend the event. She pushed and prodded until I relented. Next time, if there even was a next time, she would not get her way.

Hazelle returned with her purse and a smile on her face. I placed my hand at the small of her back and led her out of the museum. It was a beautiful night, warm but not humid. The valet pulled up with my Bentley. I opened the door for Hazelle, tipped the valet, and then slipped into the driver's seat.

I hadn't seen my night taking this unexpected turn, but I was glad that it did. Hazelle was a statuesque woman and looked great on my arm. She had a regal yet inviting air and a lovely smile to match. On our way to the lounge, we chatted easily about classical and contemporary art, our preferences, and pieces that we each owned.

We were seated at our table, enjoying our second drink and laughing at a funny story Hazelle was telling, when my phone vibrated in my pocket. I retrieved it from my suit jacket, checked the display, and asked Hazelle to excuse me while I answered.

"I left the museum over two hours ago…I'm having a nightcap and a bite to eat…Yes, as soon as I'm done." I returned the phone to my pocket. "I apologize for the interruption."

"Someone at home waiting for you, I presume?"

"No, I live alone."

"But that was someone special looking for you?"

"You're right, it was someone looking for me. But I'm sitting across from someone special and exactly where I want to be."

Hazelle looked at me as if she wanted to ask something else, but decided against it. I could have let Natalia go to voicemail, but, if I hadn't answered, she would have kept calling. I heard in her icy tone she was angry that I had left without letting her know. She'd remained calm, but she was boiling right beneath the surface.

I'd finish up with Hazelle and then head over to Natalia's place, as I had told her over the phone.

"I have thoroughly enjoyed this evening and would like to see you again, Camden."

"I'm certain we can arrange that in the very near future. Until then, would you like dessert or another drink?"

"As tempting as that sounds, I should probably be getting home."

We left the lounge at half past midnight and I drove Hazelle to her Park Avenue home. I parked in front of her building and got out to open her door. I helped her from the car, kissed her cheek and then the back of her hand. "Thank you for joining me."

"Thank you for a wonderful evening. I look forward to doing it again."

"As do I."

She sauntered into her building and I sped off to Gramercy Park to meet Natalia.

As expected, she was wide awake and waiting for answers. She had already asked three times why I hadn't told her that I was leaving, and I had already answered the question four times.

"Natalia, I had been gone for over two hours and you hadn't noticed. Why is this an issue? You were working. We didn't go to the event together. We spent five minutes in each other's company the entire time I was there. And for the sixth time, you were working."

"It's called common courtesy. I invited you to be there. The least you could do was to stay until the end. Or at least let me know that you were leaving."

"We're going in circles and I'm getting tired of it. As far as I'm concerned, this isn't an issue. You were preoccupied with work and not accessible to me. I left at least two hours before you even noticed that I was gone. Most importantly, I attended your event because you asked me to support you."

"That's true, Camden, but there were plenty of drinks and food at the exhibition. I don't understand why you needed to leave for that reason."

"I was tired of hors d'oeuvres and I'm tired of this discussion." I went over to her and stroked her cheek. "Why don't you and I take a nice hot shower together, get into bed, and talk about what a success your event turned out to be?"

She held my hand against her face and sighed. "That does sound good."

"Yes, it does. Let me unzip that dress for you." I turned her around and slowly helped her out of the body-hugging fabric, then freed her hair from the bun she was wearing.

Natalia stood on the Persian rug in the center of her bedroom waiting for me to undress. I removed my tie first and handed it to her. She waited for the next items—my suit jacket, cuff links, shirt, and then pants. I strode into the bathroom to turn on the water as she hung up my clothing.

When she joined me in the bathroom, she was completely naked. I stepped out of my boxers and into the spacious shower. We stood under our own separate shower heads, water beating down our bodies. I crept over to Natalia and backed her against the tile. I lifted her and she wrapped her legs around my waist. As the warm water rained down over us, her wetness flooded me, and I rode the waves until I could barely stand.

CHAPTER 12

Avery

Ever since I ran into Kev, I had been checking my voicemail daily. My first year in New York, I was bombarded with messages from friends wondering where I had been, checking to see if I was all right. Kev was right, I had vanished. I didn't want to be bothered by anyone. By the second year, the calls had settled down. I'd receive a message every couple of months when I crossed someone's mind. Now, the phone hardly ever rang. That was how I wanted it.

Kev had left a message the day after I saw him and a few days later. But nothing had changed. I let his calls go into the same unanswered void as all of the calls that had come before.

I tried not to reflect too much on my time in D.C. because it would only make me angry. Some called it having unresolved issues, but I preferred to call it the past. A past that shouldn't be disturbed. A past better off forgotten. I was a different person back then—with Courtney. That woman was my world, but relationships end and life goes on. You live another day to do things differently the next time. You swear to yourself that you won't get played again, that if anyone was going to get hurt, it wouldn't be you. Since then, that had been my credo and I lived by it. No exceptions.

I sat down at the table in the yellow room. I had picked up a light dinner of London broil with a green salad from my favorite restaurant. The house was quiet, exactly how I loved it. Brookville provided such an escape. My house was set back from the main road and concealed from neighbors and drivers by a dense thicket of trees and bushes. You couldn't even see up the driveway. It was complete solitude and being off the grid for a while. It was my sanity, my way of being able to manage the hectic life I was leading. I ate my dinner and thought of the busy week ahead. I amazed myself sometimes at how I was able to juggle so many things at the same time. I was a hustler; there was no doubt about it.

After dinner, I went up to the black room and unlocked the door. I turned on the recessed lights and went over to my hulking desk. I rolled my desk chair across the black hardwood floor to access the safe underneath the desk. I moved a few stacks of cash to the side, readjusted some jewelry, and slid my passport aside. I removed a yellowing picture of my mother in her high school graduation cap and gown and stared at it for a moment. She was so beautiful. Her smile said that she was ready to take on the world and no one could stop her. Unfortunately, that wasn't what life had in store for Diane Woodson. Pregnant. Homeless. Abandoning her only child. That was her reality. I tossed the picture back into the safe and locked it up tight.

I pulled my chair up and sat at the desk. There was a stack of correspondence, bank statements, and junk mail in the letter holder on the side of the desk. One by one, I opened each envelope, addressing the important items and discarding the rest. After a few hours, I went across the room to lay on the velvet sectional. The sectional matched the black velvet flocked wallpaper. I turned on the television and watched the news, dozing off in the process. It was after eleven when I awoke. I locked up the black room and headed downstairs.

It was late, I was tired, and I had a long day ahead of me. I took a hot shower, threw on a pair of pajama bottoms, and double-checked that the alarm clock was set. Right before climbing into bed, I went over to the dresser and checked my cell phones. All three had missed calls and messages from either Miko, Romel, Quinn, Roxi, Natalia, and Hazelle.

It was definitely going to be a busy week.

CHAPTER 13

I pulled out of the garage in the Audi and barreled down the driveway, screeching onto Brookville Road. I needed to get to the Long Island Expressway before the Monday morning traffic became unnavigable. The left lane was at that moment opening as the night construction crew wrapped up their work.

I had an appointment at the Department of Records on Chambers Street in Lower Manhattan and couldn't afford to be late. The information I had on my mother was limited. My search had started with the high school graduation picture. It was the only picture I had of my mother. It was in my file at the orphanage. In my file, it said that Diane Woodson was born in New York City in 1961. In the corner of the photo it read "Class of 1978." The orphanage told me that she was seventeen when she had me and that she had graduated high school five months prior to giving birth. I was three weeks old when she left me there. They also thought that my mother had used an alias and that Woodson may not have been her real name. I had been on a wild goose chase for years—trying to find old high school yearbook companies, any Woodsons in New York City, and, most recently, birth records from 1961 and 1978. Any time I thought I found a lead, it turned out to be a dead end.

I was meeting a professional historian who was going to assist in researching Diane Woodson or digging up whoever my mother may have been. I had already shared everything that I knew; it was now in the hands of the professional. I entered the Visitor Center and Mr. Charles stood to greet me. We shook hands and immediately got down to business.

"Mr. Charles, I want you to know that money is no object. I realize I don't have much information to provide and that you'll have your work cut out for you."

"This is what I do, Mr. Woodson. I love a challenge. Being able to help people at the same time is the icing on the cake. Just so you know, I have a team of investigators who work for me from private eyes to retired detectives and, of course, other historians like myself."

Mr. Charles looked like a college professor. He was wearing a tweed blazer, a pair of round glasses, and clutched a cap in his hands. Never mind that it was over eighty degrees outside.

This was the most hope I had ever had about finding Diane Woodson. "I brought you a bank check for the deposit and, as we agreed upon, the balance is due upon the completion of your research. Do you need any additional information from me?"

He thought for a moment. "I'm a researcher, so, I'm curious by nature. You never did tell me much about yourself, like what led you to this moment, your history, per se. What do you do for a living, young man?"

"I live a complicated life, Mr. Charles, and I value my privacy. I don't talk much about myself, but I'm an attorney by trade."

"Really, what firm?"

"I work for myself."

He nodded and didn't ask a follow-up question. We wished each other well and departed. He went to the archives to begin his research and I left, on my way to Brooklyn.

CHAPTER 14
Julian

I rang the bell and waited. Miko popped her head out of the window and grinned her surprise. She came down and met me on the stoop. She was wearing overalls with paint splatters decorating the fabric. Her hands, arms, and face had droplets of fuchsia on them as well. I handed her the flowers that were hidden behind my back. She took them from me and sat on the top step.

"I would invite you up, but, as you can see, I'm painting," she said, gesturing to her appearance.

"You should have asked me to help you. I'm the man when it comes to paint."

Miko laughed. "I bet you are."

"I can go change and come right back…"

"I appreciate the offer, but Romel's up there helping me and a few more of my girls will be over in a minute."

I looked up at the window. Romel was leaning against the frame, peering down. She waved at me with an expression I couldn't decipher. I called up to her. "How you doin', Romel?"

She turned and disappeared from the window.

"Don't mind her," Miko said. "She always gets a little weird when it comes to you."

"What's that about?"

"The usual. Romel likes to be the center of attention around men."

"Oh, and I chose you."

"She's not used to that. She thinks that every man wants light skin, straight hair, and big tits. I think it surprised her that you preferred my dark choc-o-late." She said that last part with a laugh.

I tugged on her overall strap and lured her to me. "So cute… Always a queen," I said, lifting her chin and placing a kiss on her lips. "I wish she wasn't up there. I want to make love to my chocolate queen."

She moaned. "I can come to your place later."

"Why don't you send her to the store for more paint or something?" I said, laughing.

"I can't do that."

"Then why don't we slip into your bedroom and love on each other for a little bit?"

"We can't." She nudged me away from her. "But I promise I'll be over around ten tonight."

I looked up at the window again. Romel was there, watching. I pulled Miko into a hug. "All right. I'll see you tonight. Don't wash off the paint before you come. I think it's sexy."

I stood and shouted up to Romel. "Good seeing you." There was no answer; she just lingered there with her arms crossed over her chest. "Bye, my Nubian queen," I said to Miko, then headed down the street. By the time I got to my car, my cell was ringing.

"You hurt my feelings," Romel said, barely above a whisper.

"I wasn't aware that you were at Miko's."

"You brought her flowers…"

"I did. I know she loves them."

"So do I," she said, sounding like a spoiled child.

"I didn't know that."

"I don't think you care to know, Julian."

"That's not fair considering our situation and the way things got started."

"I get it. I'm the bad girl and bad girls don't get flowers."

"I didn't say that," I said, pulling out of my parking space. "You're at Miko's. Maybe we should have this conversation another time."

"I came outside to call you. She's back upstairs painting."

"It's still not appropriate. We'll get together soon. If you can swing it, meet me at BAMcafe tonight at eight."

"I'll be there."

I walked into BAMcafe and found Romel at the bar already with a drink in front of her.

"You're early," I said.

"I couldn't stand to breathe in any more paint fumes."

I handed her a single red rose. "And I caught a vision of woman...golden and brilliantly arrayed, and I caught a vision of woman...and my emotions I betrayed, and I caught a vision of woman...and inherently knew that by her side, I would stay." I kissed Romel on her neck and took the seat next to her.

"That was nice," she said.

"When the inspiration hits me, it hits me."

She laid her rose on the bar. "I guess I didn't rate an entire bouquet like Miko."

"This right here," I gestured to myself and then her, "is not about me and Miko. It's about me and you. There's no comparison because they're two entirely different situations."

"I thought I would have seen you after our night together. I don't think I've ever had a man not return my calls. Calls that I was certain to make when I knew you weren't with Miko."

"I've been wondering how you got my number."

"From Miko's phone, of course. Why didn't you call me back?"

"You obviously think I do this all the time. I don't. We're in a precarious position and my behavior toward you has been a reflection of the situation we're in."

"So, I'm the only one that wants to explore the possibilities?"

"I'm not saying that."

"You're not saying anything, Julian."

"What about your friend?"

"I love Miko like a sister. But even you said that has nothing to do with us."

"That's easier said than done. This afternoon you seemed a little upset when you saw me with her."

"I was more annoyed that you weren't returning my calls."

"I don't believe that," I said, giving her direct eye contact.

"It's true. I know you're with Miko."

"I am."

"What about us?"

"And my emotions I betrayed..." I whispered, then leaned forward and touched my lips to hers. For a brief moment, she didn't react, and then she opened her mouth and gave me her tongue. We parted and she had the look of a good girl that had just been kissed for the first time.

"I can't stay long," I said.

Something in her eyes hardened. "Miko?"

"I need to get home to meet her."

Romel nodded. "You can at least stay for one drink."

"I plan to." I waved over the bartender.

"Make it two. She can wait."

CHAPTER 15

Marcel

Quinn opened the box and then looked at me. She placed the box on the counter and started to read the instructions on the back. I wasn't expecting her to do back flips, but I certainly didn't anticipate her lackluster reaction.

"You don't like it?"

"It's not that. I merely prefer to get my coffee from my favorite shop two avenues away."

"Now you can make your own at home. Do you know how much money you can save? And this machine makes single cups."

Quinn laughed. "You are too funny. I don't have many extravagances, but a daily cup of coffee is one of them."

"All right. I'll keep my gift for myself."

"Awww," she said coming around the island in her kitchen to hug me. "I really do appreciate it."

"That's okay. You're not hurting my feelings. I will put the machine to good use at my own apartment."

She put the coffee machine back into the shopping bag and handed it to me. "Are you sure you aren't upset?"

I put the bag on the counter and lifted her off her feet. "It would take a lot more than you not wanting a coffee machine to make me upset with you." I put her down. "I know how you love your coffee. I saw the machine when I was out and thought you could use it. That's all."

She stifled another laugh. "Well, thank you anyway."

"Ain't this a blip! You can't even buy a woman a gift these days."

"Marcel! You're going to make me feel bad," she said through giggles.

"I can't tell with all that laughing you're doing."

"I'm sorry."

"I don't believe you. You're going to have to show me how sorry you are." I grabbed the belt loop on her cut-off shorts and tugged them down, exposing the top of her panties. She stepped out of her shorts, then pulled her baby tee over her head and revealed her braless breasts. I walked her over to the stool next to the island and sat her on my lap, facing me. I played with her nipples, pinching them between my fingertips. "Bring it to me," I said.

She raised up and leaned back, granting me full access to her perfectly round, full breasts. I bent forward and lowered my mouth to one of her nipples. I flicked my tongue across and then blew on it until it was hard. I did the same to the other, going back and forth between them. She playfully traced her nipples around my lips, until I sucked her breast into my mouth. She let out a sharp moan. I pulled on her flesh with my tongue, rolling it around the inside of my mouth. She squirmed until I released my hold on her breast.

"What are you trying to do to me?" she said breathlessly.

"Let me show you. Scoot back a little." Quinn inched back further on my lap and I unzipped my jeans. I pulled my dick out of my boxers and looked at it, then at her. "Come here."

She placed her feet on the pegs of the stool and rose up over me. I pulled her panties to the side as she lowered her pussy onto my dick. She was tight and I had to work my way into her inch by inch. She moved her hips in a figure eight as I held on to her waist. I closed my eyes and concentrated on not exploding too soon. When she started to pop and rock down on my dick, I wrapped my arms around her waist and buried my face in her breasts. I was about to lose it. Quinn was going to have me punk out like a one-minute man. I grabbed her hips and held her still.

She looked down at me. "I know my cookie is good. Let me show you how good it is."

I let go of her hips and let her freak the shit out of me. She bounced that ass like it had hydraulics. I was counting backward from one hundred, saying my ABCs, and anything else I could think of to hold my own.

Needless to say, when the pussy's that good, there's only so much a brother can do not to embarrass himself. I had to switch it up and carry Quinn into the bedroom, where I put it down on her and had her screaming my name over and over again.

CHAPTER 16

Camden

Hazelle Mason had invited me over to see her artwork. She told me she had won most of it from her husband in the divorce settlement, but had acquired some on her own. There was a colorful painting that hung in the living that was meant to be the main talking piece. It looked like a Basquiat, but she insisted a close friend painted it. Her artist friend had apparently borrowed heavily from Basquiat's raw style.

"I hope you'll repay the favor one day and allow me to sneak a peek at your collection."

"I'd hardly call my few pieces a collection, but you're more than welcome to see what I have."

"I never cared too much about art until I realized how much my husband wanted to keep it during the divorce. I figured if he was fighting so hard for it, I would fight just as hard to make sure he wouldn't get it," she said and then laughed.

"How long have you been divorced?"

"For about as long as I was married. It will be five years this fall."

"Married for five and divorced for five."

"I married young. My ex-husband was twenty years my senior. If I knew then what I know now…"

"You'd do things differently?"

"Absolutely. I married him for all the wrong reasons."

I assumed money was the main reason considering the age gap and her seemingly obvious wealth. "That sounds like regret."

"I think of the wasted years and, yes, I have some regrets." She shook her head, then perked up. "I do not want to talk about my ex. I'm sorry I even raised the subject."

Hazelle made no mention of being a divorcée in any of our previous conversations. It didn't matter to me that she had been married, but I liked to know what kind of baggage a person was hauling around.

I transitioned the discussion away from her failed marriage. "Right. We should be talking about the here and now."

"You're absolutely right. Which leads me to what I've been wanting to ask you since you arrived."

"Which is?"

"You remember my friends, Peter and Toni Ann, whom I attended the art exhibit with the night we met?"

"I didn't have the pleasure of meeting them."

"Well, I would like to rectify that. Peter is hosting his monthly mixer this evening at their home."

"Is that right?"

She moved closer, took my hand, and led me to the sofa. "Yes, Peter graduated from Harvard and when I told him you were also a Harvard Alum, he asked a barrage of questions like what did you study, did you belong to any clubs, when did you graduate. Of course, I couldn't answer a thing. So, he insisted that I bring you with me tonight. Will you come?"

"It is short notice," I said, letting it hang in the air for a moment, "but it sounds like it would be an enjoyable evening."

"Wonderful," she said with a quick squeeze of my hand. "I'll let them know there will be one more at the mixer."

Hazelle's friends lived down in SoHo. I cruised through the moonlit streets, taking my time getting there. Though I was having a carefree conversation with Hazelle, my mind was working overtime. I stopped at the yellow lights instead of speeding through like I typically would. I needed the extra time to think. We had already circled her friends' block twice in search of a parking space.

I pulled in front of their building. "Let's wait a few minutes to see if a space becomes available," I said, putting the car in park.

"That's probably the best thing to—"

"One moment, my phone is vibrating." I reached into my pocket and answered. "Yes, this is Camden. What kind of emergency? I'll be right there." I ended the call and looked into Hazelle's expectant eyes. "I'm sorry but I have to go. There's an emergency."

She looked at me with a face full of concern. "What happened? Is everything all right?"

"I'll explain everything later. Please give your friends my apologies."

"Yes, of course. Go take care of your business." She leaned over and kissed me on the lips, then slowly grabbed the door handle. "Call me later."

"As soon as I can."

Hazelle exited my car and headed into Peter and Toni Ann's apartment building. I sped off. At the first stoplight, I picked up my phone and turned it on.

It had been off all night.

CHAPTER 17

S ix damn messages. Kev had left six messages in one day. Weeks had passed and not a word. I figured I was off his radar; then, out of nowhere, an onslaught of calls. I was going to ignore them, the same way I had the two messages he'd left the week I saw him, until I got to the last one. He was back in New York.

His message said that his father-in-law was in the hospital and it wasn't looking good. He wanted to know if I would meet him for a drink. He needed to get away from the hospital for a while. Needed to pull himself together. I sat in the white room, hunched over on the sofa, phone dangling from my hand, deep in thought. Why, I didn't know. I knew what I should do. Absolutely nothing. Turn on my television and unwind for the evening. Instead, I found myself heading to the red room, opening up my nightstand drawer, and plugging in my old cell phone from D.C.

I sat on the edge of the bed while I let the phone charge. Twice I got up to unplug it and return it to the drawer, but each time I placed it back on the nightstand and continued to wait. I reclined back on the bed and stared at the ceiling. Kev was my boy when I was in D.C. We had a lot of good times hanging out, going to games, and doing a whole bunch of nothing like homeboys tend to do.

I checked the phone. One bar. That was good enough. I punched in his number. He picked up on the first ring. After a brief discussion, we agreed to meet at a lounge in Hempstead. I threw on my pants, pulled the tags off a crisp, new shirt, then put on my suit jacket. As I got dressed, I questioned why I was bothering. Kev had his family to lean on; he didn't need me. We hadn't been cool for years. I was trying to comprehend what made him feel like I was his go-to person, but kept coming up with nothing. I grabbed my keys and headed out of the house before I changed my mind and pulled a no-show.

We sat at the bar, drinks in front of us untouched. R&B music played in the background. Dim lighting cast a mellow shadow across the half-filled room. For a weeknight, I was surprised to see the spot wasn't empty. People were on the dance floor, partying. I checked out the ratio of men to women. As usual, the women outnumbered the men as they sat in small clusters, populating the booths interspersed throughout the lounge. Some of the brothers were working the room, trying to find the one that would go for whatever they were offering.

I turned back to Kev and I genuinely felt bad for him. When I arrived, he had thanked me profusely for agreeing to meet him. It unsettled me to see how uncomfortable he was in my presence. We used to be boys, now we were practically strangers.

"So, your father-in-law is in stable condition?" I asked.

"For now. It's been touch and go for the past two days. My wife's going crazy."

I just listened because I didn't have anything to say. I didn't know Kev's wife or her family. He had met and married her after I left D.C. I lifted my glass and took a drink before the melting ice diluted it too much.

"She's convinced he's not going to make it," he continued. "I'm starting to feel the same. I had to get away for a while because I didn't want her to see that in my face. It's tough knowing you're about to lose somebody." His shoulders slumped as he voiced the last part.

"He's still here. Don't write him off yet." That was the best I could offer.

"You're right." Kev nodded, staring into his drink. "So what happened, man?"

"Kev, you didn't ask me to meet you down here for this—"

"You're telling me not to write my father-in-law off, but that's exactly what you did with all of us, your boys." He looked up from his glass and fixed me with a penetrating gaze. "I want to know why."

My expression was blank. "I don't know what to tell you."

"You can tell me why."

I took a swig of my drink. "There's nothing to tell."

"How can you say that?" he asked, his voice strained. "We were like brothers, man, and you up and disappeared without a word to anybody. How can you think there's nothing to tell? I would think there's a hell of a lot to tell. You could start with why you left. What have you been doing all this time? Why the hell didn't you call any of us? So don't give me that. There's plenty to tell, Avery."

"You asked me to meet you tonight," I said with a hint of a warning in my tone, "and I'm here. But we're not getting into all of that."

"You're not going to answer any of my questions?"

"I don't have any answers for you."

Kev shook his head with a frustrated look on his face. "I need to make a call. I'll be right back." He left me alone at the bar and went outside cradling his cell phone to his ear.

I should have stayed out of sight and out of mind. It was stupid of me to think Kev only wanted to discuss what was happening with his father-in-law. As soon as he returned, I would tell him I needed to be going.

Ten minutes had passed. I scanned the room and directed my attention to what was going on while Kev had been trying to interrogate me. I did a double, triple, eventually a quadruple take. My eyes glazed over as I stared at her beauty. I had to remind myself to blink and to close my mouth. Everything on this woman was long—hair, lashes, nails, legs—everything except the skirt. I was thanking God for such a wonderful sight when she caught me right in the middle of my unadulterated observation. She smiled and it was like the sun came from behind the clouds on the darkest day. She turned to whisper something in her companion's ear. That backside. I wanted the opportunity to rest my head on it. Suddenly, I was on autopilot. I crossed the room and stood next to her like I knew her. Up close she was nutmeg brown with lips that looked as soft and pink as cotton candy.

She extended her hand before I uttered a single word. "Indiya Spencer. I wondered if you would ever notice me the way I had noticed you. I saw you as soon as I came in. And I said to my girl, 'I saw a fine man sitting at the bar. His skin was as dark and smooth as French roast coffee beans.' Then she and I stole a few glances at your close-cropped hair, impeccably manicured, slightly glistening goatee and brown eyes that are a shade lighter than your face. And now that you've finally made your way over here, I like that you have a towering presence. You make me look dainty and I'm five-eight in flats. Tonight, with my heels on, I'm almost six feet and you still have me by five inches." She paused, touching a hand to my chest. "Your upper body is muscular, but not in a way that says that you spend all of your free time at the gym. No, you have the physique of a basketball player, but in your suit, it's a little difficult to see exactly what you're working with. Don't look surprised. You came over here; I figured I'd make it worth your while. You know exactly what I think."

I was momentarily speechless. This beautiful woman, with her hand in mine, captivated me. I licked my lips. "That was quite an introduction. My name is Cam—" A hand clamped down on my shoulder and Kev was suddenly standing beside me. I coughed to cover up what I was about to say. "I'm Avery Woodson," I said to Indiya.

Kev interrupted, "Sorry, Avery. My wife wouldn't let me off the phone. I'd better be getting back."

I let go of Indiya's hand so I could give Kev a pound. "No problem. Hope your father-in-law pulls through."

"I'll call you." Kev looked at me, then Indiya and left without another word.

Indiya looped her arm through mine and slowly led me back toward the bar. "Avery," she said as if she were considering whether she liked my name or not. "It's nice to make your acquaintance."

I smiled. "That had to be the most interesting first encounter I've ever had."

"Admit it. Wasn't it nice to hear what I thought about you from the moment I saw you?"

"I can't lie. It caught me off-guard. Most women like to play cat and mouse. They get a brother to buy them a few drinks while he tries to decipher if she's feeling him."

"I'm not most women."

"What are you drinking?"

"I'll have whatever you're having."

I nodded. "Goose and cranberry," I told the bartender.

"Only a splash of cranberry," she chimed in.

"So, Indiya, if you were thinking such flattering things about me, why didn't you come over and let me know?"

"You were with your friend."

"I was at the bar by myself for a good ten minutes."

"That's true, but I wanted you to feel my aura drawing you to me."

"Oh, no," I said with a laugh. "Don't tell me you think you sent out some sort of cosmic signal and I responded."

"Something like that." The bartender placed her drink on the bar and she tapped her glass against mine. "I prefer to think my energy inevitably attracted yours."

"And that's why we're having a drink together?"

"Certainly. I also think my energy was responsible for your friend leaving. I hope I didn't intrude."

I tried to keep the smile off my face. "I welcome the intrusion, more than you know."

"Since you're not buying into my aura theory, what led you to walk over to me?"

"My desire to be in your presence."

She frowned. "You didn't give that any thought. Move past the superficial and go beneath the surface."

I gave Indiya a probing look. "You know what? Maybe you did draw me to you."

"Now you're pacifying me. It's okay. Not many men can operate on my level." She stood up to leave. "Thanks for the drink."

I lunged forward and grabbed her arm. "Wait, what's wrong?"

"You mentioned that most women play cat and mouse. I think I made it obvious that's not my style. So, feeding me lines about why you approached me doesn't make me want to have a drink with you. In fact, it makes me think I'm wasting my time, which is too valuable to waste."

Again, I was at a loss for words. I held on to Indiya's arm, willing her with my eyes, to sit back down. "Whoa," I managed after a beat. "I was being serious. The furthest thing from my mind was to pacify you. I turned around, saw you standing there, took in your beauty and the next thing I knew, I was walking over to you."

Indiya smiled, then sat back in her seat. "Was that so hard?"

I shook my head and laughed. "You are an interesting woman."

"If you want to find out how interesting, you should invite me for dinner."

"I think I'll do that."

"Think?"

"Don't misunderstand me. I would love to take you to dinner."

"Let me see your phone." She took my cell and punched in her information. "Now you have my number and I set an appointment on your calendar for dinner."

I raised my eyebrows at her forwardness, then looked at what she had input. "Dinner tomorrow night at eight?"

"Does that work for you?"

"Most definitely."

"Good, then I'll see you tomorrow night." Indiya winked at me, grabbed her drink, and strolled back over to her friend.

I downed the rest of my vodka, took a final glance at my date for tomorrow night, and struggled to break free of her aura as I walked out of the lounge.

CHAPTER 18

W e sat in a booth in a quiet room at Ruth's Chris. The larger dining room was buzzing. Indiya objected to me picking her up at home in Rockville Centre and insisted on meeting me at the restaurant. When she arrived, twenty minutes late, I was already seated at the table. She entered with an unhurried elegance. I had been observing her with veiled curiosity from the moment she got there.

Indiya was reading the menu, trying to decide what to order. I already knew what I wanted. I had been through the menu a few times while I was waiting for her. Every so often, she would make a small noise that sounded way too sensual for what she was doing.

"I'm starving and everything looks good." She moaned again. "I think I'm going to start with the Crabtini and then I'll have the Petit Filet." She placed the menu on the table and smiled broadly at me. "You are a handsome man, Avery."

I don't think I had ever had the feeling of someone making me blush, but Indiya had clearly made it happen for the first time. "I'm just a black man with smooth skin."

She laughed at that. "Is that what it is, nice skin?"

"Now you, on the other hand, are a sight to behold."

"You're deflecting, but I'm not going to let you. I don't want to talk about me; I want to talk about you."

"All right. Shoot."

"Last night you approached me with such purpose. What were you going to say before I cut you off?"

"I was going to ask if I could buy you a drink."

"Is that all? I would imagine you to be more creative than that."

I winced. "I get it. Brothers buy you drinks all the time."

"Which I can do for myself. It's what a man says to me that counts."

"Then why didn't you wait for my lead?"

"Because sometimes I'm moved to say what I feel and I can't hold back."

"Must be a double-edged sword."

"I've been cut a few times."

"I can imagine. You're pretty direct."

"Is there any other way to be?"

"Sometimes, you have to finesse a conversation. Not every situation calls for the direct approach."

Indiya cocked her head to the side. "That sounds borderline questionable. Sort of like saying sometimes you have to tell a lie."

"That's true, sometimes you do."

"I'm not sure that's something you say to someone on your first date."

I laughed. "Didn't you tell me a moment ago that you like being direct?"

"Touché. I'm going to move this conversation in an entirely different direction."

"I'm enjoying this," I said with a smirk, "but now would be a good time for the waiter to show up."

That time she laughed. "Oh, you're looking to be saved by the bell. Don't worry, I'll be gentle. Do you like it gentle?"

I paused. She wasn't going to bait me. "Depends on the question."

The glint in her eye told me that she was amused by my response. "Okay, let's see. First question, when you went home last night, did you think about me? And be honest."

"Did you think about me?"

"Answering my question with one of your own is not allowed."

"That qualifies as a yes."

"I thought about you quite a few times last night. I was looking forward to dinner tonight, so I could find out more about you."

At that moment, our waiter came over to the table. We placed our orders, then Indiya picked up right where she had left off. "In case you can't tell, Avery, I want to know what you thought of me."

"You were the highlight of my night."

"Tell me why."

"You're intense."

"Yes, I am. In all things."

I leaned forward, putting my elbows on the table, fingers tented. This woman was exhausting and engaging all at once. I wanted to figure out what made her tick. "Last night, you were the only person that I actually saw in the lounge. I was there having a drink, but I hadn't noticed anyone until I saw you."

"Did you think I was sexy?"

"That goes without saying."

Indiya leaned back in the booth and narrowed her eyes. "Do you want to get to know me, I mean the real me, not what you see on the exterior?"

"That's why we're here."

"We're here because I made a move on you."

"I think we made a move on each other."

She nodded. "Are you single or is there a special someone in your life?"

"I do not have someone special in my life." Technically, I told the truth. The answer to her question wasn't black and white. It was gray. Extremely gray.

"Are you looking for that special someone or are you playing the field?"

"I don't play the field."

"You have an interesting way of answering questions."

"And I could say that you ask interesting questions."

We regarded each other for a minute before she spoke again. "You know, Avery, I don't spend a lot of time trying to get to know someone. I can usually tell what I think about a person after a few minutes. So far you're an enigma. I'm not sure if I like that or not."

"I think you like it."

One side of her mouth curved upward. "I'm flirting with the idea of not seeing you past this first date."

"I don't believe that."

"You should, because I mean it."

"If you meant it, you wouldn't be telling me that's what you thought. Instead, you would enjoy your dinner and your drinks, at my expense, and then give me the biggest brush-off at the end of the date. No, I think you're telling me this to gauge my reaction. So I can tell you what you've wanted to hear since last night. That I think you are the sexiest woman I've met in a long time."

"That's what you think I want to hear?"

"You've already asked as much."

"That's the obvious, and not what I want to hear."

"Well, maybe by the end of the date I'll figure it out."

"Let's hope that you do."

Our appetizers arrived and I was grateful that she had something to occupy that mouth. Indiya was throwing me off my game. I was trying to figure out what approach to take with her while she concentrated on her food.

Thanks to Kev's impeccable timing, I introduced myself as Avery Woodson, not Camden Tennyson as I had intended. At the root, Camden and I were one, but we were not the same.

"Can I taste your shrimp?" she asked, interrupting my thoughts.

"Help yourself."

She harpooned a shrimp from the sauce in my dish with her fork, then took a bite. "This is delicious," she said, wiping the corner of her mouth with a napkin. "Do you cook?"

"Not a lick."

"That's probably the reason you don't have a woman. Women love a man that can cook."

"I'm not that man."

"I can relate. I don't cook either."

"Eating at home is overrated." I took my final bite of food.

"I thought all men wanted a woman that could throw down like their mama."

"Again, I'm not that man."

"I find that hard to believe. I'm sure you've compared the cooking of many women to your mother's."

"I don't know my mother."

Indiya went still. "I'm sorry."

I shrugged it off. "It's all right."

"No, it's not. I talk too much."

"You won't get an argument out of me on that point," I said, attempting to lighten the mood.

"As long as you don't hold it against me."

"I won't, if you agree to change the subject."

"Consider it changed. I'll talk about my favorite subject—me."

"You have my undivided attention."

"Let's see. Well, I was raised in the Windy City—"

"You're from Chicago."

"Yes, indeed. I'm a Chicago girl. I love the Bulls, the Bears, and the Cubs."

"Okay," I said with a nod and a smile, "so you're a sports fan?"

"Absolutely. And let me guess, you're a diehard Knicks and Jets, no, Giants, fan?"

"None of the above."

"Not a sports guy…interesting. What are you into?"

"We're back to me already?" I said, with a laugh.

Indiya tossed her hair over shoulder and let out a hearty laugh. "I can't help it."

"I'm a book guy. I have an affinity for books, particularly historical novels. Occasionally, I dabble in genealogy."

"You're a thinker."

"You could say that," I said nonchalantly.

"What do you do for a living?"

"I'm an attorney."

"I can see that," she said, mimicking my indifferent tone. "What about you?"

"I'm a senior buyer at Saks."

"That explains your flawless style."

"Image is everything. That's been my personal motto since junior high."

"That's a great motto. Image is everything."

"But I still know how to let loose from time to time. I can be a bit of a wild child."

"Oh, yeah?"

Indiya leaned forward and put her hand on top of mine. "My eyes are up here, Avery," she said, seeing my eyes lingering on her cleavage. "Who knows, maybe one day you'll find out how wild I can be."

The waiter returned with our steaks, sizzling hot and juicy, and I wondered whether Indiya would be the same.

CHAPTER 19
Julian

I strode to the stage, giving dap to the brothers I recognized along the way. The crowd was restless. Hushed conversations and laughter continued as I grabbed the microphone from the stand. I didn't ask for silence. I didn't wait for silence. I just started to speak.

"Can you repeat the question? I don't understand what you're asking me.
Did I do it? No.
Was I there? Yes.
What was I doing there? I don't know.
One minute I was thinking about it. The next, it was in my face.
Visible, tangible and so tempting.
What's the question again?
Why did I do it?
I didn't say that I did.
I only said that I'd thought about it.
Thought long and hard. Thinking…over and over again.
Did I consider you at all?
Of course I did.
You never left my mind. You were ever-present, looming like an angel over my shoulder.
I saw your face every time I closed my eyes.
What exactly are you asking me?

I thought I answered that question.
My answer is not going to change no matter how many times you ask.
Can you repeat the question?
Yes, I swear, I'm telling the truth.
No, I didn't do it. I only thought about it…"

The response started slowly, then the room filled with thunderous clapping. I returned the mic and walked off the stage. I peeped Miko on the other side of the room, heading up front. I took a seat at one of the tables in the back as she reached the stage.

She stepped to the microphone, head bowed, bushy hair framing her face. She cleared her throat. "I don't believe you," she uttered into the mic. The audience stared. "Thank you," she whispered, then briskly cleared the stage. No one clapped.

The host for the evening took the stage, gesturing with shrugs while shaking his head. He checked his clipboard. "Thank you, sister, for that unscheduled…uh…I would call it a haiku, but it was too short for that. Y'all give it up for the sister's piece," he said with a low chuckle. "Let's bring up our next artist, who I'm sure will have a lot more to say. Give it up for Zee."

Zee took the stage and instantly engaged the crowd.

Miko plopped down in the seat next me. Her face was unreadable. I leaned over and kissed her cheek. "Hey, beautiful."

"That's all you have to say to me? Hey, beautiful?"

"What did you have in mind?"

"You could start with where you've been and why you haven't returned my calls."

I put my finger to my lips and silently shushed her. "You're talking kind of loud."

"I don't care about that, Julian."

"The brother on the stage and the people around us may care."

"Then let's go outside to talk," she said, with a slight wobble in her neck.

I reached over and clasped her hand, so that mine rested on top of hers on the table.

Miko slid hers from beneath mine. "I'm serious, Julian, we need to talk."

"All right. I'm up once more. You're obviously not enjoying yourself and I don't want you to wait for me. I'll meet you at your place in an hour." I brushed a lock of hair from her face and added a smile. "Okay?"

She visibly exhaled, shoulders relaxed. "Okay."

I gently grabbed her by the chin and kissed her softly on the lips. "See you soon."

Miko nodded, then slowly left me sitting at the table.

I wasn't too concerned by her behavior. It was as a result of wanting to spend more time with me. She was upset because I had been off the grid for the past few weeks. It wasn't like me not to cater to her and she was reacting.

I knew how to handle Miko. I'd do my last piece for the night, then jet over to her place. I wouldn't keep her waiting. She was already simmering and I wanted to put out the embers, not create a blaze.

My plan of attack was simple. I'd talk to her through an impromptu poem—all about her beauty and grace—give her a bath, bathing her body in exotically-scented bath water, and then show her how much she had been missed.

In fact, I didn't anticipate that we would be doing much talking at all.

CHAPTER 20

Marcel

I waited because Quinn wasn't done; she had merely paused for effect. I was reclined on her couch with one leg crossed over the other. She was standing near the entrance to the living room, arms folded across her chest. There was an almost imperceptible quiver in her voice when she had been speaking. So, I waited because there had to be more.

"I'm hoping that I didn't make a mistake with you, Marcel."

"Where is this coming from, beautiful?"

"Weren't you listening to anything I said?"

"I heard every single word."

"I don't share myself, emotionally or physically, with just anyone."

"I know that, Quinn. Where is this coming from?"

"You haven't been the same with me lately."

"Nothing has changed between us. I explained that I've taken on a few new clients and I thought you understood that, for at least a little while, we may see a little less of each other."

"I didn't think that meant I wouldn't hear your voice or see your face for over two weeks."

"At the time, I didn't believe so, either. You have to know that I would prefer to be with you over those knucklehead athletes. Now, come over here." I graced her with a contrite smile as I motioned for her to sit by my side. "What kind of fool would I be if I didn't want to spend every free moment I have with you?" When she got close enough, I extended my hand to her. She slowly linked her fingers with mine, sat down, and settled into the curve of my arm. I kissed her temple. "Isn't this better than you glaring at me from across the room?" I said teasingly.

"I was upset with you."

I kissed her neck. "Even if you're mad at me, I would prefer to have you by my side telling me why. I don't want there to be any distance between us."

Quinn craned her neck and looked up at me. "You can't simply say that, you have to mean it."

"I mean everything I say to you. You just need to stop doubting me."

When I had met Quinn, she shared that she hadn't dated anyone in almost two years. Her last man was in the Army reserves and had been shipped off to Landstuhl, Germany. Although he wanted to continue their relationship, she wasn't willing to endure a long distance situation. She cut him off and shut down emotionally. She focused on her career, refusing to entertain any brothers that stepped to her, that is, until I came along.

With Quinn, there was always a sense that she was struggling with some sort of internal conflict. Should she or shouldn't she give me her number? Does she or doesn't she let me come up to her apartment? Will she or won't she sleep with me? Is she or isn't she going to let her emotions run free? Am I or am I not keeping it real with her? I had been navigating Quinn's dual perceptions of our situation since day one.

That's who Quinn had become before I had even met her. Our few months together couldn't undo years of emotional and physical isolation. Nevertheless, I was doing my best to shape her into who I needed her to be—laid-back, available when I wanted to see her and non-confrontational. I did and said whatever I had to in order to accomplish that end.

"I don't doubt you," she replied.

I moved her from my side so I could see her face. "You're telling a big fat one."

Quinn let out a vibrant laugh, her first since I had arrived. "I'm not lying," she said, trying to stifle her laughter.

"You know I'm right. That's why you're laughing."

"Okay, you got me. But it's not so much that I doubt you, it's more like you make me doubt myself."

"How do I do that?"

"Because you're a charmer, Marcel. You're sexy, you always know the right thing to say, and when I'm near you, I'm melting inside."

Bingo. "You have the same effect on me. I can't understand why you still don't know that. I tell you all the time how amazing you are."

"I can't argue with that. You tell me what you think of me all the time. What you don't say is how you feel about me."

"Is that what this is about, feelings?"

"I guess it is."

"You don't know how I feel about you? I think I make it obvious."

"Most of the time I believe I know how you feel about me, but then you go missing for two weeks and—"

"And you start to doubt me."

"Yes," she said, barely above a whisper. "I start to doubt you."

I kissed the side of her face. "Don't you worry your pretty little head. When I'm with you, there's no place I'd rather be. Rest assured that when we're not together, it's only because I can't be in two places at one time."

I guess that made sense to Quinn because she snuggled closer to me. I held her tighter and figured I had better stop talking before she realized I hadn't really said anything at all.

CHAPTER 21

Camden

I had put off the inevitability of the conversation for as long as possible. I knew a public forum would be the best venue to keep Natalia in check. She could be a firecracker at times and I wasn't willing to take the risk of having this discussion at either one of our homes.

"I did not blow off your invitation or disregard you."

Natalia polished off her martini. "You made it seem that you would attend the wedding with me. The date rolls around and you're conveniently nowhere to be found."

"Let's be clear, Natalia. When you asked me on Fire Island whether I would escort you to the wedding, I informed you at that moment that I needed to check my schedule. I never confirmed with you that I could make it."

"You never said that you couldn't. I called you for weeks, only to be met by silence. Common courtesy, no, make that *decency*, would dictate some sort of response on your behalf."

"I'm not one for apologizing, but I offer you one if I gave you false expectations that I would be attending the wedding. However, I was out of the country for a few weeks, and that is the only reason why you had not heard from me. I wasn't avoiding, neglecting, or disregarding you. I was inaccessible while conducting business abroad."

"It's always business with you, isn't it, Camden?"

"Not always," I said, looking her directly in the eyes. "I don't want to talk, or even think, about business right now. Not when I'm sitting across from the most engaging woman in the restaurant. I can't keep my eyes off you. When I was in Paris, I had dinner with some business associates and a couple of them brought their wives along. All evening, I couldn't stop thinking how I wished you were by my side. I wanted nothing more than to show you off—your beauty and elegance. Their wives had nothing on you."

"Except for being wives," she said dryly.

"All right. What's it going to take?"

"For what?"

"What's it going to take for the ice to melt?"

"I have feelings, Camden. I'm not some cold, hardened ice queen."

"I know that. I wouldn't come bearing gifts for an ice queen." I reached into my suit jacket, removed a rectangular velvet box, and slid it across the table in front of Natalia.

She stared at it unmoving, a trace of a smile spreading on her lips. "What is it?"

"Open it."

Natalia grabbed the box from the table, excitement now clearly visible on her face. She inhaled. "Oh, my goodness." She looked up at me. "I love it."

"How's that for ice?" I asked.

She smiled as she delicately removed the diamond necklace from the jewelry box. "It matches the earrings and the bracelet you gave me."

"I wanted to complete the set and you deserve it." I knew I had to buy my peace when it came to Natalia. No amount of talking could make amends, but the right amount of ice always did the trick.

She touched her hand to her bare neck. "I want to wear it now. Could you put it on me?"

I scooted my chair back and walked around to her side of the table. She handed me the necklace and tilted her head forward. I put the sparkling five-carat peace offering around her neck, secured the clasp, then kissed her naked shoulder.

Natalia looked up at me and all traces of anger had evaporated. Even if she wanted to continue to complain, she wouldn't. She knew the rules of the game. I had paid generously for my infraction and she would let it go...until the next time.

CHAPTER 22

I walked Indiya from room to room, showing her around my home. I had finally decided to invite her to my house in Brookville. Over the past few weeks, I had wined and dined her, taken her to the movies and a Broadway show, gone to a couple of concerts and even a cooking class, since neither of us were cooks. I had been putting in work to impress Ms. Spencer. Of course that meant there were more than a few women who were unhappy with me at the moment.

"This is the yellow room," I said as I moved to the side so she could walk past me. "This is where I plan to dazzle you with the dinner I'm going to prepare tonight."

Indiya started laughing. "I'm sorry," she said, attempting to compose herself. "I couldn't hold it in anymore. What is with all this yellow, white, blue, and red room mumbo jumbo? This is a kitchen. Why can't you just call it a kitchen? We just left the living room. I get that everything is white, but come on, Avery. You're killing me with this pretentious pomp and circumstance."

"Pretentious? I thought you of all people could appreciate my living environment."

"See what I mean? Living environment…" she said, holding back another laugh. "I can appreciate your house. It's fabulous. I love the décor and everything you've done to it, assuming you did the decorating. But it's still a house; and that's what I'm going to call it, not a living environment."

I cracked a smile. "All right, Ms. Spencer. Have a seat at the table in my kitchen. I'm going to use my newly obtained cooking skills to make you the best dinner you have ever eaten."

"Now that's more like it."

"What are you drinking?"

"Whatever fancy wine you have in mind."

"I suppose I'm going to be subjected to nonstop jokes tonight."

"Not nonstop, but maybe a few more."

"Okay, but let me warn you, I may have a few of my own."

"Bring it. I can handle whatever you've got."

That time I laughed. Indiya was fond of double entendres. I was pretty good at not responding to her comments, but the more I ignored them, the more frequently she employed them. "I'll keep that in mind."

"You should," she said, with a wink.

"I hope you realize that I have never done this for any other woman."

"If that's the case, I hope I survive it."

"I was the one getting my hands dirty in our cooking class. You were too squeamish to touch the raw chicken."

"It was my job to cut up the vegetables and I was damn good at it."

I walked over to the counter and grabbed a knife, holding it out to Indiya. "All right, I've got some zucchini for you to slice."

"I didn't come here to be put to work."

"Don't you want to practice your newly acquired skills?"

She laughed. "Not really."

I went over to the table, pulled her from the chair, and nudged her toward the cutting board on the counter. "You're going to be my assistant tonight."

"After I'm done with this," she moved closer to me, "what else will I be assisting you with tonight?"

"Cleanup."

"You like to evade my advances."

"Those are advances?"

"You know what it is," she said, with her hand on her hip.

"The way I see it," I placed fresh dill next to the zucchini, "actions speak louder than words."

She nodded. "I can back up everything I say."

I handed her a knife. "Can you cut the zucchini in half-inch slices?"

"I can," she said matter-of-factly.

"I should hope so. You learned the proper technique in cooking class."

Indiya gazed at me for a beat. "I meant that I can back up what I say."

I went to the refrigerator and removed a package of chicken breasts. "I don't doubt it."

"I think I'm offended."

"Why? I only agreed with what you said."

"Because I was expecting you to say something flirty like 'prove it.' Not that you think I'm some sort of tramp."

"I don't recall saying all of that." I tried to stifle a laugh.

"Maybe not, but you didn't answer the way you were supposed to."

That time I did laugh. "Is that right?"

"If I say something flirty, then you should respond in kind."

"I'm a man of action, not unnecessary words."

"Here's a heads-up, Avery. You're going to need those words to get some action."

"You don't mince words, do you?"

"Haven't you learned that about me yet?"

"I'm learning."

"Yet, I don't feel I'm learning enough about you."

"What's there to learn?"

"I wish I knew. You're so damned guarded."

Definitely not the first time I had heard that I was guarded. That was the only way I was able to protect myself while growing up. I didn't have a mother to cry to when I was hurt or a father to show me how to manage my feelings and what it meant to be a man. I had myself. I taught me what it took to survive—staying two steps ahead of everyone else.

"What you see is what you get."

"Oh, I see. So there's nothing more to you than a handsome face and this nice house?"

"That's all I've shown you these past few weeks?"

"Damn, Avery!" she said, her voice elevated. "Stop answering my questions with a question."

"Then stop asking so many damned questions."

"What?"

I rinsed the last piece of chicken, then washed my hands. I dried my hands on a dishtowel and turned to Indiya, meeting her intense expression with a pointed one of my own. "Stop trying to figure me out, Indiya. This is me."

"I don't know what that means. What is you?"

"Everything I've shown you since we've met. We've been having a great time together."

"Yes, we're having fun—I'm not disputing that—but three weeks later, I'm not sure I know you any better."

"That hurts," I said, clutching my heart.

"Cut the theatrics. I'm being serious."

"I know, too serious."

"I don't think so, considering the amount of time I've been spending with you. And I still don't know your story."

"Sit down, Indiya." I went over to the table and sat, waiting for her to join me. She kept slicing the zucchini as if she hadn't heard me. "Please, come sit down."

She put down the knife and sat across from me. "Okay?"

"I'll admit that I'm not an open book like you. I don't like to dwell on the past and I hate rehashing things that have already transpired. I choose to live in the now." I paused to let what I had said sink in for a moment. "What we're doing is new. I want to get to know you as much as you want to know me. But you have to understand, this is me. What you see in front of you—right here, right now—is me. Not my past. Not my future. Not anything else you may be thinking. All I'm asking you to do is to take me as I am. Nothing more, nothing less."

I wasn't oblivious as to why Indiya kept prodding me to let her in more. She wanted reassurance. Most women wanted reassurance that the man she was about to become involved with was worth her time and effort. She wanted to know if I was worthy. Up to that point, I hadn't shown her that I wasn't, but she wanted my backstory. Well, that was a story that she would never get. I had been juggling identities for so long that I had actually become Julian, Marcel, and Camden. They had become me.

The first time I had ever introduced myself as Julian was unintentional. I had moved to New York a couple of months prior and was standing in front of my brownstone in Brooklyn, chatting with an attractive neighbor. A process server approached us attempting to execute a subpoena. He asked if I was Avery Woodson. I smiled at him, then my neighbor, and simply stated that I was Julian Efram, the new tenant. I told him that Avery Woodson must have been the previous resident because I was getting some of his mail in my box. The process server thanked me and went on his way. My neighbor ended our conversation with "It was nice to meet you, Julian" and thus he was made manifest. Out of necessity. Out of my need to protect myself and keep a low profile. At that moment, Avery had become Julian. I didn't feel guilt or regret. Instead, I felt a weight lift from my shoulders and I knew I would be all right.

"I'm accepting you at face value," she said slowly, "and I completely understand where you're coming from. I guess I'm used to something different, like having a little more context."

"That's important to you...a frame of reference."

"I need to know who I'm dealing with."

"You could see all of that if you'd stop looking backward." I reached across the table and took her hand in mine. "Get to know me in the here and now."

She smiled. "Fine, I will. Let's finish making dinner because I want to go to your blue room—or is it white room?—to watch a movie, drink your fancy wine, and see what else you have in store for me."

I didn't know what it was, but she had a way of making me feel self-conscious. I hadn't felt those emotions in a long time, not since I was with Courtney back in D.C. I shook it off and went to finish dinner, hoping I could deliver on the expectations I had set.

CHAPTER 23

I was stretched out on my back on the floor with my hands folded behind my head. Indiya was lying on the couch alongside me. She had the remote and was flipping through the channels on the flat screen. I was praying for her to find something to watch. She had been going through channel after channel for the past fifteen minutes. I closed my eyes and settled into the soft, shaggy white carpet, feeling like I was on the verge of drifting off. I opened my eyes when she climbed on top of me, straddling my body.

She leaned down and kissed my cheek. "Dinner was delicious. You should cook for me all the time."

"Did it take you this long to decide that you enjoyed it?"

"No, but I wanted to make you sweat." She gyrated her hips when she said that. "Do you like to sweat, Avery?"

I didn't respond and she intensified the twist in her hips. That elicited a smile and a low moan from me. She took that as her cue to reach for my belt buckle.

I grabbed her hand. "Indiya, wait."

She leaned forward and pressed her upper body against mine. "Wait for what? It's obvious your friend wants to come out and play." She placed her hands near my shoulders, grasped the carpet between her fingers, and ground on my hardness.

Reflexively, I grabbed her ass, pulling her down into me as I thrust against her. "Indiya—"

"Do that again." She started a syncopated popping motion. "I can feel you...so I know you want to."

I thrust again, holding her still while I ground into her. I watched her bite her bottom lip as she stared at me through partially closed eyelids. She was damn sexy. I pumped against her, steadily increasing my tempo. She let loose a high-pitched moan and my body reacted. If I didn't stop, I would come right then and there. That caught me off-guard because I knew how to control my flow.

I placed my hands on Indiya's hips and stopped moving. I lifted her and slid from beneath her, situating her beside me. "We should slow down."

She looked at my swollen dick straining against my pants. "You can't be serious."

I sat up and rested my back against the sofa. "We went from zero to a hundred in a matter of seconds."

"A hundred would be you and I naked with absolutely nothing left to the imagination."

"That's exactly why we need to chill. I don't want there to be any misunderstandings about why I invited you here."

"I know why you wanted me here—to show off your home." She grinned.

"I thought you wanted me to get to know the real you. That's what I'm trying to do."

"I get it. You're following my instruction. But you should know that the real me is not a nun."

"Apparently not."

"I think I'm offended again."

I laughed. "Don't be. I'm no saint either. Although tonight, we can both be on our best behavior."

"I was going to show you my best behavior."

"Indiya—"

"Instead, I'll resume channel surfing."

"Come over here." I patted the floor next to me.

She crawled up beside me. I pulled her closer, then turned her face to mine. I kissed her, soft and gentle. My tongue slipped inside her mouth and invited her to slow drag with me. We engaged in an unhurried exploration of each other's lips, tongues, and mouths. I was savoring the flavor of sweet wine from her lips, getting intoxicated on the taste of her. After a few minutes, I pulled away and gazed at her face.

Indiya opened her eyes. "That was nice…"

"…and slow." I finished her sentence.

"All right, we'll take it slow. So what do you want to watch on TV?"

"Whatever you choose, I'm open."

"How about a romantic comedy?"

"If that's what you want to watch."

"I don't; I just wanted to see what you'd say."

"Did I answer how I was supposed to that time?"

"Exactly."

"I guess that means I'm learning you and you're learning me."

My eyes popped open. The electronic display on the alarm clock read 2:38 AM. The room was too still. I felt the bed next to me. It was empty. I threw back the covers and climbed from the bed. I shuffled barefoot out of the room and down the hallway. The lights were off throughout the house, with the exception of the nightlight in the kitchen.

I entered the dimness and saw Indiya's silhouette near the stairs that led up to my office. She jumped when she saw me approaching.

"You almost gave me a heart attack." Indiya rested her hand on her chest. She was wearing the pajama top to the bottoms I had on.

"I woke up and you weren't there. I thought you might have left."

"I needed some water." She pointed to the bottle on the countertop. "I dropped the cap and it rolled near the steps. I couldn't find it and didn't want to turn on the light."

I looked toward the darkened staircase, then at Indiya. "You should've turned it on." I walked to the switch on the wall and flipped on the lights. She watched me as I meandered back to the staircase. I knelt down and picked up the bottle cap resting in the corner at the bottom of the stairs. I stood and tossed it onto the counter.

Indiya grabbed her bottle, finished off the water, and twisted the cap back on. "Thanks." She placed the empty bottle on the counter. "Sorry I woke you. I bet you wish you put me out when you had the chance."

"It was too late for you to be leaving. I'm glad you stayed." I took her by the hand, turned off the light, and headed back toward the bedroom. "If you need anything else, let me know and I'll get it for you."

"Anything?"

I nudged her toward the bed. "Go to sleep, Indiya."

CHAPTER 24

Marcel

Roxi was already on stage performing when I entered the club. I could hear her in the lobby doing a lively call and response with the audience. She had left a ticket for me and backstage pass to meet her after the show at will-call. The short, muscular security guard puffed up his chest when I approached. I flashed my ticket, then held out my arms for him to frisk me. He gave me the all-clear with a silent nod and I strolled into the darkened performance room.

Roxi's single was getting significant airplay and the club was packed with her new fans. I squeezed through the standing room only crowd, knocking into raised cell phones recording the show. YouTube would be flooded with shaky, amateur videos by the end of the night. I managed to make it up front and positioned myself off to the side of the stage.

The R&B diva belted out a song about feeling good and living free. I nodded to the music. She worked the crowd, stepping to the edge of the stage and touching hands while she sang. As she moved down toward the end where I was standing, she spotted me and her face lit up. Her smile broadened as she reached out to grab my hand. She gave it a squeeze, then sauntered back to the middle of the stage. I watched that saunter with reminiscent pride. Her body was tight in her fitted golden dress. It stopped mid-thigh, but had a long, flowing train that trailed down one side, stopping at her ankle. The shoes, strappy and skyscraper high. Her playful faux-hawk provided an unobstructed view of her hypnotic eyes and adorable face.

"Hold it! Hold it!" she shouted into the microphone to her band. The music came to an abrupt halt. "Let's switch it up, boys. I'm feeling kind of irie."

The band picked up the music immediately and a reggae beat filled the room. Roxi closed her eyes and swayed to the rhythm as the band played the deep island groove. "Did y'all hear what I said?" She looked out into the audience. "I said I'm feeling kinda i-riiie." She rotated her hips slower, working them to the beat. "Is anybody out there feeling irie?" The audience roared. "Who's feeling irie?" The crowd screamed again. "Is it you?" She pointed at someone in the front. "You?" she asked, walking the length of the stage. "Or maybe it's you." She stopped in front of me and held out her hand. "Why don't you come on up here and show me how irie you're feeling."

The audience went crazy. I smiled and raised my hand in a subtle gesture to decline. I recognized the song. It was the same tune that had her dancing for me in my living room.

"I guess he's not feeling irie tonight." The crowd unleashed a barrage of boos.

The dude standing next to me gave me an elbow in the side, with an expression that said I was crazy. I chuckled.

Roxi continued to scan the crowd. "How about you? Come on up here with me." A brother positioned up front at the opposite end made his way onto the stage. She led him front and center for all to see. "Show me what you got." She had a sexy smile on her face as she watched the brother begin a slow wine. "Ladies, what do you think?"

The women cheered. Roxi stepped up to the brother and

danced with him. She turned her back to him and wrapped his arms around her waist as she began to sing the lyrics to the song. He followed her every hip dip, with a shit-eating grin that signaled he was having the best time of his life. As she sang, he moved his hands from her waist and touched her hair, stroked her shoulders, even rested his hands on the curve of her hips. The brother was getting carried away.

I tensed as I watched. Roxi didn't flinch. She performed for the audience and moved with that cat like he was the man she was singing about. It wasn't until the song ended, and she escorted the brother off stage, that I realized I was clenching the backstage pass in my hand. The laminated tag was permanently bent in half after I released my grip on it.

An hour later, the show was over and the club was jumping. The DJ was spinning and the dance floor was overrun with partygoers. I went to the bar for a drink before making my way backstage to see Roxi. I eavesdropped on a couple of conversations and the consensus was that the girl definitely had talent.

I held up my pass to security and headed down the hall to her dressing room. I rapped on the door before entering.

Roxi was seated in a chair in front of a lighted mirror, taking pins out of her hair. Kneeling in front of her, taking off one of her heels, was the dude that she had pulled onstage.

I hesitated for a beat, then approached Roxi, giving her a kiss on the cheek. "Great show, babe."

The dude looked up and then at Roxi. She cleared her throat. "Thank you, Marcel. This is Dark, my manager." Dark slid off her shoe, barely paused to give me a pound, then started on her other foot. "I put on these long fingernails for the show and I can't do anything with them. Poor Dark had to put on and take off my shoes because I can't work the clasp."

Dark removed the shoe, placing one hand gently on her calf as he pulled. He placed the shoe next to the first. "Rox, I'll be at the bar. Text me when you're done changing and I'll come get you, so we can do a quick walk through the crowd before we leave."

"I can bring her over to you at the bar," I said.

"That's all right; it's my job. Text me, Rox." He turned and left the room.

Roxi smiled at me. "So, you really enjoyed the show?"

"It was amazing."

"You don't sound too convincing."

"You were absolutely phenomenal and completely in your element."

"Why didn't come onstage with me?"

"I'm a low-key guy."

"I kept it low-key." She laughed.

"Do you do that at all your shows?"

"What? Pull a guy onstage?"

"Yeah."

"Only if I know someone in the audience that I can bring up. But you turned me down, which was a first."

"Your manager was more than happy to oblige you."

Her brow wrinkled. "Well, I wasn't going to pull a stranger up there with me. Dark was my impromptu Plan B. As my manager, he couldn't say no. He knows how that part of the show is supposed to go and he knew how to play up to the crowd."

"Seems like you have the perfect manager."

"It sounds like you're jealous, but I know that can't be the case, since you haven't checked for me in weeks." Roxi smirked. "Help me with this zipper, please. These nails..." She stood up and turned to the side. A zipper ran the length of the dress from her underarm to her hip.

I stepped behind her, letting my body brush against hers. "You've been busy performing. I didn't think you would have time for me." I touched my lips to the curve where her neck and shoulders met.

She tilted her head to the side, providing me with full access. "That's bullshit, Marcel. You know it and I know it. But it's okay because I'm a big girl and I know what this is."

I unzipped her dress and worked it down her body. I should've known she had nothing on underneath—the dress had been painted on so smoothly. Her full breasts were perfectly upright as if suspended by invisible strings. She was hairless down below, which was a surprise. The last time I had seen her naked, she had a Brazilian with a small landing strip. I let her dress drop to the floor and filled my hands with her breasts. She leaned her head back against my chest, while I massaged her. My hand traveled lower, parted her lips, and began to stroke her clit. Her breathing sped up. I took that as my cue to slip my middle finger inside of her.

Roxi grabbed my hand and held it still, pressing me firmly against her. She exhaled a shaky breath. "Not now. I have to get out there."

She reluctantly moved her hand from mine and I slowly extracted my finger from inside her. She turned around and pecked me on the lips before grabbing a small bag and rushing into the adjoining bathroom.

I picked up her dress and placed it on a hanger on the garment rack. I sat in the chair she had been in earlier, my eyes surveying the room. The dressing room was filled with flowers and gift baskets, probably from label executives and family.

She emerged from the bathroom in a strapless push-up bra and a black thong. She stood in front of the mirror, applied some red lipstick, then fluffed her hair with her fingers. "I have a show in Atlantic City tomorrow night; you should join me."

"I wish I could, but I have to prepare for client meetings."

The door opened and Dark stepped into the dressing room. He tapped his watch. "Rox, let's go."

"I'll be ready in a second."

Dark went to sit on the couch across the room and pulled out his phone.

Roxi hurried to the garment rack and snatched a pair of skin-tight, leather-like leggings from the hanger. She stepped into them, jumping up and down to pull them on.

Dark looked up. "You need help?"

"Nope. I got it."

I looked from Dark to Roxi. I didn't know what was going on—if anything—but I knew I didn't like it. "When will you be back in New York?"

She pulled a tank top over her head and tugged the tight fabric over her abdomen. "After Atlantic City, I'm headed to D.C., Charlotte, Atlanta, and then Texas. Dark, when are we back?"

He didn't look up from his phone. "A week and a half."

Roxi slipped her feet into a pair of high pumps. "A week and a half." She came over to me and kissed me quickly on the cheek. "I'll call you when I get back."

Dark stood up, went to the door, and held it open for her. She rushed out of the dressing room without a second glance in my direction. Dark gave me a head nod, then shut the door behind them.

I tossed my backstage pass on the dressing table and exited stage left.

CHAPTER 25

Camden

I t had been twenty minutes since I had shouted up the staircase to let Hazelle know if she didn't hurry we would miss the opening act. We were going to the theater to see *Ma Rainey's Black Bottom*. Hazelle had a love for August Wilson's work and invited me to join her for opening night.

I could admit I wasn't the most patient man—I didn't like to wait on anyone or anything—and Hazelle was testing my limits. She had secured the tickets so she was more than aware of what time the show started. She needed to wrap up whatever prepping was going on if we were to have the slightest chance of making it on time.

Forty minutes in, I poured myself a drink from her bar. I needed to take the edge off or the evening would be unsalvageable. After fifty minutes, I was perched on the couch, bouncing my foot, glass drained. When my watch registered that I had been waiting an hour, I called up to her again. When she didn't answer, I headed upstairs.

I briskly walked down the hall, peering into rooms looking for Hazelle. I continued down the hall and heard faint laughter coming from the last room on the right. I pushed open the door and stepped into the bedroom. She was sprawled across the bed in a robe, watching television. She had a glass of champagne in one hand and a strawberry in the other. The opened bottle was chilling on ice on her bedside table.

"Hazelle, what the hell are you doing?"

"Having a bit of strawberries and champagne," she said, without even looking at me.

"I've been waiting for you for over an hour and you're up here watching TV?" I felt the heat creep up the back of my neck. "We're going to miss the opening act."

"There is no opening act," she replied casually, then took a bite of her strawberry.

I positioned myself between Hazelle and her mounted television. "What are you talking about?"

"Sit down, Camden. I can't see."

I didn't move. "I don't give a damn if you can see or not. What the hell is going on?"

Hazelle sipped her drink, then put the glass on the table. "No one likes waiting, Camden. Especially me. Weeks ago, you unceremoniously dumped me at my friends' home and disappeared like you were in the Witness Protection Program. I was concerned because you said you had an emergency and would explain later. I'm still waiting. I didn't appreciate that one bit." She grabbed her glass. "I don't have tickets for any play this evening. I wanted you to experience discourteousness at its finest."

"So you abandon me downstairs with no plan whatsoever to come out of this room?"

"I was curious to know how long you would wait."

I nodded, my nostrils flaring. "Now you know. Enjoy your evening." I turned to leave the room.

"Before you leave…"

I looked back over my shoulder. Hazelle was untying the sash on her robe. I paused in the doorway. She spread her robe and revealed a sheer black teddy. I stared at her, my anger slowly subsiding. "Hazelle, I don't like playing games."

"I'm not sure I believe that."

"Believe it."

She slipped out of the robe. "I talked an awful lot about you that night at Peter and Toni Ann's."

"Is that right?"

"My constant bragging on you had pretty much intrigued the Harvard crew and they're determined to find out more about you."

"I'm flattered," I said, my voice monotone.

"I, on the other hand, enjoy a bit of mystery. I had hoped that you would come back for me. I wanted to take you home to show you all of this." She stood up and walked over to me. "I think we've both waited long enough. Are you really going to leave when the fun is about to begin?"

"Yes." I kissed her on the forehead. "I'm not in the mood for games. Enjoy your evening."

Hazelle had left me no choice. I didn't have patience for her antics and, more importantly, I didn't like anyone poking around to find out about me. I walked out and left her standing in the middle of the room with her lingerie, strawberries, and champagne.

I gave her a reason not to wonder or wait anymore.

CHAPTER 26

"Funds transferred" flashed at the bottom of the computer screen. One hundred thousand dollars into the account of Avery Woodson. I unlocked my safe and removed my ledger. I entered the transaction along with the confirmation number, then returned the book full of my financial records to the safe. I tried to refrain, but couldn't stop myself from taking out the aging picture of my mother. I had her eyes and lips. I could only guess that my nose was like my father's, whoever he may have been. I wondered if she were dead or alive. How she could abandon her child and never look back, I'd never understand, no matter how hard I tried.

I flipped through my Rolodex, then picked up the phone and dialed Mr. Charles.

He answered on the third ring. "Charles speaking."

"Mr. Charles, it's Avery Woodson."

"Avery, how are you? I had you on my list of people to call today."

"I'm all right," I said, gazing at the photo. "I was anxious to hear whether you found anything on my mother."

"I've been able to cobble together a trail of residences for her. It seems that after she left you at the orphanage, she lived in New Jersey for a while. Next, she headed to Virginia, down to South

Carolina, and then Indiana where I found an arrest record for a domestic dispute. I think she may have changed her identity before moving on because her trail went cold."

My pulse raced. "Does that mean you won't be able to find her?"

"Oh, no, that's not what I was trying to convey at all. This is merely one limb of the tree. I have many limbs and branches yet to explore. Between my team and me, we are dedicated to providing you with some answers. It may take some time, though."

"I understand. Thanks for the update, Mr. Charles."

"I'll be in touch."

I hung up the phone and continued to look at my mother's smiling face. She had to be out there somewhere. If she was, what kind of life was she living? Was she living comfortably or out on the streets? If I ever got the chance to meet her, I didn't know what I'd say. I wasn't even sure if I wanted her in my life, but I knew that I wanted her to live in comfort. That was the one thing I could guarantee her—a life of comfort. As a teen, she obviously couldn't provide for me. I hoped that her life had improved throughout the years.

If there was one lesson I learned from a mother I never knew, it was to be self-sufficient, resourceful, and accountable to no one. I was all of that and more.

CHAPTER 27

Julian

When I walked through the door, I pecked Miko on the lips and headed straight toward the living room. Romel was perched in the window ledge with one foot up, staring in my direction. I sat on the sofa furthest from her and looked back at Miko as she came into the room.

"I thought it was common courtesy for someone to speak when they enter a room," Romel said.

"Good to see you, Romel."

"Isn't it always?"

I ignored her question and turned my attention to Miko. "You didn't tell me you had company when I called."

"I don't consider Romel company. Besides, you know she's always here."

Miko was the only one amused at her attempt at a joke. Romel's eyes hadn't left me from the moment I sat down. They were transfixed, like she was trying to bore a hole through me. Miko sat on the couch next to me, linked her arm through mine and rested her head on my shoulder.

This wasn't the type of evening I had in mind. I was going to come by, put in a couple of hours with Miko, and then head to the lounge for a little spoken word. I cleared my throat and shifted in my seat. "So what are you ladies getting into tonight?"

"I thought we could go see a movie; we haven't done that in quite a while."

"I don't think there's anything in the theater worth seeing."

"That is so not true, Julian. Let me get the newspaper and see what's playing." Miko unhooked herself from me and went to get the paper.

"She loves her some Julian."

The sarcasm in Romel's voice and smirk on her lips instantly grated on my nerves. "The feeling is mutual."

"Who are you kidding? I know better than that…from personal experience."

"All you know is that if you dangle a carrot in front of a rabbit, it's going to nibble."

"I beg to differ. You're not a rabbit. You could have chosen not to indulge."

"There aren't too many men that will pass up what's easy."

Romel opened her mouth to respond, but Miko interrupted when she re-entered the room. "You're right, Julian, there isn't anything good in the movies."

"That's what I said." I smiled. "When are you going to learn to trust me?"

"I do trust you, snookum wookums." Miko grabbed my face, leaned down and gave me an exaggerated kiss.

Romel rolled her eyes. "Really, Miko?"

Miko let go of my face and turned to her friend. "Yes, really. I can show my man affection if I feel like it."

"Do you have to be so nauseating about it?"

"I know what the problem is. We need to find you a man to get kissy-faced with."

Romel narrowed her eyes at Miko. "Oh, yeah? Well, maybe Julian can introduce me to one of his friends. He must know a fine, tall brother like himself."

"Unfortunately, I don't. My circle is tight and I don't know anyone who fits that bill."

"What a shame. I was convinced you would know someone that would love to get with all of this." She posed like she was taking a picture.

Miko looked from Romel to me. "He really doesn't associate with many people, Romel. We're on our own if we're going to find you a man."

Romel laughed. "I'm not looking. If I want a man, I know how and where to find one. It's not that difficult. As a matter of fact, it's easy. Right, Julian?"

"You're an attractive woman. You shouldn't have any problem in that department, but you don't need me to tell you that."

"You're right, I don't," she said, with an edge to her voice. "I'm smart, sexy, and I know how to satisfy a man…in the bedroom, outside of the bedroom, hell, even in a club bathroom."

"Romel!" Miko shrieked.

"I'm just being honest."

"You don't have to be so honest in front of Julian. Save that discussion for girl talk."

"I haven't said anything that he shouldn't hear. Besides, I'm sure Julian understands discretion. In fact, I would like to get the male perspective from him on that situation I told you about."

Miko shook her head. "Oh, no. Come on, Romel."

"Why not? He can tell me what he thinks I should do."

"Fine, go ahead. It's your business." Miko looked embarrassed for her friend.

I went still. There was something in Romel's expression that I didn't like. Every bone in my body told me it was time to leave. I started to get up. "I can get out of your hair if you two need some time for girl talk."

"No, sit down. I want your opinion on a situation I'm dealing with."

Miko looked at me and shrugged. Reluctantly, I eased back down onto the couch. "I'm listening."

"I'm just going to cut to the chase. I wasn't kidding when I said I can please a man in a club bathroom. Not too long ago, that's exactly what I did."

I swallowed and I would swear it could be heard clear across the room. "Okay…"

"And it was sooo good—"

"Romel."

"Let me tell the story, Miko. Anyway, it was amazing for both of us. I've been with him a few times since, but not in the way I would like. Because of the way we got together, I'm not sure if it will ever go any further."

"Don't forget to mention that he has a girl," Miko chimed in.

I silently gazed at Romel. My expression was unreadable, but, inside, my blood was coursing through my veins like a lava stream.

"Yeah, he has a girl, but I don't think he cares about her." Romel's neck rolled. "Otherwise, why would he be messing around with me? I'm convinced he knows he should be with me."

"Then why isn't he?"

"Can I ask Julian my question, please?"

"What's the question, Romel?" The bass and gravity in my voice caused Miko to look at me, her brow furrowed.

"I want to know two things. Does this man truly love his woman if he's cheating with me? You know what? Don't even answer that. I know the deal. Answer this, if you were him, would you be with me even though I sexed you when I knew you had a woman?"

"Probably not." I stood up to go.

"That's it? You're not going to explain?"

"No man wants a woman he can't trust." I looked at her for an instant, long enough to see her face crack. I reached out and stroked Miko's cheek. "I don't do girl talk. Call you later."

Miko searched my face, then eyed Romel suspiciously before she nodded at me. They may have been two very different women, but at that moment, they had one thing in common—the same uncertain look on their face.

I swiftly departed before they got a burning desire to question me further and an interrogation ensued.

CHAPTER 28

Avery

I was reclined on a lounge chair in the middle of my backyard, a small table next to me with a bottle of beer on it, sweating in the heat. I had been spending more time than usual in Long Island since I had met Indiya. I couldn't remember the last time I relaxed in the sun in my own yard.

The landscapers did an excellent job on the upkeep of the property; they were paid well enough to do so. The grass was green and well-manicured. I had to pull the lawn furniture out of the shed since it hadn't been set up since the previous summer. After lugging out piece after piece, I was hot as hell. I settled into my recliner and closed my eyes, short-sleeved shirt unbuttoned, wearing a pair of cargo shorts.

Indiya was in the chair next to me, ponytail in a knot, a pair of booty shorts, a bikini top, and glistening with baby oil. She was reading a fashion magazine. Every once in a while, she would ask me what I thought of something. I would give my opinion without opening my eyes. The harder she laughed, the more I knew my comment didn't make sense for the picture she had flashed in front of me. Only then would I peek at the magazine and end up laughing myself.

I took a swig of my beer. The only thing that was missing was a barbeque grill. I had never felt the need to have one, but sitting in the yard with Indiya made me think I should. If we were going to be out in the yard sipping drinks and chilling in the sun, a grill only made sense. It sort of completed the picture. I reflected for a moment and was a little caught off-guard. I was thinking about doing something for Indiya and me. I hadn't realized until that moment that there was an Indiya and me.

Admittedly, I hadn't spoken to Roxi, Hazelle, Miko or Romel in a couple of weeks. Quinn and Natalia, I texted a few days ago. Yet, I spoke to Indiya every day and had been increasingly spending more time with her. When I was with her, the others rarely crossed my mind.

"What are you smiling about?"

I looked over and she was peering at me. "I didn't know that I was."

"Well, you were." She closed her magazine and sat up. "I just had a great idea. We should go to London Fashion Week."

"When is it?"

"In a couple of months."

"Let me know the specific dates and where you want to stay and I'll take care of the arrangements."

"It's like that?"

"I don't know of any other way."

"I hope you're not giving me lip service."

"Why would I do that?"

"Maybe you're just big talking and we won't end up going any-where."

"You want to go; we're going. Get me the information." I closed my eyes and returned to my state of silence, but not before catching a glimpse of her beaming as she sat back with her magazine.

Fashion Week didn't mean a thing to me, but, as a buyer for Saks, it had to be a can't-miss event for Indiya. I'd fly her to London and show her an amazing time. Maybe the trip would help get my mother off my mind. Thinking about her too much was never a good thing. London would be a welcome distraction.

"This heat is brutal."

I opened my eye a sliver to see her fanning with her magazine. "Do you need another bottle of water?"

"No, but I would love some ice cream."

"There's vanilla in the freezer."

"I'm a strawberry girl. I'm dying for three scoops of strawberry ice cream with whipped cream and nuts."

"Does that mean I have to get up from my comfortable chair to go on an ice cream run?"

"Come on, Avery. All you have to do is put your chest away, I mean button your shirt, and take me." She laughed.

"You got jokes."

"You might as well say yes or I'll keep right on bugging you."

"There are fresh strawberries in the fridge and whipped cream; you can make your own. I even have nuts."

"I know you do and I bet they're big ones, too."

"Let's go." I started buttoning my shirt. "The quicker I take you, the faster I can get back to my relaxation."

"I should have known that all I had to do was say something kinky to get you to do what I want."

"I'll show you kinky…"

"I wish you would. I've been waiting long enough."

"C'mon. Let's get this ice cream."

There was no disputing it was one of the hottest days of the year. I ended up getting a pint of chocolate ice cream for myself. Indiya headed straight to the kitchen for a spoon and I hoped she didn't forget to put my ice cream in the freezer.

The mailman had apparently come while we were out. He haphazardly left letters sticking out of the box, hadn't even bothered to close the door on the mailbox. Before we walked in, I grabbed what was in there and tucked it beneath my arm. While Indiya busied herself in the kitchen, I quickly flipped through the envelopes.

I passed through the kitchen, giving her a wink, then headed upstairs to my office. I unlocked the door with my key and immediately closed it tight behind me. I tossed the letters on my desk to open later. If Indiya was over, I didn't spend any real time in the office. A few minutes here, a few minutes there. I checked the messages on the phone, jotted down a couple of notes, and then locked the door on my way out.

Indiya had already vacated the kitchen and was probably out back in the yard. I checked the freezer and my ice cream wasn't in there. I shook my head. Indiya must have taken my ice cream out back with her and had it sitting in the hot sun, melting away. I went to the back door and was about to step out when I realized she wasn't in the yard. I called out to her, but didn't get a response. I traveled back down the hallway, looking in each room, but didn't see her. When I got to my bedroom, the door was closed. I eased it open and stepped inside the room. My eyes scanned down, then up, and down again.

Indiya cleared her throat, then let her towel drop. "It was too hot outside. I took a cool shower and now I'm ready for my ice cream. I brought yours in here too. It's on the dresser."

I stood speechless, taking her in. We had been dating for a minute and she stayed over frequently, but I hadn't seen her in all of her glory. At least not like that. We had been playing it safe, respecting one another's boundaries, merely taking our time to learn each other. The vision that stood before me was nothing short of perfection. Toned voluptuousness was the best way to describe what was flooding my field of vision.

I inched forward, moving further into the room. "I think I need a shower now."

Indiya approached me, with measured steps. She reached out and started undoing the buttons on my shirt. I was still, looking down on her nakedness. Admiring how her hair cascaded over her shoulders. I shrugged my shirt off as she pulled the sleeves down my arms. She was gazing at me, but I kept my eyes on her breasts, how they moved gently as she worked the drawstring and zipper on my shorts. She pushed them down, letting her breasts brush against me. My dick flexed.

She bit her bottom lip and smiled. "The ice cream is melting," she said, pushing me toward the bathroom. "Hurry up."

I looked back over my shoulder before going into the bathroom. I didn't rush, but I moved with purpose. All sorts of thoughts ran through my head as I showered. This was probably the longest I had waited to be with a woman—ever—and I didn't have the usual sense of excitement. It was a different feeling altogether. If I didn't know better, it almost felt like I was nervous. That couldn't be. I didn't get nervous about having sex with a woman for the first time. That wasn't my style. I shook it off and washed the soap from my body. Clean and dry, I wrapped the towel around my waist and entered the bedroom.

Indiya was sitting at the foot of the bed, legs crossed, palms flat on either side of her. "You don't need that towel." She uncrossed her legs. "Come closer."

I stood directly in front of her. She untucked the towel and tossed it aside. My body reacted and my dick was on the rise. She stood up and hugged my body to hers. My heartbeat sped up. She wrapped her arms tighter around me and I pulled her against me. Every inch of her body touched mine. The softness of her breasts made me lean back, so I could touch them.

"Your breasts are beautiful." I bent down to suck one of them into my mouth. "And they taste good, too."

"Let me get the ice cream." She went over to the dresser, filled her mouth with the melting dessert, and then returned to me. She shared her strawberry kiss with me. She licked my lips, sucking any remnant that her cool kiss had left behind.

The ice cream was cute, but I wasn't in the mood to play. I had kept myself in check and bottled up my desire for Indiya since we had met, ever since she asked if I wanted to get to know the real her. We had toyed with one another, usually her taunting me, but never crossed the line. I was done with holding back.

I pulled her down on the bed, positioning her on top of me as we sank into the softness. I raked my fingers through her hair, smoothing it to the side, over her shoulder. I lured her closer, touching my lips to the nape of her neck. Gently, I licked her throat, then lightly sucked on her skin. She nudged my face with her own. I kept sucking until she craned her neck to the side, giving me total access. A subtle smile settled on her lips. I lay back and watched her. Eyes closed, expectantly waiting for what was next, it was the most beautiful I had ever seen her.

Her lids fluttered open. "Is something wrong?" she asked, voice soft, barely above a whisper.

I stared into those questioning eyes and couldn't speak. I reached up, cupped the back of her head, and showed her that everything was right. My kiss drank from the deepest part of her. Unhurried yet urgent, I drank and I drank. When we pulled apart, her expression told me that she felt everything I didn't say.

I rolled her over, pinning her body beneath mine. Indiya spread her legs and I nestled between them. I was knocking on her door and she was ready to open it. I held my penis and entered her gradually, in one steady push, until I filled her up completely. Her wetness, combined with her tightness, made me want to stay inside of her. I didn't want to withdraw. I laid my chest against hers and pushed deeper. Her pussy was so warm and comforting; I didn't want to come out.

Again, I pushed and she tightened around me. A whimper-type sound escaped me and I almost didn't realize that I was the one who made it. I thrust a little harder, then shakily drew out to my tip. She reached up and captured my face between her hands. She kissed me as I re-entered her, wrapping her legs around my waist. I dipped in and out with an upward swing. She moaned into my mouth. I pulled away from her kiss as my breathing became more labored.

Without breaking stride, I placed her legs over my shoulders—I wanted to hit that spot. She tensed slightly, then relaxed with each thrust. I wouldn't go too deep or too hard, not in this position, unless she asked me to. The faster I pumped, the wetter she got.

Indiya moved her legs from my shoulders and I rolled us over. She straddled my body and immediately eased down on my dick. I grasped her hips and watched as she rolled them to an unheard rhythm. I closed my eyes because feeling her ride me was enough. If I looked at the sway of her body and the sensuous way she tossed her hair, I wouldn't be lasting long.

"Let me give it to you from the back," I said in between breaths.

"Not yet. This feels so good."

Indiya was definitely working it. I toppled her to the side so that she was lying beside me. She threw one of her legs over my hip and we rocked back and forth. The pressure was building; I wanted to come so badly. I pulled her to the edge of the bed. I stood at the foot as she got on all fours. I slid inside. She gasped and I pulled her into my dick, making her scream out. I clutched her waist and drew her to me over and over. I thrust at a steady pace, my knees starting to buckle. I looked down at my dick getting swallowed in her pussy. It was glistening. She contracted around me, then released her juices all over me. I continued pumping until I couldn't hold it anymore. I came in a mad rush of heat.

We collapsed next to each other, our breathing sounding louder than it was. I stretched my hand out and linked my fingers with Indiya's. "Are you good?" I asked.

"Damn good."

"Next time, it'll be better."

"You mean you were holding out on me?"

"Not quite. More like struggling to keep it together."

Indiya laughed. "I couldn't tell. I am more than satisfied."

Again, she had me doing the male version of a blush. I couldn't put a finger on why I was responding to her like I did. I was actually lying beside her wondering if she really enjoyed the sex. I made her come, but did I rock her world? I couldn't ask again because that would make me look insecure. The only thing I could do was to hit her with round two and freak her like she had never been freaked before.

I awoke to the smell of something burning. I sprang up, scanning the room quickly as I jumped from the bed and ran out of the room. The smoke alarm was chirping and Indiya was in the kitchen, fanning smoke with a dish towel. A skillet with a singed salmon filet was in the sink, water running over it.

I rushed to open the window, coughing while trying to let some fresh air in to clear the smoke away. The sun was setting, so a warm breeze flowed through the screen. I turned to Indiya and looked her over. She was in one of my T-shirts, hair up, feet bare. "Are you alright?"

"This is what I get for trying to make you dinner. I don't belong in a kitchen."

I went over to the sink and turned off the water. "What happened in here?"

"I called myself making you pan-seared salmon. I was going to wake you up with a delicious dinner. Obviously, that went wrong." She came up beside me at the sink. "I thought I had everything under control. I rinsed off the fish. Turned the pan on high and dropped it in."

My head cocked to the side. "High?"

"Yes, isn't that what I was supposed to do?"

"You didn't put a little olive oil in the pan like we did in our cooking class?"

Indiya cringed. "I guess I forgot that part."

I drained the water from the pan, then took it over to the trash can to scrape the remnants of burnt fish into the bag. "I know I'm not an expert in the kitchen, but you have to watch food closely while you're cooking. What were you doing?"

"I was watching it," she said, looking down at her feet like a scolded child.

My eyes traveled around the kitchen. Everything seemed to be in place.

I tossed the pan back into the sink, squirted a little dish detergent in it, and added some warm water to let it soak. "You got a brother butt-ass naked in the kitchen, throwing away some black-ass, burnt-up fish."

We both laughed.

"I'm sorry, Avery."

"It's alright, babe." I dried my hands on the dish towel and kissed the tip of her nose. "Even though you almost burned my house down, I appreciate the effort."

"I really was trying to make you a delicious dinner."

"Was there anything else to go with the burnt fish?"

"Avery!" she shouted, stomping her foot at the same time.

"Well, was there?" I wasn't planning to let her live the incident down.

"I cut up lettuce and tomato for a salad. It's in the fridge." She was pouting as she motioned toward the refrigerator.

"Then it sounds like we're having salad for dinner. I think there's Italian bread in the breadbox and I'll open a bottle of red wine. Don't worry. We can salvage your first attempt at making dinner. Let me throw on a pair of shorts and I'll be right back."

I left Indiya in the kitchen and laughed to myself all the way down the hall. I think I was better off that the fish burned. No seasoning. Dry pan. That meal was destined to be a major flop. Luckily for me, she couldn't do much damage to lettuce and tomato; at least I hoped not. I supposed anything could be ruined.

CHAPTER 29

Marcel

I knocked again, growing a little impatient, because I heard voices and there was no mistaking Quinn's lighthearted giggle. The lock turned from the inside and the door opened a crack. Quinn peered through the opening, then threw the door open. She was holding a cell phone to her ear and the smile she was wearing quickly disappeared.

"Let me call you back, okay?" She ended her call, then wearily peered at me.

A large, floppy stuffed dog was tucked beneath my arm. "Happy Birthday, Quinn." Silence. "Can I come in?"

She stepped to the side so I could enter the apartment. I took it upon myself to head into the living room. She followed behind me. I propped the overstuffed animal on her sofa.

"What are you doing here, Marcel?"

"I promised to show you a good time for your birthday."

"That was months ago."

"I keep my promises."

"I haven't heard from you in nearly a month. Why would you think I was going anywhere with you on my birthday?"

"Well, you're in that black dress and those high heels. Your purse is over on the table. It's obvious you're going somewhere. I figured it had to be with me since we had plans."

Her mouth fell open. "You're kidding, right? I would not and do not want to spend my birthday with you. Obviously, you've been pre-occupied these days and didn't have time for me. Well, now I feel the same about you."

"Then why are you all dressed up?"

"You are not the only person I know, Marcel. I'm going out tonight, but, of course, you can see that."

"Where are you going?"

"To dinner and then a lounge."

"Would you like an escort?"

"No, thank you."

A rap on the door halted our discussion. Quinn went to find out who was persistently knocking up and down the door frame. She came back into the living room with company. Dude was a little beneath my height, wearing a well-tailored suit and carrying a bouquet of roses.

He handed her the flowers. "These are for you, happy birthday." A hug and a kiss on the cheek was her thank you.

I watched the exchange and wondered a few things, but I was about to get the answer to my biggest question. I extended my hand to him. "Hey, bro, I'm Marcel."

He exaggeratedly looked down at my hand before reciprocating the gesture. "Tony." He turned to Quinn. "So this is Marcel?"

I was at a disadvantage and slightly annoyed. "How do you know Quinn, Tony?"

Quinn jumped in, "Tony, you don't have to answer that. Let me grab my purse and I'll meet you down in the car."

Tony nodded and left Quinn and me to settle our business.

"So you're rolling with that dude?"

"You're a little late with this performance, Marcel."

"Performance?"

"Let's not go there, okay? It's a little too late for any of this."

"I just wanted to make sure that you were all right and didn't want to leave you hanging on your birthday."

"You left me hanging a long time ago."

I resignedly smiled. "So, you're good?"

"I'm more than good."

"That's all I wanted to know." I leaned over and kissed her cheek. "You and Tony have a good night. Enjoy your birthday."

Dude was double-parked in front of the building. He was staring at the door when I came out. He rolled down the passenger window and as I passed by, he shouted, "Is Quinn coming down?"

I looked at him and kept going. I knew Quinn wasn't going out to celebrate with me. I just didn't feel like being the bad guy. I wanted her to feel like she had ended our situation on her own terms, not that I had dumped her without a second thought. She was a sweet girl and I didn't want to be responsible for her losing all hope in men.

CHAPTER 30

Camden

I scanned the racks. I didn't necessarily need new clothes, but I figured it couldn't hurt to pick up a few things. I was trying to decide between a pale yellow and a tangerine polo shirt. I wasn't sure if I was a fan of either color, but thought maybe I could make it work with a pair of white shorts.

"Either one would look good on you, Camden."

I spun around. "Natalia. What a surprise."

"You certainly look like it is."

I hung the shirts back on the rack and gave her a hug. I didn't have all day to trifle with her. I needed to make our inconvenient meeting as quick and painless as possible. "I ran in to grab a couple of items for an upcoming trip to London."

"That's rather casual attire for business meetings."

"Who knows, I may also catch a polo match or two."

"You had better hurry, the season ends soon."

"There's always Fashion Week."

"I never took you as a Fashion Week type."

"I'm not into polo matches or fashion, but you only live once."

"You know I'm not good at small talk." Natalia paused, then reached out and touched my arm. "Have you missed me at all?"

I escorted her by the arm over to two club chairs in the men's suit salon. We sat angled toward each other and I grabbed her by the hand. "If there's anything you know about me, it's that I'm not a sentimental guy. My work has never afforded me the time to leisurely stroll through life. It has, however, allowed me a few moments, every so often, to enjoy your company. I have truly enjoyed the time we've spent together."

"You're basically telling me that you haven't missed me one iota since you've last seen me."

"It's not in my nature to miss someone. Instead, I appreciate the experiences we shared."

"That silver tongue of yours is always at work. You must be quite a force to reckon with in the boardroom."

That had to be Natalia's greatest flaw. No matter how much she said she wanted *me*, she couldn't separate the power from the person. She would protest about how I treated her or devoted so little time to her, yet she would stay because of who she thought I was and what I could give to her. "I'm a force to be reckoned with at all times."

"I was thinking the other day, how nice it would be for us to take a trip to Seychelles. Do you remember our trip to Tahiti? The lagoons and white sand? We'll certainly need to top that."

I intently watched her while she spoke. Natalia was high off the idea of taking a magnificent vacation.

"In fact," she continued, "why don't we leave here and head to the travel agency to book something?"

I shook my head. "I don't think so."

"You don't want to see the travel agent?" She seemed puzzled.

"I don't want to go on a vacation."

"At all, or with me?"

"I don't have the time."

I refrained from being brutally honest with Natalia. I wanted to tell her to stop ignoring the inner voice screaming inside her head. If she had to ask whether I wanted to go with her on vacation or not, then she already knew the answer. There was a greedy desperation to her that I knew I was responsible for. I had created that monster. The best thing I could do for her was to put an end to it. "With all of the business travel I have coming up, I won't have the time for any personal jaunts. I'm sorry."

Natalia sighed. "Well, how do you intend to make it up to me?" She smiled and then slickly added, "We are in the perfect place for you to buy me a trinket to show exactly how contrite you are."

"Head over to the jewelry department and pick out something you like. I'll be over there as soon as I finish up here."

Natalia squealed and airily ran off toward the jewels.

I returned to the rack I was searching before she had surprised me, picked up both the pale yellow and tangerine shirts, paid for them, and then exited the store. When I got to my car, I called the jewelry counter and gave them authorization to process a purchase for Natalia up to two thousand dollars. By the time she realized that I wasn't going to show up, she would have a nice new gift to make her feel better.

CHAPTER 31

Avery

Indiya peeked into the oven for the third time. I held my tongue because I knew she was trying her best to redeem herself. She was making dinner for me. I had teased her relentlessly about almost setting my house on fire the last time she cooked. She went out, bought a few cookbooks, and had been practicing at home. Tonight, she was unveiling her *specialty*— baked ziti. She claimed it was quick and easy and there was no way she could mess it up. I had been forced to stay in the kitchen the entire time, to make sure there would be no more accidents.

She browned the ground beef, made the sauce, cut up cheese, and constructed the dish—all without incident. The only problem I saw was her incessant opening of the oven door while it baked. If she wasn't opening it, then she was turning on the oven light and peering through the small window. It looked and smelled good, but I was sure she was prolonging the cooking process.

I poured myself another glass of wine. My fourth. "I'm impressed, Ms. Spencer."

"You haven't tasted it yet."

"I know, but you had a near disastrous occurrence in here, yet, you're trying again."

"You're trying to be funny."

"No, I'm serious." I raised my glass. "Cheers to you for not burning down my house this time." I took a sip, then erupted in laughter.

"Just for that, you're not getting any. And I'm not talking about dinner."

She came over to the table and took a drink from her own glass. I pulled her down on my lap, holding her tight around the waist. "Now why would you say something you know isn't true? I will be getting plenty tonight."

"Don't be so sure, Mr. Woodson."

"I'm more than sure. In fact, I'm willing to bet you that you'll be begging me to give you some."

"I'll take that bet. What do I win when I prove you wrong?"

"You win breakfast in bed for a week."

"Wait a minute, is that supposed to be a prize or a punishment? You cannot cook."

"I'm getting better. And you can't deny I have more skills than you."

"Okay. What about the fact that I don't live here? How am I going to redeem this prize?"

"All right," I said, gracing her with a faux grave expression, "you have two options."

"Let me hear them."

"You can either stay here for the week to get your hot, delicious breakfast every morning or I can come to your house, bright and early every morning, to bring you breakfast in your own bed."

Indiya tensed. "I'll take the first option."

"Somehow, I knew you'd say that." She started to get up, but I tightened my hold on her. "So, what is it? Why don't you want me to come to your house?"

"What makes you think I don't?"

"You've never invited me."

"That's because I'm always here." She shifted nervously. "Let me check the ziti."

"It's fine. You need to leave the door closed for a while, anyway."

"Now you're the expert telling me how to cook?"

"Don't try to change the subject, Indiya. I've been wondering for over a month when you'd have me over. In the beginning, I figured you were being cautious, but now it's obvious you're avoiding it. What's up?"

"Nothing's up. Really."

I let go of her waist. "Go check your ziti."

She got up from my lap, but lingered in front of me. I stood, took my glass, and headed from the kitchen.

"Where are you going?"

"To watch a little television in the white room."

"Don't you mean living room?"

"Same thing."

"But dinner's almost ready."

"Come get me when it's done."

I went into the white room and propped up on the sofa. I wasn't going to mention anything to Indiya about not having been to her home. I was going to wait and see how long she would take to invite me, but it had started to plague my thoughts. After the first time she visited my house, it immediately became an established norm that she came here. I didn't mind because if she was comfortable being in my space, then I knew she'd come back again. What I didn't realize was that I would never get the invitation to see her living environment, her home. It seemed she was avoiding it, but, until tonight, I didn't have confirmation.

I turned on the television and went from channel to channel, not really paying attention to what was on the screen. My mind wandered. I could have played things more cool. I knew how to finesse a conversation, but I saw an opening and steamrolled through. She must have been rubbing off on me—saying whatever, whenever. I chuckled to myself. I was making an issue out of nothing. As long as she was here with me, I had nothing to complain about.

Indiya wandered into the room, her head turned toward the television. "What are you watching?"

"Just surfing the channels."

She sat on the floor, taking up a post next to my legs, leaning her head against my knee. Spontaneously, my hand started smoothing stray wisps of hair away from her forehead.

"The ziti will be done in a few minutes."

"Good, I'm starving."

She raised her head and smiled at me. "It's not that I don't want you to come to my house." She hesitated and I waited silently. "It's what I don't want you to see when you get there."

"You live in Rockville Centre. What could possibly be wrong with your home?"

"There's nothing wrong with the outside; I'm ashamed of what's inside."

"If it's not a dead body, then I'm sure I can handle it." I was curious, but I was going to let her talk at her own pace.

"I have a problem, an addiction, and my house is where I hide that I have this problem."

"Whatever it is, you can tell me."

"My house is a cluttered mess."

"Do you mean like you need to do a little cleaning?"

"No."

"Like those people on that television show that have a problem with hoarding things?"

"Damn near. I mean, it's not dirty or nasty. I don't have vermin.

It's not like that. I have a shopping addiction, Avery. I'm addicted to buying things. New things."

I was confused. "Okay, you like to shop. Is this really a problem?"

"You can barely walk from room to room because of all the stuff I've bought."

"Like what?"

"All sorts of things—clothes, furniture, electronics, toiletries, books. I can go on, but I won't. I am so embarrassed."

"So your house is filled with all sorts of stuff?"

"Each and every room. It looks like a warehouse."

I wasn't sure what I should say. Obviously, she had a problem and based on what she was saying, she was pretty far gone. "Have you sought any professional help?"

"I started seeing someone for it a few weeks before I met you."

"It sounds like you're on the right path."

She stared at me with searching eyes. "You think there's something wrong with me now, don't you?"

I frowned. "Why would you say that?"

"Because I can tell by the look on your face."

"I don't see you any differently than I did ten minutes, an hour, or a day ago."

"I don't believe that. I just told you that my house is a cluttered warehouse and you don't think any less of me?"

"I'll be honest. If you said there were rats and roaches running rampant, then, yes, I would." I started to laugh, but she didn't. "I'm kidding, I'm kidding."

"That's not funny, Avery. I shared something very personal and extremely private with you."

"All right, I'm sorry." I pulled her up on the couch next to me. "Believe me when I tell you this does not tarnish what I think or how I feel about you. I'm here for you however and whenever you need me. And when you're better and ready to get rid of that stuff, I'll help you. At least I know I'll get invited over."

Indiya leaned forward and kissed me full on the lips. "You can't imagine how much I appreciate you right now."

"It feels good to be appreciated." I kissed the back of her hand. "Let's go check on dinner before we have another smoky situation."

After dinner, I was back on the couch trying to keep my eyes open while Indiya finished up with the dishes. Her ziti wasn't half bad. It could have used more sauce and salt, but I would never tell her that's what I thought. I wanted to encourage her to continue cooking, not throw in the spatula, so I told her it was excellent.

I opened my eyes to Indiya snuggling up next to me. She was planting tiny kisses along my neck while unbuckling my belt. I kissed her forehead and whispered, "I guess this means I won the bet."

CHAPTER 32

Avery

I strolled into the bank and waited to be acknowledged by the chit-chatting personal bankers. Three women surrounded the desk of a fourth as they giggled at something on the computer monitor. I looked at my watch and cleared my throat loud enough to get one or all of their attention.

All four looked up and exchanged a few words, yet only one sprang into action—the one who appeared to be the youngest of the group. Clearly, she had the least seniority. She gestured for me to have a seat at her desk up front, closest to the customer waiting area.

I took a seat and read her name tag. "Good morning, Emma. You must be new."

"Good morning, Mr. Hudson. Yes, I am."

"You know my name."

"Yes, Avery Hudson. The ladies just told me."

Her personable demeanor made me smile. "Well, Emma, I need to check if a wire came in this morning. Your website was having technical problems this morning and I couldn't access my account."

"I'm sorry about that, Mr. Hudson. I think the problem has been resolved now and you shouldn't have any additional trouble if you need to visit the site later. Do you have your account number or social security number?"

I gave her my account number. "Do you need to see my ID?" I was careful to fish out my identification that said Avery Hudson, not Avery Woodson.

"No, it's fine. The ladies know you."

I slipped the ID back in my wallet. "Can you also tell me my balance?"

"Okay. It looks like your wire in the amount of two million dollars came in this morning and your balance, including the wire, is thirteen million. Is there anything else I can help you with?"

I thought a moment. "One more thing, Emma. I need to do an international wire transfer in the amount of eight million." I unfolded a slip of paper from my wallet and handed it to her. "This is the account information of where it needs to be sent."

"One moment, Mr. Hudson. I know I need to contact our wire desk to complete your transaction, but you're my first customer that's actually requested to send an international wire."

Emma went to confer with the other ladies still gabbing around the computer. One of the older women took Emma to her desk and walked her through the process.

I hadn't planned to send a wire when I entered the bank, but there was no reason for me to have thirteen million dollars sitting in a commercial bank. Maybe I was paranoid, but I liked to keep my money moving. Emma came back with an authorization form for me to sign, then gave me a copy for my records.

"Thank you, Emma. You have yourself a wonderful day."

I left the bank and hopped into my car. I had a little over an hour to get from Long Island to Connecticut. It was a beautiful morning with low humidity, radiant sunshine, and a soothing summer breeze. I was casually dressed in a pair of slacks with a short-sleeved, button-up shirt and a pair of boat shoes with no socks. I opened my sunroof, put on my sunglasses, and hit the road.

I tuned into smooth jazz and hummed along with the instru-mental that played. I crossed the Throgs Neck Bridge and hit traffic at the I-95 split. I would never make it on time if cars didn't start moving. I honked my horn at a tractor-trailer that almost strayed into my lane. I sped up and maneuvered in front of it. If he was having problems staying in his lane, I definitely didn't want to drive next to him. I saw a couple of more openings and darted from lane to lane until the traffic abated. I looked around for any state troopers, then gunned it. I had to make up some serious time if I were going to make it by noon.

I pulled into the parking lot at Oak Estates at three minutes before twelve. I did a light jog from my car to the reception desk. The desk attendant was hanging up the phone as I approached. "I'm here to see Robert Hudson."

"Your name?"

"Avery Hudson."

"Relationship to the resident?"

"Son."

She typed in my information to verify against the approved visitor list. "Mr. Hudson, you do realize it's lunchtime? There are no visitors permitted from noon to one-thirty."

"Yes, ma'am, I know. Unfortunately, I got caught in traffic on my way from Long Island. If you would let me see him for a moment, I promise I won't take more than ten minutes. I can wheel him to the lunchroom myself when I'm done." I added a schoolboy smile at the end of my plea.

She sighed as if I were disrupting her day. "All right, go on up, but you have him down here for lunch no later than twelve-fifteen."

I thanked her profusely, then hurried to the elevator bank. I took the slow-moving elevator, which was large enough to accommodate a couple of stretchers, to the third floor. I picked my way through the meandering nursing home residents to room 302 at the end of the hall. I tapped lightly before I entered.

Sitting in a chair, next to the window with a picturesque view of the grounds, was my foster father, Robert Hudson. I walked to the window and stood next him. He was staring in the direction of the pond. Visitors were milling about on the lawns and through the flower garden, probably waiting for resident lunch to end.

"How are you, Sir?" He had insisted that I call him that since I was fourteen, the age he had taken me in.

He looked up at me as if he hadn't noticed me standing there. He turned his head to the side, eyes squinted as they inspected my face. "Is it time for lunch?"

"I'm going to take you down for lunch in a few minutes, okay?"

"Good, because I was getting hungry."

"Sir, do you recognize me?"

Again, confusion registered on his face. "Of course, I do."

"I'm Avery."

"That's what I was going to say."

"Are you feeling all right?"

He smiled wistfully. "I've never felt better. How are your wife and the kids?"

"I'm not married, Sir. Remember?"

"Right, right. Now I recall."

I didn't have much time before I had to have him downstairs. "Sir, I need you to complete some paperwork." I reached in my back pocket and removed the folded single sheet of paper. "I need your signature like before, remember?"

"Yes, yes."

I handed him the paper and a pen. "Sign here," I said, pointing to the bottom of the page.

He shakily clutched the pen and scanned the document. "Five hundred thousand dollars? Is this my money?"

I pointed again. "Sign right here, Sir."

He shakily signed the document. I folded it and returned it to my pocket. "Have you seen my wife around here?" he asked.

"Mrs. Hudson passed away a few years ago." I didn't think what I said had even registered. He was once again staring out of the window, as if he hadn't heard me. "I'll take you down to eat."

I wheeled Robert down the hall and past reception for her to see that I brought him down. I waited outside of the cafeteria for one of the aides to come get him.

As a female attendant came to take him inside, he looked up at me and smiled. "What was your name again, young man?"

"Avery."

"My wife had a foster son named Avery. He wasn't helpful like you. She insisted on dragging him home. Wanted me to adopt him, but I refused. I didn't want him having my last name. I was convinced he would never amount to anything. Those kids never do."

I wordlessly watched as he disappeared into the room. Each time I came to the nursing home, he was progressively worse. I didn't know how much longer he would be able to cooperate with me.

Robert Hudson hadn't made life any easier on me growing up. It was his wife, Beatrice, who wanted to bring me home to stay with them after she met me at a charity event at the orphanage. He wasn't inclined to have a parentless, teen boy living under his roof. I struggled trying to adapt to the rigors of life in a house with a man who ran his home like a military base. I was up before dawn daily, even during summer breaks. I had a curfew, that if I broke it, I would be punished for months on end. Although he had no affiliation with any branch of the service, we had to use military time around the house. He was a rich man, but didn't flaunt it. The only outward manifestation of his fortune was his home. Robert owned a string of car dealerships and gas stations. It wasn't until I got older that I understood the depth of his wealth.

He and Beatrice were middle-aged when I came to live with them. They never had any children of their own. She was kind enough to me, but there was no emotional connection between us. I could tell that she genuinely cared that I was taken care of and had what I needed; however, I didn't feel that she loved me.

I lived with the Hudsons from the age of fourteen until I completed my undergraduate studies. I went away to college, but I would return to their home for breaks and vacations. If it weren't for Beatrice, I wouldn't have received an education at all. She insisted that her husband pay for my schooling. The older I got, the less time I spent with them. I stayed on campus, went home with my boys or a couple of times with girls I was dating.

It seemed the older I became, the more harshly Robert treated me. In his eyes, I never did anything right. When he took me to any of the dealerships, he introduced me as his wife's foster kid.

I studied hard and kept my nose clean because somehow I thought it would make him proud, maybe claim me as his son. It never happened. He always treated me the same. Back then, I couldn't figure it out. Now, I didn't want to know. I made a promise to myself that I would take what I deserved in life. I hadn't deserved a mother who abandoned me and a father I didn't know. I didn't ask for foster parents who gave me little more than a place to stay. I was forced to adapt to survive at an early age. I was still adapting. Every day of my life.

I got back in my car with my signed document and headed to the investment bank. Robert Hudson had made yet another sizeable contribution to the Avery Woodson Survival Fund. He would do so until the day he died—physically or mentally— whichever came first.

CHAPTER 33

I t was Friday night and I had not seen Indiya all week. She told me that after our discussion about her addiction, she decided to spend the week cataloguing what she had in order to determine what to get rid of and how to do it. I offered to help; however, she told me it was part of her process of getting better and needed to do it alone. I didn't mind because after my visit to the nursing home, I was battling my own demons.

Going to see Robert Hudson always stirred up memories that were best left forgotten. His face was a reminder that I had been a loner for most of my life. I had learned to never get attached because people and things were easily snatched away. I remembered being about six and living at the orphanage. At the time, my best and only friend was a boy we called Squirrel. I couldn't recall his real name—I wasn't sure I ever knew it—but he was like a brother to me. We had shared a room together since we were three. We played together, ate together, and were even in the same class at school. We did not make a move without one another.

We both had families that were interested in us, but none would take us home to stay. Until one day the principal came to our classroom in the middle of a lesson to get Squirrel. He didn't come back to class for the rest of the day. I remembered thinking that he must have been in trouble for something and I couldn't wait to ask him about it when I got back from school.

When I returned to the orphanage, I hurried to our room. Squirrel's bed was stripped and all of his belongings were gone. I checked the closet, under the bed, even behind the curtains, to see if he was playing some sort of game with me. I heard someone walk in and turned around, expecting to see him. It was the social worker. She stood at the door and told me that a family had come to adopt Squirrel and that he wouldn't be coming back.

She didn't sit me down or even ask how I was feeling. She delivered her cold news and then said I would have my own room for a while. I curled up on my bed and cried. I haven't cried since.

I shook those old thoughts out of my head. I wanted to have a better state of mind before Indiya arrived. We were planning to do dinner and a movie. I wanted to stay home, maybe break in the grill I had finally bought, but she insisted we go out. She wouldn't let up if I refused, so we compromised. She picked the restaurant; I picked the movie.

I went to the bedroom to check my cell phones for text and voice messages. Nothing from Miko, Quinn, Natalia, Romel, Roxi, or Hazelle. I was relieved. They had not reached out to me and I had not been reaching out to them. I was actually feeling lighter, less heavy. I hadn't noticed that I even felt like I was carrying a load until it was unloaded.

I slid the phones back into the drawer and went to retrieve my cell phone from my D.C. days from the nightstand. I plugged it up to get a small charge, then headed to the kitchen for a bottle of water. I leaned back against the counter and leisurely sipped my water. I felt content. I would almost say happy, but I didn't know happy. Happy had never been a friend of mine. At that moment, I was good with content and embraced it. The doorbell rang and drew me out of my contemplation. I left the water bottle on the counter and went to answer it.

I opened the door for my brown-skinned beauty and inhaled the breeze carrying the sensuous notes of her perfume. Indiya's eyes could slow time—I was suspended in the moment. She stepped into the foyer and I pulled her into a hug. I held on. When she tried to pull away, I continued to hold her.

She craned her neck to see my face. "Is everything all right?"

"Everything's fine," I said, releasing her from my arms.

"I guess daddy missed his baby this week."

I had to laugh. Indiya had a way with words. "You could say that."

"No, why don't you?" Her hands went to her hips and she fixed me with a playful glare.

"I missed you, Indiya."

"I know you did because I missed you too."

I pulled her to me again and kissed her breath away with a smoldering expression of my sincerity.

"You really missed me." She stepped back and wiped her smeared lipstick.

"That's what I said."

She walked toward the door. "Thanks to that panty-stirring greeting, I almost forgot my overnight bag on the front porch." She grabbed her bag, then headed to my bedroom. She called back over her shoulder, "I decided we should go for hibachi tonight. Hopefully we'll sit with other sexy couples and have a lively time."

I came into the room behind her. "Why do they have to be sexy?"

"It's a better experience watching a hot man or woman with their tongues out, trying to catch food that the chef tosses. Wouldn't you rather see food land in a perky set of Cs or full double-Ds rather than a saggy pair of triple-Es?"

"And I guess you would rather see a shrimp bounce off of a rock-hard chest rather than roll down a potbelly stomach?"

"Of course!"

"You make a good point."

"Don't I?"

We laughed at our own silliness. I didn't care who was at our table. All of my attention would be on the hot woman with me. Her strapless jumpsuit pretty much guaranteed it.

Indiya was taking clothing out of her bag when my cell phone started ringing. My head jerked toward the nightstand. I had forgotten that it was charging. I momentarily froze.

"Um, your phone…"

I took my time walking around her to get it. By the time I reached the nightstand, it had stopped ringing. I picked it up to shut it off, but it began to ring in my hand. *Damn*.

I answered. "Hello? Hey, Kev, what's going on, man? You're back in town? Oh, only for the weekend. I don't know if I can get up with you tomorrow. I sort of have plans with my lady. Bring her? No, I don't think we can."

"We can make it, Kev!" Indiya shouted loud enough for him to hear. "We'll be there."

I turned and gave her a look of incredulity. "All right, what time? Okay. See you there." I powered off the phone. "What the hell, Indiya? Why would you yell that we're going to meet someone you don't know?"

"I know who Kev is. He's your friend you introduced me to the night I met you."

"Yeah, but you don't know if I wanted to meet up with him or not. We're not going."

"What is the big deal, Avery? That's your boy. From what I could glean from your conversation, he's visiting for the weekend. You and I don't have any real plans for tomorrow, so why not?"

"Could it be because I didn't want to?"

"You know, Avery, we have been dating for months now. That is the first time your phone has ever rung when we've been together. Aside from the Bat Phone in that office of yours upstairs that rings occasionally, I didn't think you ever got any calls."

"And that's an issue for you, my phone doesn't ring enough?"

"That's not what I'm saying. I just thought it would be nice if you caught up with your friend."

"*You* thought?"

"Yes, I did. I would have to be blind if I didn't notice that you keep a tight, almost non-existent, circle." She sat down on the edge of the bed. "I don't know, maybe I did get a little carried away and I'm sorry. But you did tell him we were coming…"

"Let's get to dinner or we'll never make our movie."

I left Indiya sitting on the edge of the bed. As far as I was concerned, the conversation was over.

Our ride to the hibachi restaurant was in complete silence. I opened Indiya's car door when we arrived, offered my hand to help her out and she mumbled a thank you. With the exception of one boisterous group, the restaurant wasn't busy and we were seated at a table by ourselves. I was drinking sake and she was sipping green tea.

The hibachi chef came over with his selections of seafood, meat, and vegetables and greeted us. He dramatically assessed our table. "What's the matter, no friends?"

He laughed at his own joke. Indiya looked away and I took a drink from my sake.

"It's just us," I eventually replied.

"I hope you bring your appetite." He dumped a large bowl of rice on the grill along with shrimp and beef.

I dipped my head and glanced at Indiya from the side. "All right. We'll go tomorrow night."

She tapped her tea cup to my sake cup. "Okay then."

"You know, it's not like I've met any of your friends or family either."

"My family is in Chicago."

I nodded. "They don't come to visit?"

"Maybe once every two years."

The chef tapped the grill with his spatula, ready to toss a shrimp to me. I shook my head. Indiya opened wide and caught one. I smiled.

"How often do you go home to visit?"

"Probably about the same. Every other year."

"Why so infrequent?"

"I don't know, really. My family has never been big on traveling and Mom and Dad don't care for New York. They usually try to convince me to come home before they commit to coming to see me. I think when I left Chicago for New York, I fell in love with this city. It's strange. As much as I love Chicago, sometimes I don't want to go back."

"Going back can be hard sometimes. I would imagine family complicates that even more."

The chef placed plates of steaming hot fried rice in front of us. I went for my fork, Indiya grabbed her chopsticks.

"Can I ask you a question?" she said, rubbing her chopsticks together to remove any pieces of splintered wood.

"Go ahead."

"Why is it that you don't know your mother?"

I stopped eating my rice. "Good question."

"You don't have to answer if you don't want to."

"No, it's all right." I took a swig of my sake. "My mother had me at a very young age. She was seventeen, had just graduated from high school and decided the best thing for her to do was to abandon me at an orphanage."

"I'm sorry, Avery."

"I've asked myself a million times why she never came back for me. I wondered where was her family, her parents. Did they throw her out on the street when they found out she was pregnant?"

"Anything was possible back then. Teen pregnancy had a terrible stigma attached to it."

"How about my father? Where was that good-for-nothing?" The beginning of anger was seeping out of me.

Indiya clasped my hand in hers. "Did the orphanage have anything useful to share with you?"

"Not enough. I'm using what I do have to try to locate her. It's not much, so, as you can imagine, it's not easy."

The chef quietly plated the rest of our dinner without any tricks or unnecessary flair. He seemed to have taken a cue from our demeanors that we weren't in a celebratory mood. He excused himself with a stiff bow and moved on to a new table.

"Will you be all right if you don't find her?"

"I'll have to be. I have been for my entire life. It's funny. I used to think, 'How can you miss what you never had?' That may be true in regards to material things, but not when it comes to your mother. I want to find her; however, if I don't, I'll continue going on just as I always have—without knowing."

I was hoping that by sharing a bit of my history with Indiya that maybe she would understand me a little better. No, I wasn't an open book; my story wasn't for everyone. Very few knew it and I liked it that way.

"Do you want a family of your own someday?"

I thought about it for a moment. "I honestly don't know. I'm not sure what family is."

"I might have to take you to Chicago and show you."

CHAPTER 34

S unday afternoon. I had finally broken in my gas barbeque grill. I kept it simple and grilled a few hot dogs, hamburgers, and Italian sausages. I had already decided that I would step it up next time with salmon and chicken cutlets, providing I could find the right marinade recipes.

I was on the patio, sitting at the table with the umbrella concealing me from the sun rays. I squirted mustard on my second hot dog and took a bite that left about half.

Indiya was on the lawn in a lounge chair. She called out across the yard, "If you keep eating, what are you going to do when it's time to have dinner with Kev?"

"I'm a big man, if you haven't noticed. It takes a lot of food to fuel this body." I took another bite. "And we're not meeting for dinner. We're going to a champagne and cigar bar."

"No dinner?" She popped up from the chair and traipsed over to the table. "Let me get one of those burgers. I thought we were going out to eat."

"That's what happens when you eavesdrop." I laughed before polishing off my last bit of hot dog.

"I wasn't eavesdropping and you know it."

"Just eat your hamburger."

"I am now that I know stogies and drinks are on the menu later."

I chucked her beneath the chin. "I'm going in to take a shower. Come join me after you finish eating."

"I'll think about it."

"Don't take too long."

I smoothed my hand down Indiya's long leg. I couldn't resist the lightly oiled, glistening chocolate next to me and kept glancing over while trying to keep my eyes on the road. She was wearing white shorts and a tight, cropped white blazer with no shirt underneath and plenty of cleavage on display. I glanced at her black strappy sandals and oversized black bag. She knew how to do sexy.

I was sporting white linen pants with a matching suit jacket and white shirt underneath. She reached around the gear stick and put her hand in my crotch, tenderly massaging my package. I started to get stiff. "Don't start something you can't finish."

"What makes you think I can't?"

I downshifted. "I'll pull this car over right now."

"No, don't," she said, snatching her hand away. "We'll be late."

"The next time I say meet me in the shower, you need to show up."

"You finished too quickly," she said with a laugh.

"You were playing games, but, when we get home later, I'm going to take care of you."

I zoomed up to the valet in front of the cigar and champagne bar. We stepped from the car, visions in white, and entered the building. It was dark and inviting inside. Black carpet, leather and velvet seating, glass tables, and ambient lighting.

Kev was already seated in a corner pod with a puff of smoke surrounding him. He stood, cigar clenched between his teeth, and gave me a brotherly handshake. I introduced him to Indiya.

Kev removed his cigar and kissed Indiya on the back of her hand. "I never forget a beautiful face. Nice to see you again."

I held back a laugh. Kev had always tried to be charming with the ladies. Unfortunately for him, it usually fell flat. "Where's your wife? I had assumed she would be with you."

"Even though he's doing much better, I can't convince her to leave her father's side when we come to visit."

"That's understandable. He had a close call."

"Believe me, I'm not complaining. These are the only times I get to go out without her giving a damn about where I am or what I'm doing. I got here a little early just because I could." He motioned to the empty seats. "Sit, sit. The concierge should be right over for your cigar and champagne orders."

"Concierge?"

"That's what they call them here. Indiya, you are a tall drink of water. How tall are you, if you don't mind my asking?"

"Tonight, in my heels, I'm about six-feet-one-inch. I'm five-eight without."

"Very nice."

Kev must have been waiting for a long time and had a few drinks in the meantime. I redirected his attention from Indiya's stature to something he should have been thinking about. "Are you driving back to D.C. tonight, man?"

"We decided to leave tomorrow afternoon. My wife wanted to stay for her father's doctor appointment in the morning."

The concierge interrupted and ran down the menu for us. I ordered a cigar and scotch and Indiya ordered a glass of champagne.

"Kev, are you from D.C.?" Indiya inquired.

"Born and raised. I wouldn't move if you paid me. Although, my wife is starting to get a few ideas about living up here ever since her father got sick."

"You wouldn't consider it?"

"Not unless I absolutely had to, and we're not quite there yet." He puffed his cigar. "Though, I'll admit, finding out that my boy Avery lives here made me think twice."

The concierge returned with my cigar and scotch on a tray. He handed Indiya a champagne flute and slipped back into the darkness.

"How did you two meet?"

I started shaking my head and Kev laughed as I began to recount our first meeting. "I went to college in D.C. and decided to move there permanently after undergrad. Needless to say, I didn't have much money and the apartment wasn't in the best neighborhood. So I pack all of my belongings into my car and drive over to the building. I have my keys, I have my signed lease and anything else I needed to move in. When I get to my apartment door, there's music blasting from the apartment. I use my key to go in and there's this fool chilling in a fully- furnished living room." I started laughing at the recollection. "So I ask who the hell he is and what is he doing in my apartment. He tells me, he's Kev Ski and he rented the apartment a week ago and somebody in the leasing office must have screwed me over. So we get to arguing, pushing, and shoving until one of the other neighbors hears the brouhaha and comes to break us up. To make a long story short, I sleep in my car overnight in front of the leasing office because first thing in the morning, I wanted some answers and a new apartment."

Kev wiped tears from his eyes and picked up the retelling of the story. "Fast forward to the next morning. I'm in the shower washing my ass, and this dude bursts into the apartment waving two sheets of paper. One was his lease and the other was mine. His apartment was 518 and mine 618. I was in the wrong damn apartment on the wrong damn floor." Kev started laughing so hard he couldn't finish.

"When this idiot moved in, he got off on the wrong floor and walked down to 518. The cleaning crew was just leaving. He told them he was the new tenant and they let him walk on in with all of his junk."

"Once I was in there, my mind didn't even think 618 and I didn't have a reason to look at my lease again."

Indiya chimed in. "But what about the key? It couldn't have worked for both doors."

"That's the kicker. The next day, I left the apartment and couldn't get back in. I saw the cleaning crew and asked if they could let me in and later I'd go to the leasing office for a new key. The lady was so sweet; she gave me her key and said she would get a new one from the office."

We all burst into laughter.

"So, after I came in with the leases, I pulled his soapy ass from the shower and went off. I told him he had fifteen minutes to get all of his crap out of my apartment. After watching him dragging around in a towel packing his stuff, I started to help him. We started talking and eventually laughing at our predicament."

"We were as thick as thieves ever since," Kev added. "At least until a few years ago."

We silently acknowledged one another. I stuck my fist out for dap and Kev tapped it. Indiya watched not quite sure what was being discussed through silent means.

"Well, what happened a few years ago?" she finally asked.

"Avery disappeared without a trace."

Indiya looked at me. "Why would you do that?"

I threw back my scotch. "I don't want to talk about this; it's old news."

"I still think you need to come back to D.C. to visit with the crew. We miss you, man."

"I'm real busy these days, but I'll think about it. Now, who needs another drink?" I waved the concierge over to our area.

There was only so much reminiscing I was willing to do and I had had my fill. Kev was my boy and we had great times together over the years, but there are times when you have to put yourself first and do what's in your best interest. Walking away from my life in D.C. was an act of self-preservation. I wasn't expecting anyone to understand it then or even now. My time with Courtney had come to an end and I was feeling as alone as ever. There was nothing Kev, or any of my other boys, could have done to make me stay. It was time to get away to start a new chapter, written by me. That's what I did.

Kev didn't push. "I think I'll have another drink and another cigar."

"And I'll have another glass of champagne."

We stayed a couple of hours, had a few drinks, then parted ways. Indiya and I left Kev enjoying his last smoke. He must not have been kidding when he said it was rare that he had such a long leash. I guess sometimes you just don't want to go home.

CHAPTER 35

Avery

The radio was on softly in the car and Indiya hummed along to almost every song that played. We hadn't said much since leaving Kev. I didn't know what she was thinking about, but I couldn't wait to get her home. Her head was turned toward the passenger side window. I squeezed her knee to make sure she was still awake.

She looked at me and sighed. "Why don't you want to go back to D.C.? Does it have to do with a woman?"

"What?"

"Is the reason you don't want to go home because of a woman?"

"No, Indiya," I snapped. "D.C. is not my home."

"Sorry I asked."

I took her hand in mine and brought it to my lips. I didn't mean to bark at her. Her questions, always direct, could push my buttons at times.

"When we get back to the house, I want you to go straight to the bedroom and take off everything except the heels." She offered no response. "I apologize for snapping at you."

She lifted my hand to her lips, placing a delicate kiss across my knuckles.

We cruised to Brookville, hands intertwined. I pulled into my driveway and turned off the car. "Give me those luscious lips." I received a measly peck. It was obvious I had some warming up to do. "Bedroom. Nothing but heels."

We went inside the house. I loitered near the living room, taking my time to remove my shoes. I wanted to see whether Indiya was mad at me or if she was going to the bedroom to get naked. She set off down the hallway to my room. I waited in the living room for a few minutes before following behind her.

The door was closed. I turned the knob and stepped inside. Close enough. G-string and heels. She was standing at the foot of the bed, legs crossed at the ankles, one hand on her hip, loose curls pulled to one side and cascading over her shoulder with tendrils framing one of her breasts. Those breasts—nipples erect and waiting to be tasted.

I was unbuttoning my jacket while poring over every inch of her body. "No panties."

Indiya slid her panties over her ass, let them drop to the floor, and stepped out of them.

I unzipped my pants and my dick was already protruding from my boxers. I swiftly removed my clothes and advanced on her. "Stand in front of the mirror."

With a slow stroll, she walked over to the decorative floor mirror. Her body was perfectly framed in the high, arched mirror. I came up behind her and pressed my chest against her back. She bumped her ass back into me, rubbing herself against my erection. I bowed my head and kissed the side of her neck, watching us in the mirror at the same time. Her eyes fluttered.

My lips traveled down to her shoulder. I nibbled on her and she leaned her head against mine. When I reached my hand around to stroke her kitty, she purred for me, then gave me a wicked smile that turned me on even more. I caressed her left breast as I stroked her clit with my right hand. She rested her head against my chest, but kept her eyes on the mirror. She sucked her bottom lip into her mouth and moaned. Her hips began a slow twirl, the roundness of her ass sliding on my dick.

I moved my hands across her abdomen to her hips, gripping firmly as I angled my hardness against her. Indiya backed her ass up slightly; I dipped down, then slid up inside her. We grunted in unison. I held her still as I thrust upward again and again. Her legs trembled as I kept her upright while working her pussy.

I wrapped my arm around her waist and used my other hand to pull the blanket rack from beside the bed. I set it in front of Indiya. "Put your hands on here."

She grasped the top rack, steadying herself as I picked up the tempo. I turned us to the side and bent her over so we could see my dick working her pussy. My hands were on top of her back as I drilled her long and deep. With each thrust, Indiya cried out. The look of ecstasy on her face made me pump harder. She popped her pussy hard in response. My moans got louder and I drowned her out.

In a swift move, I swept her up and deposited her on the bed. I rolled her over and climbed on top, pushing myself back inside. I thrust my tongue in her mouth and sucked her into me. I couldn't get close enough. She raised her legs high, but that wasn't where I wanted them.

"Bring them down," I said in between breaths. "Hold them close to your chest."

I pounded harder until I hit that spot. The spot where I couldn't go any deeper. We weren't moaning anymore, we screamed with each dive I made into her wetness.

"I'm coming, I'm coming, I'm coming, I'm coming, I'm coming...Avery, I'm coming." Indiya let loose a glass-shattering scream.

Sweat poured down my back. I pushed her legs up, leveraging my body for the long stroke. I faltered; it felt too good. I pulled out to the tip and dipped back in, my climax building. I was close. I long-stroked her pussy. She came again, her legs violently shaking.

Her wetness enveloped my dick and I couldn't hold it anymore. I came hard, my body convulsing with each wave. I collapsed beside Indiya, pulling her into my arms as the last spasms racked my body. I held her tight, my face resting on the top of her head.

I lay still as I caught my breath, my heart racing. I realized I was probably holding her too tight and loosened my grip around her shoulders.

"What was that?" she asked, with a weak smile. "I can't move."

"I hope that's a good thing."

"It's an amazing thing."

I kissed the top of her head. Her hair was plastered to her back and forehead. I pushed some of it away from her eyes. "Do you want some water?"

"Yes, but I don't want you to move right now. Let's just lay like this for a minute."

I woke up hours later, Indiya sprawled across my chest, hair covering her face completely. I slid from beneath her, my body stiff from knocking out in that position. I peered toward the end of the bed and smiled. I slipped off her heels and covered us with the blanket. Those shoes may get a starring role in all of our sexcapades.

CHAPTER 36

I stretched myself awake, moving every single body part before I opened my eyes. Indiya was lying on her side, her head propped up on her hand, staring down at me. I quickly shut my eyes as if I hadn't stirred from my sleep.

"Cut it out. I know you're awake." I didn't budge, but the slight curve of my lips was betraying me. Indiya straddled me. "You know what I was thinking as I watched you sleep? I'm going to make you breakfast."

My eyes flew open. "Don't you have to get ready for work?"

"I'm not going. And I knew you weren't sleeping."

"You're taking the day off?"

"If I can convince you to as well."

I pulled her down on my chest. "I'm convinced." She stretched her body along the length of mine, tucking her arms against me. "How'd you sleep last night?"

"You gave me the knockout pill. I barely remember getting tired. One minute I was awake, the next, unconscious."

I laughed. "It was a good night."

"Umm-hmm. And I really enjoyed Kev. He seems like a good guy."

"Yeah…"

She raised her head and looked into my face. "Are you all right?"

I thought a moment. "Chilling with Kev last night made me realize that I do miss him."

"Maybe you should think about going to D.C. to visit like he asked."

I sat up and shifted her to the spot next to me. I propped the pillows against the headboard and leaned back. "You were partially right last night."

"About what?" she asked, her brow wrinkled.

"I left D.C. because of a woman." Indiya waited for me to continue. "And that's part of the reason why I didn't return."

"What happened?"

"Too much or maybe not enough. I don't know."

"Well, obviously something happened if it drove you from there."

"Right before I moved to New York, I had been in a relatively long-term relationship with this woman. It was definitely the longest situation I had ever been in."

"How long were you together?"

"Five years."

"Did you love her?"

"Yeah, I did. I loved her, her family, some of her friends." The last part I added with a chuckle. "Yes, I loved her."

"Then what went wrong?"

"Everything." I shook my head thinking about it. "One minute I was part of the family, the next, I was an outsider looking in." I went on to recount how I had met Courtney at an after-work networking event for lawyers. "Her father was a founding partner in the firm that hosted the event. Courtney wasn't a lawyer, she was a teacher, yet she attended the monthly get-togethers with her father. I didn't go to the event every month, but I took notice that Courtney was always there, chatting with the various groups of attorneys. I didn't know it at the time, but she and her father were probably husband-hunting for her. Wouldn't that be something? Matchmaking designed as networking meetings? I wouldn't put it past her father.

"Anyway, one week she made her way into a discussion I was having with a few colleagues on Brown versus Board of Education. She was on fire, talking about having the right to get a good education and how so many schools were falling short in the current day. We had a spirited dialogue that night, and after, we went to grab a drink. We met for a couple of dinners, but nothing serious developed. We'd see each other at the networking events, have great dialogue, and it was guaranteed that we would have a drink together at the end.

"We liked each other, but neither one of us pulled the trigger. About six months had passed when, one night after a meeting, her father approached us when we were getting ready to leave. He asked if he could tag along for a drink. Of course, I didn't mind. He was a respected partner at one of the best law firms in D.C. He treated us to dinner at a swanky steakhouse, all the while asking me about my education, current position, and future goals. It felt like I was on a job interview, rather than at dinner. Essentially, I was right because he called my office the next day and offered me a job at his firm with a sizeable raise.

"I was no fool, at least I thought I wasn't, so I accepted his offer and gave two weeks notice to my boss. On my first day at the new firm, Courtney's father sat me down and told me that he saw my potential and would be grooming me for bigger and better. I was honored that he wanted to groom me." I paused briefly while Indiya shifted so that she was facing me.

"Go ahead. I'm listening."

"Consequently, he took me under his wing. In addition to working at the firm, he invited me to events, galas, and family functions. Courtney and I were spending more time together, getting closer. I was cautious dating my boss's daughter, but her father encouraged both of us to take stock of one another. We did. Eventually, we fell in love. You know what? I don't even know why I'm telling you any of this. It's irrelevant."

"No, it's okay. Please continue."

I exhaled the breath I didn't know I was holding. "All right. Well, Courtney and I had known each other a little over a year before we determined that we had really strong feelings for one another and acknowledged that we were in love. Her family embraced us—me—and it was the first time I ever felt like I belonged. At work, things couldn't be better. I was learning from the best of the best. In due course, Courtney and I moved in. Her father bristled a bit because we weren't married, but he knew I loved his daughter; therefore, he didn't try to stop us.

"For three years, I advanced at the firm and had become quite fond of my colleagues. I was making great money and, for the first time in my life, felt a sense of security. Courtney had started hinting about marriage and, even though I wasn't ready, I was considering it. But the strangest thing began to happen with her father. The more I proved myself to be diligent, reliable, and trustworthy, the more he gave me glimpses that *he* may not have been.

"I'd be in his office and he would be on the phone. I didn't know who he was speaking with, but I gleaned from his side of the conversation that their business dealings may not have been on the up and up. Although, I wasn't one hundred percent sure. He would eyeball me the entire time he was on the phone, yet, once he hung up, he never explained, and I never mentioned what I had heard. This went on for at least a year, until one weekend when Courtney and I were at her parents' house. He told me he wanted to talk to me in private. He took me to his office and offered me a drink. He sat behind his desk and I in the chair in front of it. We talked sports, the stock market, and everything else under the sun. Finally, he broached the subject for which he needed privacy. I remember our conversation like it was yesterday. He said, 'It's obvious you're going to be a part of my family and I couldn't be happier with Courtney's choice.' Now, mind you, Courtney and I weren't engaged and I hadn't expressed to anyone that we were about to be. So I waited to see where he was going with his conversation. He spoke about responsibility, being a man, and providing for your family. He went on to say, 'There are some deals I want you to handle, that I would not entrust to anyone but family. Mainly estate and trusts business abroad, which requires skilled, yet discreet, handling. I'm putting you in charge.'"

What I didn't tell Indiya was that the business Gregory Francis wanted me to handle had vaulted, not crossed, the line of legality. He briefed me on the deals—laundered funds and offshore accounts. I was at a crossroads. The man I respected, the father of the woman I loved, wanted me to spearhead illegal activity. He gave me access to the client information, accounts, and points of contact. I was uncomfortable with what he wanted from me. I didn't want any part of it. If I were caught, it would be on my head. It would be my license.

A few days after my conversation with him, I went to his office. I let him know that I preferred to resume my old duties and that I wasn't cut out to run his special offshore interests. That set him off. He went ice-cold, telling me that I wasn't a man of vision, a visionary like him, and I would never excel in life. He said I knew too much and he would ruin my career if word got back to him about any of it. He stated that I could forget any type of future with his family, especially Courtney. I tried to rally back and tell him that he had no jurisdiction over my relationship with his daughter. He told me, 'Don't kid yourself.'

To make matters worse, he brought me up on false ethics violations and I was disbarred, lost my license to practice. He fired me, and his daughter did the same shortly thereafter. She did what her father told her—turned her back and discarded me. I had no job, no woman, no family, and no future. Just a threat hanging over my head that I better keep my mouth shut or things could get worse.

I continued telling Indiya a modified, slightly abridged version of the story. "He followed that up by asking me when I was going to propose to his daughter. When I responded that I didn't know, he visibly started. He was upset. He ranted about the opportunities he had afforded me and accused me of shirking my obligation to his daughter. He gave me an ultimatum. Marry his daughter or kiss my career goodbye."

"What did you do?"

"Well, I'm not married."

"And what did Courtney have to say about all of this?"

"Her father was a powerful and persuasive man. He told his daughter what was good for her and it wasn't me. She turned her back on me like I never existed." That part was true.

Indiya stroked my face. "I can understand why you don't want to go back."

I preferred not to go back. I couldn't risk it. I refused to give anyone the opportunity to make good on a threat. Reminiscing about Courtney was never good. It put me in a space that I didn't like to be in.

I was already regretting sharing that history with Indiya. It served no purpose. If anything, it made me appear weak. I could only hope that she had learned something about me—I hated rehashing and I didn't like to over-talk a subject. I was not planning to discuss Courtney, regardless if a whim hit me. I did not want to hear it used against me in an argument. I wanted this to be the first and final discussion about Courtney and Gregory Francis. That was a dark time in my life and I've had many. I was not returning to the dark.

"I apologize for unloading that on you."

"Sometimes we have to share our histories."

"I'm officially done sharing for the day, hell, maybe the month."

"Don't be that way. Let your spirit move you and don't let old walls block your path ahead."

"I'm working on that."

"I'll help you. But first, why don't you help me in the kitchen. I was serious about making you breakfast."

"Can I shower first?"

"We both can and then I'll hook up some cereal for you."

"Cereal is not making breakfast."

"I'm kidding."

I reached for her and tugged her off the bed. "Let's hit the shower."

Indiya was getting another chance to prove herself in the kitchen. I left her down there trying to make a big breakfast while I went up to my office to check on a few financial transactions. The money I transferred from Robert Hudson posted to my account. I logged on to my investment account and scanned my portfolio. I would call my money manager later to discuss making a couple of new investments. There was an energy company that had a promising outlook and I wanted to get some shares before they took off.

I had a stack of unopened letters, bills, and bank statements. Some addressed to Avery Woodson, others to Julian Efram, Marcel Mercer, Camden Tennyson, and even Avery Hudson. Each one of those identities, characters, served a purpose. My world had become confused when I left D.C. I was paranoid about being me—Avery.

From that first moment when I told the process server that I was someone else, I was. I became Julian. And when the situation arose that I needed to be Marcel, I was Marcel. And the same with Camden. If I thought about it, I never knew who Avery Woodson was, but I knew he wasn't enough. Not for his mother to keep, not for his foster parents to want or love, not even for Courtney to faithfully support through adversity. The men I created had become an integral part of the lives I lived.

There was too much mail to go through, especially with Indiya expecting me for breakfast. I would have to wait until later, after she went home. I turned off the lights and locked the door behind me before trudging down the hallway. As I neared the stairs, I could hear the incessant banging of pots and pans. I hurried down the steps, feeling like maybe I had left her to her own devices for too long. I breezed into the room. The air smelled of cooking ham and bread.

Indiya spun around, taking her eyes off the food, spatula dangling from her hand. "I've got everything under control."

"I didn't say you didn't."

"You ran in here, looking scared, as if I was burning down the kitchen."

"The thought crossed my mind while I was upstairs."

She frowned. "What were you doing up there?"

"You know my office is up there."

"That doesn't explain what you're doing."

"Going through some mail."

"Why haven't you ever showed it to me? I remember when I came over here for the first time, you gave this grand tour, with the exception of the office."

"It's just an office. There's nothing to see. It would be like me showing the inside of closets; I didn't show you those either because there's nothing worth seeing inside."

"You are so damned secretive."

It was time to shift the discussion. "How's breakfast coming along?"

"Great." Indiya turned back to the pan with the cooking ham. "I'm getting good at this."

"I'll be the judge of that."

"You enjoyed my ziti."

"Each meal rests on its own laurels." I laughed.

"I'll show you, Mr. Woodson. I will be the master of this kitchen."

"You won't get an argument out of me; the kitchen is yours to master."

Indiya reoccupied herself with our breakfast. I went to wait in the living room before she decided to grill me, instead of our ham steak, some more.

CHAPTER 37

Avery

We had enjoyed the cigar and champagne bar so much the week before, we decided to go out the next weekend. Indiya wanted to try a new club in Manhattan and I agreed that it would be cool to shoot into the city on Saturday night.

There was no valet parking, but we found a spot two blocks from the club. Indiya's heels were high and we were walking slowly to the venue. It was a warm night and we weren't in a hurry. I held her hand in mine as she navigated the sidewalk cracks to avoid her heels getting stuck. A line of about fifty people was in front of the establishment. Some were chatting, others were silent, but they all waited patiently for the bouncers to let them in.

Indiya and I strolled to the front of the line. I slipped the bouncer a hundred-dollar bill, he held the door open, and we walked right in. Classic R&B played throughout the club. The place was full, but it was a laid-back crowd. Long, snaking couches and curved tables filled the room; it had a communal vibe. It was inevitable that you either sat next to or across from someone you didn't know. Every inch of the dance floor was occupied with a moving body.

"Do you want something from the bar?" I asked.

"I could use a drink and I think there are a few seats at the bar too."

I grabbed her hand and led her through the clusters of people standing around talking. I nudged her to an open seat at the bar, then stood next to her chair. "What are you drinking?"

"Vodka and a splash of cranberry."

"Your usual." I laughed. She could have asked for vodka on the rocks because the splash was almost nonexistent.

She elbowed me. "Don't worry about me. You're the driver, so you can only have one."

"I know my role." I leaned in and kissed her temple, then felt a tap on my shoulder.

I hoped this wasn't the type of place where people were crawling all over each other at the bar, trying to get a drink. I turned around, about to tell the person we hadn't ordered yet and they had to wait just like us, but I stopped short. Roxi smiled brightly at me.

"Marcel!" She pulled me into a hug. "I thought that was you."

"Hey, Roxi, how are you?" I separated from her and put a little space in between us. "Shouldn't you be off touring somewhere?"

"I just got back. I was sitting with some folks from my label up there in VIP," she pointed off to the left, "when I saw you walk by."

"It's good to see you."

"You too." She peeped around me at Indiya. "Hi, I'm Roxi."

I reluctantly moved to the side to give Indiya an unobstructed view of Roxi.

Indiya offered her hand. "Indiya."

Roxi immediately diverted her attention back to me. "Why don't you join me in VIP? I want to catch up with you."

"I appreciate it, but—"

"Definitely, thank you," Indiya chimed in. She smiled at me and then got up from her seat.

We followed Roxi to the elevated VIP section. It overlooked the rest of the club. The deejay was spinning from up there, keeping a pulse on the crowd. Roxi led us to her table. Dark was seated front and center, giving me the eye. Roxi quickly rambled off introductions of the others at the table. "And this is Marcel and Indiya."

Indiya gave me a sideways glance as we joined their party. Bottles were open all along the table. We sat down with me sandwiched between Indiya and Roxi.

Indiya whispered in my ear. "Why is she calling you Marcel?"

"Marcel is my middle name."

"I didn't realize you went by your middle name." She held a plastic smile in place.

I didn't respond because she hadn't asked a question. Roxi lifted a bottle of champagne. "Indiya, would you like some bubbly?"

Indiya reached for a bottle of Ciroc. "This is more my speed." She filled a glass with ice, then the vodka. She raised the glass to Roxi and took a sip.

"No splash of cranberry?" I asked. She ignored me and took another drink.

"I can't believe I ran into you," Roxi gushed. "Dark, you remember Marcel, right?"

Dark nodded, or maybe he was bobbing his head to the music, who could tell. The situation was tight. I calculated my options, trying to come up with a way to get Indiya away from Roxi.

"We'll stay for one drink. We're not trying to crash your party."

"Nonsense. I invited you to join us. We have plenty to drink and no crowds." Roxi leaned closer, speaking into my ear. "You look good."

In my peripheral vision, I saw Indiya craning her neck, attempting to hear what Roxi was saying to me. It had to be near impossible with the music playing. Dark, seated next to Indiya, commented to her and when she nodded, refilled her glass. They began talking and I turned to Roxi to discreetly beg off for the night.

"We're going to finish these drinks and then get out of here."

"We're adults, Marcel. Relax. Have a glass of champagne and enjoy the moment. I came out to have a good time tonight. I can only assume you did the same." She handed me a glass. "She's pretty."

I silently agreed with a nod. "How was the tour?"

"It was amazing. I could not believe the love I've been getting."

"Your music is hot. You deserve it."

"Just my music?"

Indiya pivoted in her seat, giving Dark her back, then leaned forward so she could see Roxi. "Roxanne, right?"

"It's Roxi."

"Sorry, girl," Indiya responded with feigned remorse. "You're working that dress."

"Thank you! The designer is a girlfriend of mine."

"I may have to get her number."

"I can give it to Marcel for you."

Indiya wrinkled her nose. "So, how do you two know each other?"

"I see y'all out there doing your thing," the deejay shouted on the microphone, cutting off any possibility of talking over him. "That's right. We came here to party tonight! Who came here to party?" The crowd yelled. "I want to give a shout-out to my girl, Roxi! She's in the house tonight!" The crowd screamed again and Roxi smiled. The deejay threw on her single that was getting all of the radio airplay. "That's right, my girl Roxi is in the building!"

Dark came over to whisper something in Roxi's ear. She nodded, got up from her seat, and went to the railing that overhung the dance floor. She waved down to the masses and the crowd went wild. Dark hustled over to the deejay and got the mic. He handed it to Roxi and she began to sing along to the music, adding riffs and ad libs that weren't on the record. She could sing her ass off. She rocked to the music, singing along with her fans that there was no love better than her love.

She turned to our table and playfully sang to one of the label executives at the end of the table. Indiya looked at me when she sauntered closer to our end. Roxi stopped in front of us and sang directly to me, hand outstretched in my direction. I bopped my head to the music, but refrained from taking her hand. Indiya had propped her elbow on the table, hand beneath her chin, and watched Roxi. The R&B diva chuckled, then grabbed the hand of a guy standing near the table. She led him over to the rail and sang the rest of the song to him.

"That's right, give it up for Roxi!" the deejay shouted. "My girl, Roxi. She put it down!"

Roxi went to return the mic. She hugged the deejay and came back to the table. The label execs flanked Roxi, handed her a glass, and toasted to her.

I threw back the rest of my champagne and stood up. "Come on, let's go," I said to Indiya.

She took her time getting up. I wanted to make a swift exit, preferably before Roxi returned. Indiya grabbed her purse from the table and made a beeline toward Roxi at the other end of the table. I kept my gait slow and steady and came up next to them, catching the tail end of their conversation.

"Is that so?"

"Yeah, that's so. Oh, and nice performance."

"I know." Roxi beamed at me. "Don't be a stranger." She tugged on my hand, then rejoined her party.

I guided Indiya toward the stairs that led to the main floor. "Maybe we can find a table that's not too crowded."

"I'm ready to go."

I stopped at the bottom of the steps. "Are you serious? It's still early."

She walked past me, heading toward the door. I shook my head and followed her outside. I hastened to keep up with her brisk stride. The line to get in the club was longer than it was when we arrived. She shot by it, not answering the waiting people who inquired how it was inside.

"You want to slow down?"

"That was some bullshit, Avery. I mean Marcel." She stopped in the middle of the sidewalk, turning to face me. "What the hell was that about? That bitch was acting like she was in heat. Who the hell is she anyway?"

"Would you stop shouting," I said, approaching her coolly.

"I did not appreciate the way she was acting with you."

"What did I do?" I reached for her hand, but she it yanked away. "Nothing."

"I didn't do anything."

"Yeah and it pissed me off." She was yelling again.

I was not fond of making a scene in public. "Can we talk about this when we get to the car?"

"That chick has one song and she's acting like some sort of diva."

"Indiya, calm down."

Her eyes stretched wide, then she pivoted and marched off in the direction of the car. She was a half block ahead of me when she stumbled forward, hopping on one foot. She bent over, balancing on one leg, reaching down to the sidewalk. I caught up and peered down at her heel stuck in a sidewalk crack. I knelt down, brushed her hand to the side, and twisted her shoe until it came loose. I held it for her to step into as she placed her hand on my shoulder to steady herself.

I stood up. "Can we walk to the car together now?"

Wordlessly, we traveled the remaining distance to the car. I opened Indiya's door for her and then walked around to my side. I took a deep breath before getting inside.

"Are you sleeping with her?"

I closed my door. "No, I'm not."

"Then what the hell was with her singing to you like you're her man?"

"Indiya, she's a singer; she was performing. She sang to a few other men, not just me."

"How do you know her?"

"We're acquaintances."

"There you go with that secretive bullshit. What does that mean, Avery?"

"I don't understand this reaction. We came out to have a good time, not deal with this nonsense."

"Maybe if I start calling you Marcel, then I'll get some answers."

"Don't call me that."

"Why not? It's your middle name, right?"

"Middle name or not, don't call me that."

"All right." Indiya strapped in to her seat and stared out of the front window.

I recognized that Roxi was probably laying it on thick for Indiya's sake. She didn't have to sit next to me nor perform in front of me, but Indiya accepted her invite to the VIP.

I cruised down Second Avenue to the Midtown Tunnel. I turned the radio on and tuned into Power 105.

"I don't want to hear hip-hop and R&B." Indiya changed the station to reggae down the dial.

I switched it back to my hip-hop. I wasn't about to let her bully her way through the night. She may have thought something was up with Roxi, but I refused to prove her right. "We could have stayed at the club, you know."

"I bet you would have enjoyed that," she countered. "Private shows by big-haired chicks, of course you didn't want to leave."

I turned up the music and stepped on the gas, hugging the curves as I sped through the tunnel. I slowed only to go through the toll, then gunned it down the Long Island Expressway back to Brookville.

Indiya was climbing out of the car before I had even come to a complete stop. She carried her shoes to the front door and waited for me. She was mumbling as I came up the porch. "Taking all day with the key."

"What's that?"

"I said can you move any slower with the key? Like I want to be standing out here all night."

I unlocked the door, pushed it open, and stepped to the side. She stormed past me and went into the living room, dropping her shoes on the floor and purse on the couch. I locked the door behind us, set the alarm, then slowly walked into the living room. I bent over and picked up her shoes and went to put them in the shoe rack in the foyer. She watched me like a hawk, arms folded across her chest.

"Do you want to watch a movie?" I grabbed the remote from the coffee table.

"You can't be serious."

I froze, the remote pointed at the television, and turned around. "You wanted to do something else?"

"Oh, I don't know, you mean like maybe talk about what the hell just happened?"

"Indiya—"

"Don't Indiya me. It was obvious you and that woman had something going on."

"You're wrong. We don't have anything going on."

"I don't believe that."

"Roxi is a performer. You cannot think that I'm sleeping with her because she sang to me. She was entertaining the audience. That's all."

"Explain to me why she's calling you by some pet name or middle name or whatever? I only know you as Avery. Why don't I know that you like to be called Marcel?"

"Indiya, you are trying to find fault where there is none. I'm sure you have friends or family who refer to you by other names."

"Yeah, I do, but—"

"Exactly and if I met them and they referred to you by another name, I'm not going to flip out over it." I sat on the couch and stretched my legs out in front of me. "I don't see why this is a problem."

"She just seemed real familiar, Avery."

"I don't agree."

"You don't have to because I know what I know."

I chuckled. "Okay, Madame Zenobia."

"Oh, you think shit is funny."

"What I think is you need to calm down."

"You know what? You're right. I do. And I'm going to do that at my own house." She turned in a blur and started out of the room.

"You're leaving?" I asked, jumping up from the couch.

"That's what I said," she called out as she moved down the hall toward my bedroom.

I wandered into the bedroom. "Over this nonsense, you're going to leave?"

She grabbed her overnight bag and began tossing in items. "I don't see it as nonsense when I tell some chick that I'm your girlfriend and she asks, 'Is that so?'"

"Why did you feel the need to say anything to her?"

"I told her thanks for the drinks and next time, she needs to sing to a man that isn't with his girlfriend." She stopped and looked at me. "Why would you have a problem with me saying something to her?"

"It was unnecessary."

"Yeah, okay." Indiya snatched up her bag and tossed it over her shoulder. She stalked past me, her bag bumping into my stomach.

"Come on, Indiya. Where are you going?"

"I'm out, Avery."

I stood in the bedroom calling to her. "Indiya."

"Goodbye, Avery."

"Indiya, come on." I went out into the hallway and she was stepping into her shoes.

She grabbed the doorknob. "Goodnight," she said with a dismissive flip of the hand.

"Indiya, please don't leave!" I shouted as I ran up behind her, pushing the door closed. "Don't leave, please," I implored, my voice strained.

She turned around, her body trapped between mine and the door. My hand nailed to the door prevented her from moving.

"Don't leave me, Indiya," I whispered. "Please." I pressed my lips to her forehead.

She stared at me, the anger on her face dissipating. She shrugged her bag from her shoulder, letting it slip down her arm. I slowly reached for the strap and took it from her. She begrudgingly let me grab her hand and lead her back into the living room. I dropped her bag on the floor and pulled her into my arms. It took a moment, but eventually she hugged me back.

She lifted her head from my shoulder. "Maybe we can find a good movie on cable."

I smiled and drew her over to the couch with me. We settled in the chair, Indiya leaning back against my chest. "Promise me you won't try to leave like that again."

She nestled her head in the crook of my neck. "I promise, I won't."

CHAPTER 38

Avery

I rolled over and reached for Indiya, scooting closer to her side of the bed. I squinted as my eyes adjusted to the morning sunlight filtering into the room. The covers were thrown back and she was not next to me.

"Indiya," I grumbled, my voice deep with sleep. "Babe, where are you?"

I sat up, eyes searching the room. Her bag was gone and I didn't see any of her other belongings on my dresser. No jewelry, perfume, or hair accessories. I looked at the clock. It was five minutes past seven. I climbed from the bed and ambled down the hall to the front door. I peered out to the driveway. Her car was gone. I shook my head. She slipped out without even waking me.

I went back into the bedroom to get my phone. I dialed Indiya's number and waited for her to pick up. I got her voicemail. I hung up and dialed again. Voicemail. I waited for the tone to leave a message. "Good morning. I missed you when I woke up and you weren't here. Call me back."

I went into the bathroom to relieve myself, wash my face, and brush the pearly whites. I lay back across the bed and waited for the phone to ring. The night before, Indiya and I didn't do much talking after she had almost left. We watched a couple of movies on the couch before going to bed. I mostly stared at the television and thought about everything that had transpired over the course of the night: running into Roxi, Indiya questioning me about who she was and why she called me Marcel, but especially my reaction to Indiya wanting to leave me. I panicked; that's what I did—panicked. I got anxious when she was about to walk out.

Last night on the couch, I held her tight and kept her close to me. The thought that a coincidental encounter with Roxi almost exposed a side of me that I didn't want Indiya to know, startled me. Indiya knew Avery and that was the way I intended to keep it. She didn't need to know about Marcel, Julian, or Camden. She would never understand. No one would. Half of the time, I didn't understand it myself, but it was my life and I accepted it for what it was. Complicated but necessary. I hadn't lied to Indiya last night. I wasn't sleeping with Roxi, at least not anymore. There was no need.

Ever since Indiya had come into my life, I noticed slight changes in myself. For the past three years, Avery had played the background. It was almost as if I was slowly erasing that part of myself. My true self. I hadn't been in my own skin in such a long time I had almost forgotten what it was like. I began to realize I appreciated that Indiya had met Avery, not Camden. It could have been that I needed to spend more time as myself. I had been living with darkness surrounding me for so long that I shied away from and didn't embrace the light.

I enjoyed being with Indiya. She challenged me in a way that I wasn't accustomed to with other women. Her say-anything nature threw me for a loop at first, but I had pretty much learned how to roll with the jabs, and there were plenty.

I picked up my phone and dialed her again. When my call went to voicemail for the third time, I started to get annoyed. Why did she leave so early and without telling me? I was going to make her breakfast in bed to show her how it's supposed to be done. I smiled despite myself. Our competitiveness when it came to cooking was cute. Neither of us was really good at it, but we were learning together and trying to one-up each other at the same time. I got up and went to the kitchen. I was going to make myself something to eat, anyway. Indiya would just have to miss out.

I looked at my watch. It was five o'clock and I had been in the backyard drinking beer and listening to music all afternoon. I had not heard a word from Indiya all day and I was fuming. After placing about seven calls, I stopped. She knew where to find me when she wanted me. The problem was I didn't know where to find her. I had already Googled her weeks ago, trying to find out where she lived, but couldn't find anything.

The song playing on my Bose docking station changed to Roxi's reggae cut. She looked fine the night before. I knew better than to acknowledge it in Indiya's presence, nevertheless, her hair, outfit, and that radiant smile was on point. I bobbed my head to the music.

I checked my watch again, then ran inside the house. I came back out to the yard a minute later, with my other cell phone in hand and restarted Roxi's song. I reclined back in the seat and went through my address book until I reached her name. I gazed at the number while the song continued to play. She hit a long high note and I pressed "call." She answered on the first ring.

"Guess what I'm listening to?"

"Your favorite singer?"

"How'd you know?"

"I can hear her amazing voice in the background."

We both laughed.

"I love this song," I said.

"Really, why?"

"It reminds me of an afternoon a few months ago when someone danced and sang for me in my living room."

"That was an incredible afternoon."

"Yes, it was."

"I didn't expect to hear from you, Marcel. Your friend, Indiya, I believe, made it clear that you're her man."

"I wanted to talk to you. We didn't have much of a chance to speak last night."

"Well, it was tough with so many people around."

The song ended and I clicked the remote to replay it. "Every time I hear this song, I picture those eyes of yours."

Roxi giggled. "What are you doing tonight?"

"I don't have any plans."

"You know, that song sounds much better when it's sung live."

"So, what are you saying?"

"I'm saying, why don't you come to my place for an exclusive performance?"

"I think I can do that. What time is the show?"

"Showtime is eight o'clock and audience participation is a must."

"I'll be there."

"Bye, Marcel," she said in a kittenish purr.

I ended the call and took a swig of my beer. I replayed the song from the beginning. She was ready to give me a command performance. Apparently, she wasn't fazed by her interaction with Indiya last night, even after Indiya told her she was my girlfriend. I found it ironic that my girlfriend was nowhere to be found. I pushed the thought out of my head. If Indiya wanted to be missing in action, I'd let her. I nudged her from my mind and listened to the rest of the song.

I decided it would be a good idea to get a fresh haircut before I set off to Roxi's. A brother needed to be sharp. I turned off the music, snatched my beer, and went into the house. A few minutes later, I was on my way to the barbershop before it closed.

I walked in and my barber was finishing up with a guy. "How you doing, Chip? Am I too late for a cut?"

He nodded for me to have a seat in his chair. "What's good, man? You waited until the last minute to come up in here," he said with a laugh.

"I'm sorry, man, I know you want to get home to your family for that Sunday dinner."

"You never come in this late. That can mean only one thing. You got a date with some honey." Chip was an old school cat who had been cutting hair for a long time. Many brothers had sat in his chair and listened to his tall tales.

"I have someone to meet, so, make it snappy and cut whatever story you're about to tell in half."

"I don't have any stories to tell today, except that you young dudes better be careful out there."

"In what way?"

"With the ladies."

"I think I've got that covered."

"So did that knucklehead that just left out of here. His woman found out he was cheating and smashed up his car, everything from the windshield to the bumper."

"That's messed up."

"Yeah it is. He was driving a piece of junk, but that was still that man's property."

I started to laugh. "That's cold, Chip."

"I'm speaking the truth, that's all. Y'all gotta treat the ladies right."

"Thanks for the advice, but I'm relatively sure that no one will be smashing my car up."

"I hope not because you keep a clean ride at all times. What's that you're driving today?"

"An Audi A8."

"That's tight, man. You better keep that in the garage at all times."

"Chip, nobody wants to smash up my cars."

"You better keep your head still before you walk out of here with a smashed-up haircut."

Chip was a trip. He kept everyone entertained and most looking good. He finished up my haircut. I paid him and gave a hefty tip for being swift and for delaying his Sunday dinner.

I walked in the house and went straight to the bathroom to take a quick shower. I soaped up and washed my hair. I thought back to what Chip said about taking care of the ladies. That was a two-way street and women should be expected to do the same. I turned off the water and stepped out of the shower. I took my towel, dried off, and then wrapped it around my waist as I went to my closet for something casual to wear.

I stepped into a pair of black chinos and pulled a fitted black V-neck tee shirt over my head. It was seven o'clock and if I was going to get to Roxi's by eight, it was time for me to head out. I took my black loafers out of the closet and carried them into the living room. I set them on the floor in front of me and picked up my cell phone.

No missed calls while I was in the shower.

I leaned back against the cushion and rubbed my hand back

and forth over my freshly cut hair. I had a private show to get to, yet I sat. I reached for the remote and turned on the metro traffic channel. The traffic was moving on all highways; still, I didn't move.

I listened again. The doorbell had rung. I stood up, my body stiff from the position I had been in. The bell rang again. I hobbled to the door and checked the peephole. "What the hell?" I opened the door no more than the width of my body.

"Let me in, Avery."

I glanced at my watch, half past ten. "I'm surprised to see you."

"Can I come in?"

I stepped aside, opening the door wide enough for Indiya to enter, but still have to squeeze past me. It was childish, but I didn't care. I left the door open and kept her standing in the foyer. "What's going on, Indiya?"

She looked me up and down. "Are you on your way out?"

"I was, but I changed my mind."

"Where were you going?"

"To a show."

"Do you mind if I come in to talk to you?"

I closed the door and gestured for her to go into the living room. With the exception of the light coming from the television, the room was dark. She went over to the lamp and turned it on.

"I know you're probably upset with me."

"Why would you think something like that?"

"Avery."

"Could it be because you left out of here this morning without so much as a word? Then you didn't answer any of my calls or even think to call me all day long. Could that be why you would think I'm upset?"

Indiya eased down on the chair closest to her. "I needed a little break."

"Yeah?"

"Don't sound like that, Avery. I needed some time with my thoughts."

"Then what are you doing here?"

"I missed you today and I probably should have told you what was going on."

I stared down at her waiting for her to finish.

"Last night really got to me," she continued. "I felt like I still don't know you and you are perfectly fine with that."

"You're not going to learn something about someone overnight."

"We've been seeing each other longer than overnight."

"It takes time to get to know someone, Indiya. It's not something you force."

"It just seemed that you weren't taking my concerns seriously."

"I know that I'm not sleeping with Roxi, so maybe I was some-what unresponsive to what you were saying, but you blew everything out of proportion."

"I can concede to that. I get a little crazy sometimes, but it's just because I'm a passionate person. I got mad when I felt like that chick knew more about you than I did."

I kneeled in front of Indiya's chair. "You know the real me, Indiya. Why can't you accept me at face value—what you see right here in front of you?"

"I'm working on it." She smiled and stroked my face. "I'm sorry for not calling you back."

"You were trying to make me as crazy as you." I laughed. "It almost worked."

Indiya had driven me crazy. As much as I had tried all day to put her out of my mind, I couldn't. With each passing hour, I fumed a little more than the previous one. But when it came down to it, I didn't act on emotion. I had every intention to go to Roxi's, but when it came time to walk out that door, I still wanted Indiya. I wanted her to call. I wanted to see her face. I wanted to feel her next to me. Not anyone else. So, I waited on the couch with my phone on the coffee table. I nodded off waiting.

I left Roxi hanging, but somehow I knew the R&B diva had a plan B. She had a lot going on in her life and my no-show wouldn't stop her world from turning. That didn't excuse my behavior; however, we were both better off for it.

"We'll have to work on not making each other crazy," she said.

"Are you staying?"

"I left my bag in the car in case you threw me out."

"I'll go get it." I held out my hand. "Give me the key."

"My bag is in the back seat."

I went out to the driveway and felt a sense of relief. If I had left to be with Roxi, this moment would not have been happening. It was where I had wanted to be all day long, from the minute I woke up. I smiled at the thought that I hadn't complicated the situation any further.

I went back into the living room with her bag and a lighter mood. "I have some news for you about our trip."

"You mean you're still going to take me after today?" she teased.

"Of course, and we've got a suite at the Mayfair Hotel in London."

"That's near all the great shopping, isn't it?"

"I figured you would appreciate that. When I get tired of Fashion Week, thankfully, I can go horseback riding or golfing. There's also a casino in the hotel, so we can do some gambling when we get back from the shows."

"I can't believe it's in two weeks."

"I've got the tickets for our flight to prove it."

"Thank you, Avery." She got up to hug me. "I wanted to go to London Fashion Week, but you made it happen."

I kissed Indiya and started to undress her in the middle of the living room.

What she didn't understand was I wanted to make her happy and that her happiness was starting to rub off on me.

CHAPTER 39

I was parked outside of the Long Island Rail Road Hicksville Station, waiting for Indiya's train. Instead of going home to get her car to drive out to my house, she was coming straight from work on the train. The Friday evening frenzy was in full swing—cars doing pick-ups, darting in and out of spaces; people rushing across streets, trying to beat traffic; droves of commuters descending from the platform. Her train could not arrive soon enough. I was ready to return to the comfort and solitude of my home.

I received a text from Indiya that the train was running late, but it was one stop away at Westbury. The car in front of me pulled out and I crept closer to where she would be coming down the stairs. A few minutes later, I saw her in the crowd carrying a small bag. She put it down at the bottom of the steps and wheeled it to my car. I popped the trunk and got out of the car.

"Hey, babe," I said, greeting her with a hug.

She passed me the bag. "Hey, handsome."

We jumped into the car and I jetted into traffic on Route 107. "What do you want to do for dinner, beautiful?"

"I'm so tired. We can go to Johnny Rockets right over there and take it back to your place."

"If you want a burger, I can grill you one when we get home."

"I know you love your grill and all, but a turkey burger and onion rings from Johnny Rockets would hit the spot."

"All right," I said resignedly.

Indiya laughed. "Awww, your burgers are good, too."

"It's too late. Don't try to spare my feelings now."

We got Indiya her food and while we waited, had to suffer through a tired lip-syncing-to-the-oldies act by the kids who worked there. Indiya sang "Shop Around" by the Miracles the entire ride home and was not doing Smokey Robinson any justice. I ushered her into the house, begging her to stop with the song.

By the time we went to bed, I was singing it to Indiya and driving her crazy.

The next morning, we were up early having coffee at the table in the kitchen. Indiya sat across from me in a pair of my boxers and a tee shirt, with her bare foot in my chair between my legs. She was trying to convince me that instead of drinking coffee, we should be juicing.

"Kale is especially good for you. We could juice it with a few oranges. Trust me, you'd love it."

"I'm with you on the orange juice. You lost me with the kale."

"Be open to trying something new."

"I am. I made you this coffee, didn't I?" She tapped her foot and I scooted back. "Watch the jewels."

"I know how to handle your jewels."

I stopped laughing with Indiya and cocked my head to the side. It was faint, but I heard the phone up in my office.

"The Bat Phone is ringing," she said sarcastically.

I thrust back from the table and bounded up the steps. I felt along the top of the doorframe and retrieved the key to unlock the door. I slipped inside, closing the door behind me. I dove across the desk to answer the phone before it stopped ringing.

"Good morning," I answered, lightly panting.

"Avery? It's Mr. Charles."

"Hello, Mr. Charles."

"I apologize for calling you early on a Saturday morning."

"It's not a problem. I was already up."

"I wanted to schedule a day to meet with you. I have some information I want to share. Are you available on Monday?"

"You found something out about my mother?"

"Possibly."

"I don't want to wait that long. I can meet you in two hours."

"All right, young man. Meet me at The Comfort Diner on East Forty-Fifth at ten. We can talk over breakfast."

I hung up with Mr. Charles and rushed downstairs.

"You almost broke my leg off to get to that phone. Is everything okay?"

"I may have a lead on my mother."

"Really?"

"I have to run out for a bit, but I'll be back as soon as I can."

"Don't worry about me. I'll find something to occupy myself."

I was heading out of the room before Indiya completed her sentence. I took a quick shower, threw on a pair of shorts and a polo shirt, kissed Indiya goodbye, then jumped in the car on my way to the city.

I was driving faster than I should have been, but I couldn't wait to hear what Mr. Charles had found out. For the first time in my life, I felt that maybe, just maybe, my mother and I would be together soon. It was an alien feeling. I had always hoped to meet her, but I never had the feeling that it could be tomorrow or the next day. I always thought it would be someday. That was a familiar feeling to me. Always wanting to know my mother, but not knowing if it would ever happen. I questioned whether she wanted to know me in the same way. Did she look for me? If so, why hadn't she found me?

I desperately longed to know more about Diane Woodson. Was life better to her than it had been to me? I had cobbled together an existence that brought little happiness. I had experienced happy moments and times, but that wasn't the same as being truly happy. Maybe I never deserved to be happy. I wasn't dealt the best hand in life, but there were many ways to play the hand I had been given. I definitely could have played mine differently, although, there was a time when I played with more integrity, more honesty. After I learned that those who were dealing the cards had a few tricks up their sleeves to always win, I adapted my game. I lied, connived, and cheated to make sure I would always win too.

I thought for a moment, *What would Diane Woodson think about the things her son had done to get by?* The potential answer concerned me.

I found Mr. Charles sitting at a corner booth in his usual tweed blazer. He was scanning the menu and drinking a cup of coffee. He looked up when I slipped into the booth.

"Avery," he reached over and shook my hand, "good to see you."

"I appreciate you meeting me on a Saturday."

"Breakfast at The Comfort Diner is a Saturday morning ritual for me. I figured I could talk to you here just as well as I could at the office. Would you like to order something?"

"Maybe a cup of coffee."

The waitress came over to take our orders. I asked for coffee with cream and sugar. Mr. Charles had a healthy appetite; he ordered eggs, pancakes, bacon, and sausage.

He started polishing his silverware with his napkin. "Avery, I have an unusual piece of information for you. I want to caution you in advance that I don't know how useful it will be."

I leaned forward anxious for him to continue. "I'm listening."

"I managed to find out that your mother married a man in Detroit close to thirty years ago, named Delroy Gross. I don't have much information. What I do know is that Delroy is now deceased, but his sister, Ruthie, is alive and still lives in Detroit."

"So you don't know where my mother is?"

"Not yet, but there's a chance that Ruthie has some information that could help us locate her."

I weighed what Mr. Charles was telling me. There was a possibility that this woman could lead me to my mother. "Well, what's next?"

"This is highly unusual, Avery, and in any other situation I would not advocate this approach. However, this could be a pivotal cog in our search."

"What is it?"

"Ruthie would not talk to me. When I told her who I was and what I was looking for, she insisted on only speaking with you."

"All right, fine. What's her number? I'll call her."

"In person."

"I've got to go to Detroit?"

"If you want to hear what this Ruthie person has to say, yes."

I sighed, rubbing my hand along my chin. "Then, I have no choice. I'm going. In fact, I'm going today."

Mr. Charles reached into his jacket pocket and took out a slip of paper. "This is Ruthie's address in Detroit." He slid it across the table to me. "I want you to call me as soon as you get back. I don't care how late it is." His breakfast arrived at the table.

"I will." I took out my wallet and tossed a twenty on the table.

"No, keep your money. You didn't eat. You didn't even touch your coffee."

"I intruded on your weekend ritual. The least I can do is treat you to breakfast." I stood up to leave and then sat back down. "Mr. Charles, there's something else I want you to look into for me."

"Certainly."

CHAPTER 40

Avery

I called my travel agent from the car. I had a two o'clock flight out of LaGuardia to Detroit. There wasn't much for me to consider in deciding to go to Detroit. If I wanted to find my mother, I had to be willing follow every decent lead. If Ruthie knew Diane Woodson, I needed to hear what she could tell me.

I was going home to pack an overnight bag, in case I had to stay an extra day, then head right back out to the airport. Indiya was in the living room dusting the coffee table when I came in.

She popped her head up. "When is the last time you dusted in here?"

"Forget about that," I responded as I grabbed her hand and pulled her to the bedroom. "I'm going to Detroit."

"What?"

"I should be back tonight or tomorrow afternoon at the latest." I took my bag from the closet and placed it on the bed.

"What's in Detroit?"

"I'm going to see a woman that may be my mother's sister-in-law. I'm hoping she can fill in some blanks for me, maybe even lead me to my mother."

"Do you want me to go with you?"

"No. She insisted on talking to only me and I don't want to

rock the boat." I snatched her up in a brusque hug and placed a rough kiss on her cheek. "But thank you for offering. My flight is at two, so I have to get out of here. I want you to stay, though. If you need to go out or decide to go home, take the BMW. I'll leave the keys on the table in the mudroom."

"I hope this woman has some information you can use."

"I do too."

I hurried through the house. I thought it would be a good idea to take my picture of Diane Woodson to show Ruthie. I ran up the stairs to retrieve it from the safe in my office. I reached for the key and then grabbed the doorknob. It was already unlocked. I paused outside the door and tried to remember whether I had locked it before going to meet Mr. Charles. I figured I was rushing and must have neglected to do it. I hurried inside, opened up the safe, and pulled out my lone picture of my mother. I pressed it to my lips before tucking it in my wallet. I exited the office and closed the door behind me, turning the knob to confirm that it was locked.

I went to grab my bag from the bedroom. Indiya was back in the living room with the television on. "You going to be all right?"

"I'll be fine."

I planted a hurried kiss on her lips. "I'll call you later."

"Have a safe trip."

CHAPTER 41

Avery

The plane touched down and the flight attendant welcomed us to Detroit. She announced that the local time was four p.m. As we taxied to the gate, I sent Indiya a text letting her know that I landed. I was seated in first class and my bag was in the overhead compartment. I anticipated being off the plane in a couple of minutes.

One of the flight attendants slipped me her number as I exited the plane. Her name was Candi and she did look sweet. Unfortunately for Candi, her timing was all wrong. I was turning over a new leaf. I got to the top of the jetway and tossed the paper with her number written on it in the first garbage can I came to.

I followed the signs to car rentals and waited on a short line to get to the counter. I told the rep that I would need a GPS because I was not familiar with the area. She told me to be careful because there had been an increase in crime lately in some areas. She had no idea; crime was the furthest thing from my mind.

I found my car in the lot, a mid-size that was way too small for my long legs. I pushed the seat back as far as it could go and squeezed myself behind the wheel. I hooked up the GPS, plugged in Ruthie's address, and drove out of the airport.

The GPS guided me off the highway and into a neighborhood filled with old and shuttered homes. I passed block after block of houses with lopsided porches and tattered fences. I made a right on to Ruthie's street and drove slowly down the block, checking house numbers to see which one was hers. I stopped in front of number twenty-seven. It was a small, single-level house with olive green siding. A couple panels of the siding were hanging off and blowing along with the breeze. Four children played in the front yard. One of them chased the others with a long stick, wildly swinging it from side to side. I sat with the engine idling for a few minutes, watching the kids play. When one of the kids stopped to look and the others followed suit, I parked the car and got out.

I walked up to the weathered white picket fence and stood outside of it. One of the kids, a little boy no more than six, started to approach me. The one with the stick grabbed his shoulder and flung him back.

"What you lookin' at?" he asked, with young bravado.

"Hey, little man. Does Ms. Ruthie live here?"

"Who wants to know?" he asked. The others stood by with wide-eyed curiosity.

"Avery."

"Grandmaaaa!" he yelled from where he was standing. A little girl ran up the two steps to the house and went inside.

A gray-haired woman, supported by a cane, limped out of the door. The little girl peeped from behind her housecoat. The woman pushed her glasses closer to her eyes. "Who's that at my gate?"

"My name is Avery Woodson. Are you Ruthie?"

"That's what my birth certificate say. Come on in."

I opened the gate and it squeaked for some oil. The three boys trailed behind me. "Hey, fellas," I said, rubbing the head of one of the boys.

"Y'all stay on out here and play." She shooed the little girl down the steps. "Go on, Diamond."

I walked up the crumbling stone steps and followed Ruthie into the house. The blinds were open and sun streamed into the living room. Worn plaid furniture, covered with throws, and oak tables filled the small but neat room. A floor-model television blasted an old episode of *Martin*.

Ruthie shuffled over to the TV and turned down the volume. "Have a seat, Avery."

I sat in a recliner across from the love seat. A glass of soda was on the coffee table in front of where Ruthie had been sitting. She sat down and took a sip of her beverage. "You want something to drink?"

"No, thank you. I appreciate you taking time to talk to me."

"I didn't expect to see you this soon." She wiped her top lip with the back of her hand. "I only spoke with that Charles man yesterday."

"It was important for me to come see you."

Ruthie picked up a pack of cigarettes. She waved the pack in my direction. I shook my head. She lit a cigarette, took a drag, and blew a stream of smoke across the room. "So, you're Diane's son?"

"She's my mother."

"How old are you?"

"Thirty-four."

"Where do you live?"

"In New York."

"New York's a big place. Where specifically?"

"Long Island."

"I had a cousin that lived in Long Island. I think it was somewhere called Wine Dance. You know where that is."

"You must mean Wyandanch. Yes, I know where it is."

"Are you married?"

"No."

"Any kids?"

"Not yet."

"How do you make your living?"

"I'm a lawyer."

"You're doing good for yourself."

"I do alright."

Ruthie mashed out her cigarette in the ashtray. "I used to want to be a lawyer or something like that, but after I graduated high school, my family couldn't afford to send me to college. I had to get a job as a cashier at the local food market. I would try to save up my money to maybe one day take a few classes, but there was never enough. Now, my brother, Delroy, he could save a dollar. He was good like that. Resourceful, I think they call it. Since I was his baby sister—he was five years older than me, you know— he would buy me things and give me money from time to time. He would always say, 'Ruthie, you have to learn how to save and not spend so much.' I wished I was more like my big brother. When he graduated from high school, he went and got himself a trade. Got himself a job at the Ford plant and worked his way up the ranks to management. He was making good money. Bought himself a big ol' house out in the suburbs. Once he moved, I didn't see him as much, but he would send checks for us."

Ruthie stopped talking long enough to take a drink from her glass. I started to think there was more than just soda in it.

"Eventually," she continued, "I got married. I was only nineteen. I didn't want to get married so young, but my parents thought it was time for someone else to take care of me. My husband, he didn't have the sense God gave him. He worked all week, then got drunk on Fridays and spent all his money playing cards with his fool friends. I can remember crying to my brother that we didn't have enough money for food and he would send one of his workers over with a bag of groceries or an envelope with enough money to get us through to the next week. I loved my brother. He was always there for his baby sister. That's what he called me too—Baby Sister. I started stashing some of the money he would send me because I was set on going back to school. I knew I was meant for greater than the life I was living. But then I found out I had a baby on the way and I had to put that dream on the shelf. Before I knew it, I had four kids running around this house by the time I was twenty-five."

I cleared my throat. "Ruthie." If I didn't interrupt, she would be talking about herself all night. "Would you mind taking a look at this picture?" I reached into my wallet and handed her the picture of my mother. "Is that the Diane Woodson you know?"

She brought the picture close to her face. "Well, look at that. All decked out in her graduation clothes."

"Is that her? Was she married to your brother?"

"That's her."

"Are you sure?"

She handed the picture back to me. "There's no doubt about it. I know Diane. Everything changed once she came around. She was my brother's second wife and much younger than he was."

"How old was she when they got married?"

"Well, if he was nearing forty, Diane had to be 'bout twenty-five. He met her down at the plant. She was working the line and he was her boss."

"Is she still in Detroit? Do you know where she is?"

"Now, you came here to find out what I know about Diane and I'm gonna tell you. But I'm gonna tell it in my way."

I held my tongue. Ruthie was the only person I encountered that could tell me anything about my mother after she left me at the orphanage.

"Where was I? Oh, yeah, I had four kids at twenty-five and my brother did a great deal for us. He helped buy clothes for the kids, pay doctor bills, and even buy Christmas gifts. As me and my knucklehead husband was reaching our eighth anniversary,, two things happened. We got divorced and Delroy married his first wife, Kim. Now that was a sweet woman. She would let me send my kids to their big house in the suburbs for weekends and sometimes for weeks in the summer.

"I was able to get myself a part-time job to take care of them kids, 'cause Lord knows I couldn't rely on their daddy. It was tough, but we made it through. I kept a roof over our heads and food on the table and they all were getting their education. I told them they were going to do better than me. I wanted them to be like their uncle—with a good job, a big house, and nice cars to drive. I made sure they had a positive role model to look up to and taught them to set their sights further than that gate out front. I told them to look at how their uncle was living and strive for the same. And you know what? All my kids are doing good. They could be doing better, but they got steady jobs, they don't have to live with me, and they give their mama a little money every once in a while."

"I'm glad to hear your family is doing well and prospering—"

"I know; you want to hear about Diane. Well, my brother had that sweet wife with a heart of gold at home. I considered her a sister to me. I never knew them to be having any problems. Neither one of them complained about any troubles. Then one day, out of the blue, Delroy tells me that they split and that Kim was moving away, out of state. I couldn't believe my ears. I tried to convince him to hold on to that woman, but he told me there was no going back; they were getting divorced. A few months later, I met Diane, your mother. And as I mentioned, everything changed."

Finally. I moved to the edge of my seat. "How did they change?"

"Well, for starters, she moved into my brother's house. I can remember it like it was yesterday. I called him to see if I could send the kids over for the weekend and he told me it wasn't a good time. His *lady* was staying with him and four kids may be too much to handle. I couldn't believe my brother was telling me that his nieces and nephews weren't welcome. That was just the beginning. Two months later, they were married. I tried to get to know Diane, but she kept her distance. She was pleasant enough, but she was no Kim. Unless my brother was around, she didn't want to be bothered with me and my kids. There was always something sad about her. Sometimes I could see a little fire in her when she spoke to Delroy, but usually she didn't seem happy."

I flinched. There was that word. *Happy.* "So my mother wasn't a mean person, you two just didn't connect?"

"Diane seemed cold to me, which I couldn't understand because my brother loved her to death."

"Maybe you misread her."

"All I know is that once your mother married my brother, he didn't have no time for me and my kids. All these years later, I still think Diane was the reason he divorced Kim."

"You blame her for that?"

"Delroy was happily married, then this girl fifteen years younger than him starts working at the plant and he's getting divorced. I ain't get the best grades in school, but I can do that math."

I didn't want to argue with Ruthie and tell her that her brother was a grown man and grown men make choices. He chose the path he wanted to travel. She shouldn't blame Diane for his decisions. "Did Delroy and Diane have any children?"

"No, but my brother had one child from his previous marriage. That poor baby was only four years old when Kim moved away.

My brother rarely got to see his own child. On top of that, Diane was keeping him from mine. We fell on some hard times too and Delroy didn't do nothing to help us. He was never like that, not until Diane. We didn't get no Christmas gifts, no school clothes, nothing. It was like he didn't even care about us no more."

I had to redirect Ruthie. "How long was my mother married to Delroy?"

"Until the day he died. My poor brother died young. He was only fifty."

"So they were married for about ten years."

"Um-hmm."

"That would mean Diane was about thirty-five when he passed."

"Sounds right to me."

"How long ago was this?"

"Let's see." She looked up as if the answer were on the ceiling. "March made nineteen years since Delroy went on to glory."

"When was the last time you saw my mother, Ruthie?"

"Nineteen years. Not since the day of the funeral."

"You never saw my mother again?"

"Haven't laid eyes on her. She got his insurance money, sold the house, and disappeared. Didn't share the money with his family or nothing. Not even his only child. I kept in touch with Kim over the years and she told me she never saw a red cent."

"Ruthie, you don't have any idea where she may have gone?"

"Nope."

"Do you remember their old address?"

"Like the back of my hand. They lived at 210 Fairfax Street."

"Did she ever talk about her family?"

"Not to me. All I knew was that Diane told Delroy she gave up a child when she was younger. A boy named Avery. He would use that as an excuse when my kids couldn't come around. He said having them over reminded her that she had a child out there somewhere that she didn't know and it made her depressed."

I shook my head. "Thank you for talking to me, Ruthie."

The sound of an ice cream truck bell ringing came through the window.

Shouting from out front soon joined it. "Grandmaaaaa! Ice creeaaaam!"

The little girl bolted through the front door jumping up and down. "Grandma, can we have some money for ice cream, please?"

Ruthie snapped, "Girl, get on outta here. I don't have no money to be wasting on ice cream."

The little girl looked down at her feet. "Please, Grandma."

"What I say?"

I reached into my pocket and pulled out my wallet. I took out five hundred dollars and handed it to Ruthie.

Ruthie looked at me with surprise on her face. "God bless you, son. You ain't nothing like your mother. God bless you." She turned to Diamond. "Here, girl, take this twenty and get y'all one thing each and bring me back my change."

"You keep that, Ruthie. I'll get them something on my way out. Come on, Diamond." I turned to leave the house.

"Bless you, Avery. Diamond," she shouted, "y'all make sure y'all thank Mr. Avery."

I walked Diamond and the boys to the curb and ordered their ice cream. I patted them on their heads, told them to do well in school, be good for their grandmother, and then sent them back into the front yard with their ice cream.

As I pulled away from the curb, the kids waved. Ruthie watched from the door with a grin on her face while I drove off down the street.

CHAPTER 42

Avery

S eatbelt fastened, I lay my head back on the headrest. There was a dull throbbing sensation near my temples and my eyes were weak and watery. I let them close as the rest of the passengers boarded the plane.

With minutes to spare, I had managed to catch the last flight of the night back to New York. My brain was running a sprint and I kept trying to slow it down. I wanted to replay everything that happened from the minute I touched down in Detroit. I couldn't help but feel like I had failed. I wasn't any closer to knowing what happened to Diane Woodson than before I arrived.

When I left Ruthie's house, I drove over to Fairfax Street. The only assumption I could make was that the neighborhood had changed drastically since Delroy and my mother resided there. The block had fallen into shambles. When I looked at the big colonial homes, I could imagine what they looked like during better times, but there was nothing impressive about them now. Peeling paint, rotting porches, and lopsided columns was all I could see down the entire street. The house at 210 was actually boarded up and had an overgrown lawn with refuse strewn across the front. I sat in the car for a good hour wondering why I couldn't have grown up in that house. According to Ruthie, it was only the two of them. Diane could've come to find me and brought me back to live there with her and Delroy. For ten years, she lived in that home and never came for me.

To hear Ruthie tell it, my mother was the cause of all of her woes. She took away her brother, possibly chased away his wife and child to another state, then after he died, ran off with all of the money without a trace. No matter what I heard Ruthie say, I didn't want to think those things were true about Diane. It had to be possible that Ruthie just didn't know her at all. Maybe Ruthie didn't want to get to know her since she loved Delroy's first wife, Kim, so much. I could see Ruthie not giving her a chance, thinking that my mother would get everything she felt she deserved from her big brother. It sounded to me that Delroy was her gravy train. Wasn't it possible the gravy dried up because he was more concerned about taking care of his young new wife?

I exhaled loudly. It was speculation. All of it. I didn't have a damn clue what transpired between my mother, her husband, and his sister. All I knew was what Ruthie told me and it wasn't flattering. If it were true—that Diane was a cold woman—I had to know what happened in her life to make her that way. I wanted to know the circumstances of her pregnancy. I yearned to find out where were her parents and what they thought about their seventeen-year-old daughter having and giving up a baby. I wanted an explanation why she didn't come back for me. I had so many questions and so few answers.

Maybe I should have asked around the neighborhood if anyone knew Diane Woodson or Diane Gross. I could have gone to the Ford plant. There had to be some people who had been working there for a long time that would remember who she was. My head throbbed harder. I knew I was dealing with a lot of maybes. The one maybe I tried to ignore was that maybe this would be the closest I would ever get to finding my mother.

Ruthie's account would be the first and last one I'd ever get. If that were the case, I would have been better off not knowing anything at all.

I nodded off during the flight and had an unrestful sleep. I kept waking up and thinking that locating Diane was an impossible feat and I should give up. She hadn't come for me and I didn't have to look for her. Each time those ideas invaded my thoughts, I pushed them back. I needed to know her; it was that simple.

When my flight landed, I texted Indiya to let her know that I didn't stay overnight in Detroit. I dialed Mr. Charles as soon as I got in my car. I would have sworn that I awakened him, but he reassured me he was up watching television. I shared everything I learned from Ruthie in hopes that he could pick up where I left off. I asked him to send someone to canvass the neighborhood and possibly the Ford plant. It could not hurt to ask around. If I were lucky, someone might remember something and share an entirely different picture of my mother. Mr. Charles told me to hang in there and assured me that he still had leads he was following. I appreciated that he was not deterred. He was convinced we would find out more information.

I checked my phone after my call with Mr. Charles. Indiya had not responded to my text. It was late, so it was likely that she had fallen asleep. When I pulled into my driveway, the house was completely dark. There were no lights on inside. I went in and went straight back to the bedroom. Indiya wasn't there. I checked the garage and the BMW was gone. I figured she must have gone home. I would call her in the morning. I wanted to be still, anyway. There were too many thoughts and emotions competing inside of my head. If I could lie down and think until I found a little clarity, that would be best. I had hoped in the morning I would feel better about the entire experience I'd had in Detroit.

I called Indiya as soon as I awoke and got her voicemail. I left her a message to call me or come by whenever she was ready. It was almost noon. I didn't fall asleep until four in the morning. I kept thinking how close I had been to a piece of my mother's past and yet I came away with next to nothing. She had vanished almost twenty years ago and Ruthie had no idea where she had gone.

I got up, showered and dressed, then went to the kitchen to make coffee. While my hazelnut decaf brewed, I went to get the Sunday paper from the doorstep. The gray skies and dark, heavy clouds matched the mood I was in. I shut the door on what looked like an imminent thunderstorm and took my paper into the living room.

I half smiled, half frowned to myself. I never used to refer to the white room as the living room. I had Indiya to thank for that. I had gotten so used to putting on facades that I had even been doing it for myself. I had never let a woman come to my Long Island house. I hadn't been showing anyone around my place to need to call each room by a color, yet I did it because it fit my many personas. I had money in the bank, clothes in my closets, and cars to drive. I vacationed when and where I wanted and had my choice of women to take along with me.

But what did it all mean? Questionable gains via questionable means with questionable behavior. I lived a questionable life. An empty life. One filled with superficial relationships and moments. Temporary pleasures that never quite satisfied me. No matter what it was, it was never enough. Never enough money. Never enough cars. Never enough women. Until Indiya. The more time I spent with her, I realized she was flipping the switches I had shut off after Courtney Francis.

I had survived most of my life by being emotionally disconnected. I refused to get attached to anyone, so, if they left, it would mean nothing to me. Courtney and her family changed that. They methodically integrated me into their lives. I let them in and they destroyed my fragile sense of family, shattered my perception of finally having a foundation. Callously, they screwed me over and turned their backs. I struggled for a while, not only emotionally, but also financially. My law license had been revoked and my ability to earn a living how I intended was gone.

When I fled to New York, I was plowing through my savings. The cost of living was through the roof and after seven months of paying bills with no job, I was anxious. Every month, I stared at my stack of bills and wondered how much longer I would be able to pay for my car note, credit cards, rent—in New York and D.C. since I couldn't break my lease—and food. I thought about the life that Gregory Francis and his family were living, compared it to mine, and I was infuriated. I reflected on the money he had, how he was getting it, the illegal account information I had been shown, and I saw an opportunity. At first, I was hesitant, but I eventually convinced myself that I had nothing to lose.

I would never forget the day I called Gregory Francis. His assistant had put me on hold and I waited more than five minutes for him to accept the call.

He finally got on the line. "Greg Francis."

"I was thinking; you owe me."

"Who is this? My assistant told me my alma mater wanted to interview me."

"You ruined me. My career. My life. My future…"

"Avery?"

"I'm honored you still know my voice."

"You have five seconds before I hang up. What do you want?"

"If you do, you will regret it."

"I don't think you're in a position to issue threats."

"I haven't threatened you. I merely stated your reality."

He laughed. "You didn't know your own reality. I created it. How are you going to tell me mine?"

"Let's cut to the chase."

"All right. You're down to zero seconds, but I'll float you a few more."

"What you're going to float me is money."

"Money?"

"Lots of it."

"And why would I do that?"

"I already said you owe me."

"Son, I don't have time for this."

I cringed when he called me son. "I suggest you make time, because if you don't, it will cost you significantly more than what I'm seeking."

"You've got balls calling my office with this bullshit."

"Two million dollars quarterly."

"Are you crazy?"

"Wired into an account I've set up."

"Why would I do that?"

"Because you've got plenty of money stashed in offshore accounts, from so-called important clients, that you've guaranteed you could discreetly manage under the radar." There was a stillness on the line. "Think of me as the radar."

"Is this supposed to be your attempt at blackmail?"

"Why don't you think of it as my salary? Two million quarterly for my career you destroyed."

"That's ridiculous. You want me to pay you eight million dollars a year? You barely made one percent of that!"

"Correction, it was about one-and-a-half percent. I would say I'm past due for a raise."

"I don't have that kind of money."

"We both know that's a lie. I'm asking for a fraction of what you're raking in. In fact, I have the records to prove it. You thought I didn't take precaution and cover my ass before I told you I wasn't cut out for your illegal activities? Well, I did. I copied every single account record in which you gave me access. All this time, I've been wrestling with whether I would use the information to ruin you or to benefit me. I guess it's painfully clear which one I chose."

"Son, I know you were hurt by everything that transpired, but it was only business. I had groomed you to follow in my footsteps. I entrusted you with vital information and you shunned me. You turned your back on my family. I wanted to know that when I'm long gone, my daughter and her progeny would be provided for. I thought you were the man to fill my shoes. You loved my daughter. You should have been willing to do anything for her."

"I don't want to talk about Courtney, that's over. Let's stick to the business at hand. Two million. Quarterly. I have the account information you'll need and I'll be expecting my first wire transfer within a week."

"Let's say I agree to this." His voice was full of gravity. "What assurance do I have that you won't sound the alarm?"

"I haven't thus far, have I? It wouldn't benefit me to do so. How would I get my salary if I did?"

"Two million quarterly," he barked, "for five years."

"I didn't say anything about a cap."

"Don't mistake my acquiescence for weakness. It's five years or nothing. I'm agreeing to this now, but I can change my mind at any minute. You better watch your ass at all times, Avery. I don't want to see you in D.C. and if I even think you whispered any of this to another soul, you'll be paying me the ultimate price."

"You don't need to be concerned about me talking. It won't happen."

"That's right. You're a loner bastard with no family. Give the account information to my assistant." He clicked off without transferring me to his assistant. Made me have to call back to provide the account details.

I needed a minute to regroup before I dialed his assistant. I thought about walking away from the entire scheme. I had bluffed my way through that entire call with Gregory Francis. I wondered how much more I could have gotten out of him if I had actually copied those records.

I'd had my coffee, but nothing to eat. I wasn't in the mood to cook or go out for anything. It had been raining steadily for a few hours, but it finally sounded as if it were easing up. I was stretched out on the carpet watching a documentary on global warming. My phone rang. It was Indiya. Three hours later.

"Where have you been?"

"Hello to you too, Avery."

"I've been wanting to talk to you since I got back last night."

"I was asleep when you sent your text and out early this morning. I figured you were still in bed when I left my house at seven."

"Where did you go?"

"For a ten-mile run with my running club, to brunch, and then a little shopping. I didn't buy anything, though. I'm really working on my problem."

"You couldn't take a minute to check in?"

"Naturally, I left my phone in the car while running and then I forgot to take it with me into the restaurant. We headed straight into the mall after we ate."

"Sounds like you've had a busy day."

"Avery, let's not go down the wrong path. I'm calling now to talk to you."

I took a deep breath. "I wanted to tell you about my trip."

"How did it go?"

"Not so good."

"So you didn't find out where your mother is?"

"Unfortunately, I don't have much more information than before, which is almost nothing."

"Did you get any useful information out of that woman?"

"Nothing more than an unflattering portrait of my mother as a husband-stealer who caused him to leave his wife and child."

"You know, Avery, some stones are better left unturned."

"Not in this case."

"I'm just saying maybe you need to move on with your life and leave the vision you have of your mother intact."

"I can't do that, Indiya. I need to know her."

"Some people aren't meant to be in our lives. Maybe that's why you can't locate her. It may be the universe's way of letting you know you're better off not knowing her."

"I don't believe that. It's just going to take more time. That's all."

Our disagreement manifested in temporary silence.

Indiya cleared her throat. "I'll bring your car back to you this evening, after I shower and go get my hair done."

"The salon is open today?"

"Yes, my Dominican sisters work on Sunday. As soon as I finish there, I'll come out to you. I'll be in pin curls because of the rain, so no jokes."

"There's no hurry to bring the car to me. It's not like I don't have anything else to drive. You go on home after the salon. No sense in ruining your hair in this weather."

"Are you sure?"

"Positive."

"All right. I'll call you later."

We ended our call and I held the phone in my hand. I wasn't going to stop looking for Diane Woodson. The universe never told me anything, definitely not to look for my mother. I was bothered by Indiya's response. I had expected her to be supportive, not discouraging. That was the last thing I needed after my fruitless trip to Detroit.

I needed to get this weight off my chest, and since I couldn't talk to Indiya, there was only one other way for me to do it.

I got up, grabbed my car keys and headed out.

CHAPTER 43

Julian

I'd been composing my thoughts since my drive into Brooklyn. I had an idea about what I wanted to say, but knew it would end up being more organic. I was only partially paying attention from my table in the back. I scanned the crowd. The room was full, considering it was the Sunday afternoon spoken word set.

"And we haven't seen this brother in a minute," the emcee said. "Come on up here, man, you know I'm talking about you."

I got up from my seat and started toward the stage. A few hand claps sprinkled the room. When I stepped onstage into the lights, the clapping ramped up. The emcee gave me a pound.

"That's right, y'all, give it up for this brother right here."

I approached the microphone. "Thanks for making a brother feel welcome. I haven't been up here in a minute."

"We know," a female voice shouted from the crowd.

"Bless that mic," a brother called out.

"Thank you," I said, my deep voice low and even, "I'll do my best."

"All right, now!"

A flitting smile graced my lips.

"Am I yours?
I thought I was.

A bouncing baby boy, should have been your joy, but no, I was your albatross.

Holding you down, preventing you from soaring.

Disrupted your plans of being all you can be. Oh, wait, that's the Army."

A few chuckles came from the audience.

"A heavy decision weighing on a young mind.

What were you supposed to do with a child?

A black male child already born with one strike against him.

Were your actions meant to erase that strike or add two others?

Left at an orphanage with nothing or no one.

With three strikes I'm out and I haven't even gotten up to bat yet.

Alone in this world filled with so many people.

But I don't belong to them, I belong to you. Or don't you remember?

Your only begotten son, oh, wait, that's Jesus—not me. I'm still waiting to be saved.

I'm waiting for a mother, who forgot she had another, and moved on in this world.

Living different lives, building family ties, all without me.

Your firstborn.

The one you forgot was yours."

I bowed my head and heaved a big sigh. The microphone carried that sigh through the room. When I lifted my head, the applause overwhelmed me. It was like a comforting embrace.

The emcee returned to the stage and gave me another pound. "That was deep, my brother." He took the mic. "I don't need to tell y'all to give it up some more. I need to you to simmer down. That brother knows how to stir up a room."

I left the stage and the crowd was still showing their appreciation. I nodded my gratitude as I made my way back to my seat. I had spoken my pain and released some of what I was feeling. I reached my table and hesitated. Miko looked up at me. She typically didn't attend the Sunday set. I slid into the seat beside her.

"That was great, Julian, but I'm sure you already know that. You are so talented with your words." She said that with a wistful smile.

"Thanks, Miko."

"Was any of that true?"

"It was just a performance piece."

"It felt so raw, so real."

I shook my head. "I'm sorry to disappoint you."

She gazed at me wearily. "I wish that was what disappointed me about you."

I stared straight ahead, in the direction of the stage. I had enough on my mind; I couldn't deal with what she was about to lay on me. "Now is not a good time, Miko."

"Maybe not, but I don't know when I'm going to see you again, so, I'm going to take advantage of this moment. You're not going to look at me?"

I slowly pivoted in my seat to face her. "What's up?"

"As if you didn't know."

"If you have something to say, just say it."

"I'll state the obvious first. I have not seen or heard from you in ages." She waited for me to respond and when I didn't, she continued. "It's clear that you don't care about me or the relationship I thought we had."

I flinched. Miko was a good girl. I never wanted to see her hurt from getting tangled up with me. Meeting Indiya had disrupted everything that had been running smoothly in the past. I no longer desired to spend my time with Miko or any of the other women. I wanted to be with Indiya.

"I've had a lot going on lately."

"It's always been about you. You fitting me in around your

schedule and my waiting around for you to do it. I wasn't a priority for you. Even now, you look like you want to be anywhere but right here with me."

I didn't have anything to say to make her feel better, which was unfortunate, because she was such a caring and giving person. As mad as Miko was, she was still hoping that I would tell her that everything would be all right and things would change between us, for the better. It was in her eyes.

Her expression turned cold when I failed to respond. "You don't even care enough to attempt to contradict me. I should have known that Romel was telling me the truth."

"Romel?"

"Yes, Romel. You know, my friend you slept with?"

"It's not true," I said without missing a beat.

"I don't believe you," she said, looking off into the surrounding audience.

I firmly grabbed her by the chin and looked her directly in the eyes. "It's not true. I wouldn't do that to you." I knew Romel couldn't keep her mouth shut. She wanted "us" too bad. She couldn't stand that I wanted Miko rather than her. She'd hurt her own friend—and I used the word *friend* loosely—instead of accepting the reality of the situation. The irony was that she pushed up on me. I bet she left that detail out of whatever tale she had shared with Miko.

Her eyes softened and it looked like she wanted to believe me. "I guess it doesn't matter who's telling the truth since you already walked away. Well, now I'm walking away too."

"I understand. Do what you have to do. I only suggest that you lose Romel as well."

She nodded, holding back the tears that were filling her eyes. After a few seconds, she stood and left the table.

I watched her as she left the club. Seeing Miko broken up was not what I needed at that moment. I waited a few minutes and then left myself. As I walked back to my car, I wondered what Romel had told Miko and when she had told her. Whatever or whenever, she was better off without me.

CHAPTER 44

Avery

I t was nearing seven in the evening when I returned home. Being on the stage had been cathartic. It had helped me to remember that finding Diane would be a journey, not a quick jaunt. I realized I was still toting her picture around in my wallet. I pulled it from my back pocket and removed the image. I was meant to know the lady in the photo, universe be damned.

I needed to return the picture to my safe and then make myself something to eat. I hadn't had anything all day and my stomach was grumbling. I went upstairs to my office and sat down at my desk. I started to open the safe, then stopped. I surveyed what was on top of the desk. One of my bank statements was in the center of the blotter, not in the organizer on the corner where it was usually kept. I stood up and thumbed through the documents in the organizer. I pulled out a stack of documents and flipped through each page. I snatched up the next stack from the organizer and did the same. I didn't see what I was looking for; it wasn't there.

I went through the next section and the one after, scattering papers across my desk. I grabbed the final stack, crumpling pages as I ripped through them and, at the end of the pile, there it was. The power of attorney form giving Avery Hudson power of attorney over Robert Hudson. That form allowed me to transact on his behalf for all of his banking, real estate, bonds, business, insurance, retirement, healthcare, and tax matters. It should have been in the first slot in the organizer. I collapsed back in the chair and shook my head at the mess I had made.

It wasn't like me to have things out of place. I neatly re-organized my documents and replaced them in their appropriate slots. I opened up the safe and returned my mother's picture. I peered inside. Everything seemed to be in place—passports and driver's licenses for Avery, Julian, Marcel and Camden; my original birth certificate; several pieces of jewelry; and a stack of cash. I did a quick count—fifty thousand—it was all there.

I went over to the door and inspected the lock and door jamb. There were no scratches or signs of forced entry. I could acknowledge that I had been rushing quite a bit lately and not paying as much attention to detail. In trying to not take myself so seriously, I had relaxed my norms. I needed to understand that I could be a more relaxed Avery, but still be as aware as I had always been.

I slid my desk chair into the corner of the room and stood on it. I reached up and turned on the miniscule surveillance camera concealed beneath the crown molding. I knew I was being paranoid, but old paranoia dies hard. I stepped from the chair, then opened the closet that housed the monitor. I turned it on to make sure the camera was functioning properly. An image of the room displayed on the screen. I checked the back-up recorder; it was on and recording. I closed up everything and headed down to the kitchen.

There wasn't much in the refrigerator. I had been doing much better with food shopping, but I hadn't perfected a system yet. I took out some turkey and cheese. It seemed that I would be having a sandwich. I remembered on my first date with Indiya, she commented that all men wanted a woman that could cook like their mother. That was something I never considered. I lacked a point of reference in which to judge the cooking skills of the women I dated. As I slapped together my sandwich, I wondered if my mother was a good cook. Indiya certainly had a lot of learning to do. Diane could probably teach her a few things—if I ever found her.

I took my sandwich and settled in front of the television in the living room. It was going to be an early night; my eyes were already feeling heavy. I dialed Indiya while I munched on my dinner. She answered on the first ring. We chatted briefly about how her hair turned out and what I was watching. I neglected to mention that I had gone out. She offered to bring my car back after work the next day and I told her not to bother. Unless she was planning to stay here during the week, she could return it over the weekend. She blew me a kiss through the phone and told me goodnight. I hung up and lounged on the couch. I was exhausted. I called myself watching television. Within minutes, the TV was watching me.

CHAPTER 45

Indiya was in my driveway, blowing the horn like a mad-woman. I came out the front door and held my hands up in surrender. She had the top down on my Bimmer and was waving for me to hurry. She was wearing dark sunglasses, a flowing yellow halter dress, and the broadest smile.

I smiled in spite of myself. Her energy was infectious. I stood next to the car. "Do you want me to drive?"

"No, I told you, I'm taking you out today to cheer you up. Get in."

I climbed into the passenger seat. "I didn't know I needed cheering up."

"Come on, Avery. Ever since you returned from Detroit, you haven't been yourself. So, today, I'm going to show you a good time, chauffeuring included." She leaned toward me and flamboyantly puckered her lips.

I placed a hand on the back of her head and drew her to me. "Hey, baby." I planted a vigorous kiss on her luscious red lips.

She pulled away. "That felt like you missed me."

"I did. All week long."

"You're not the only one. We can show each other how much later."

"That's a given." I caressed her neck. "Unless you want to go inside for a few?"

She stepped on the gas. "We have plans." She drove out of the driveway and down Brookville Road. She looked beautiful with her hair blowing in the wind.

I took her hand in mine and kissed it. "What are you getting me into today?"

"You'll be with me and you're going to love it. That's all you need to know."

"I guess I better sit back, relax, and enjoy the ride."

"That's exactly the point of today."

I tucked a lock of her hair that was whipping in the wind behind her ear. "You look good behind the wheel of my car."

"You really missed me."

I fiddled with the radio. "FM or satellite?"

Indiya looked over at me. "Oh, I see. I have to pry your feelings out of you."

"What? I told you I missed you."

"You did, when prodded."

"I meant it, though."

Indiya chuckled. "I feel like we should be having this conversation next to our high school lockers."

"Wow...high school." I couldn't go out like that. "All right. You know what? Here it is. You throw me off my game."

"We're playing a game?"

"That's not what I meant," I quickly rebutted. "When we're together, I'm in your element; not the other way around. I'm accustomed to the other way around."

"You're saying I'm pushing you out of your comfort zone."

"You're making me feel and it's been a long time since I allowed myself to do that."

"And I'm not going to stop."

I put my hand over hers and linked our fingers. "Good."

At that point in my life Indiya was what I needed. I couldn't say why, but I felt it. From our first encounter to the current moment, she was working on me.

Indiya merged onto the L.I.E. East. I tried to figure out where she was taking me. There were plenty of restaurants out East. I doubted that we were going to the outlets; she was trying to steer clear of unnecessary shopping. I convinced myself to chill. I'd find out soon enough.

I turned up the music. The sun was high in the sky and beaming down into the car. I took my sunglasses from the glove compartment and put them on. Indiya glanced at me. We were a handsome pair. I observed the way her light cotton dress clung to her curves. Her breasts were round and full, firmly held in place by the halter around her neck. I fantasized about what I would do to those breasts later. After half an hour, she exited the expressway at Route 24. I turned down the music and we enjoyed light banter as she cruised to Route 27. Wineries peppered the highway. She turned behind a tour bus into the drive of one of the wineries.

"This is a great idea."

Indiya held her hand up for a fist bump. I lightly tapped my fist against hers. She parked the car. I got out to stretch my legs while she fixed her hair and makeup. Convertibles were fun, but for women they could really obliterate a hairstyle. Indiya raked her fingers through tousled curls.

"Be ready in a sec. You don't want to walk around with a wild woman, do you?"

"Is that a trick question? I like a wild woman."

"We'll see about that later."

She finished sprucing up and we went inside. There were wine

tastings going on at an expansive rectangular bar, people per-
using the vineyard's bottles of wine, and others dining outside on
a patio overlooking the vineyard.

She turned to me. "We have a private tour and lunch scheduled.
We have to meet our guide by the gates past the patio."

I followed her outside. She glided in her flat thong sandals, her
dress billowing in the breeze as she walked. We approached a
twenty-something woman wearing a billed cap, fitted tee shirt
with the vineyard's logo emblazoned on it, a pair of khaki shorts,
and white sneakers. She had to be the guide.

She extended her hand. "You must be Indiya and Avery."

We exchanged pleasantries, then began our tour. Acres upon
acres of lush green grass stretched ahead of us. Our guide walked
us through rows of grapes discussing their varieties, growing
conditions, how they're harvested, and tastes. She discussed the
art of winemaking and how each bottle should be a memorable
experience. We were allowed to sample each of the grapes to
distinguish the nuances between the different types. I held Indiya's
hand throughout our vineyard walk.

We came upon a lone bistro table set for two. There were two
wineglasses, a bottle of red and a white wine, plates, utensils, and
linen napkins.

"This ends my portion of the tour. Please have a seat and sample
the wines. Someone will be along to serve you lunch shortly."

We thanked our guide and she left us among the grapes. I
pulled out Indiya's chair as she got situated, then sat across from
her. The fragrance from the grapes, paired with the gentle breeze,
seemed like aromatherapy.

"This is nice, thank you."

"Are you enjoying yourself?"

"I am. Now I can say that I've been educated on the intricacies of grape growing. I may have to use this knowledge to start my own small winery."

"You could, couldn't you?"

"I was kidding, Indiya." I chuckled.

"I know, but you could if you wanted to?" There was an intense curiosity in her eyes.

I uncorked the white wine and poured some in her glass. "If you mean can I afford to start a winery, then, yes, I can." I filled my glass.

"The amount of capital you need is nothing to sneeze at."

"I'm aware of that. I've done all right for myself." I tapped my glass against hers and toasted. "To this moment."

We sipped our wine. "Mmm," she hummed, "that's good." She placed her glass on the table. "I can see you've done well. You're an attorney, you have that amazing living environment in Brookville, a few nice cars, and you're always impeccably dressed. You must work extremely hard or have some high-powered clients."

"I work smart."

"I know a lot of people that make smart career choices and they aren't rolling like you. Especially considering you work for yourself from home and not with a big law firm."

"You don't need a big firm to be successful. There's an abundance of successful people in the world that work for themselves."

"True. How many clients do you have?"

"Two."

"How can you afford your lifestyle with so few clients?"

I leaned back in my chair. "I made a lot of money thanks to the firm I was with in D.C. I invested wisely and I continue to do so. I make choices that are meant to guarantee I'll be taken care of in the future."

"Smart man." She raised her glass to me.

"What about you? You have a job you love as a buyer, you zip around in a Mercedes, live in Rockville Centre—which isn't cheap—and have a warehouse full of stuff in your house."

"Are you making fun of me?" She laughed. "I told you about my stuff in confidence."

"I haven't told anybody." I started laughing, too. "I'm sorry. All I'm saying is we're both doing well."

"You and I are in two different leagues. You're rich, Avery."

"I don't remember ever saying to you that I was rich."

"I never told you I was a woman, but it's obvious."

"I wonder where our lunch could be." I said, looking around to see if anyone was coming.

"All right, I get it. I'm talking too much and asking too many questions."

"Yes, Lord, you do answer prayers!"

We laughed.

"I'm learning you, Avery Woodson. I know when it's time to pull back, so I don't drag you out of that damn comfort zone."

"My comfort zone and I thank you for cutting me some slack."

"You are so sexy. If they weren't coming with our lunch, I'd have my way with you right here in the vineyard."

She did it again. Had me blushing. "I'd take you up on it too, but there he is."

A server wheeling a cart was coming up our row.

He stopped beside our table. "Indiya, Avery, lunch is served." He placed mixed green salads with pecans, blue cheese, and grapes in front of us. Then, he placed a long covered dish in between us. "Here's your entrée, and I'll leave your dessert on the cart. Whenever you're done, just leave everything as is and we'll take care of it. Feel free to continue to enjoy the vineyard and come back to the tasting room when you're ready." He briskly disappeared in the vineyard.

"I'm famished," Indiya said, bringing a forkful of salad to her mouth.

"This looks good. I wonder what's under the lid."

"Let's see." She lifted the lid from the entrée. "Pan seared salmon filet with capers and lemon, asparagus, and baby red potatoes."

"Thank you again, Indiya. This is wonderful."

She smiled and went back to eating her salad. I truly appreciated the afternoon. It was rare for someone to do something special for me. With the lives I led, I was always doing for others—wining and dining, taking trips, buying jewelry, and so much more. The simplicity of the day I was having with Indiya was pure perfection. The fact that she had planned it for me, priceless.

Indiya cleared our salad plates and served the entrée. "I wonder if I could make this at home."

"I think you could."

"A better question is would it be edible?"

"I'd eat it, baby."

"I like when you call me that."

"Baby?"

"Yes."

"You are my baby. I'm realizing it more and more."

"You're a good guy, Avery."

"Not always, but I'm trying."

"You've never shown me any different and I appreciate that."

"You're special, Indiya, and I want to show you that's how I feel about you. I may not express myself all the time, but I will attempt to show you through my actions. Our trip to London next week is one of those ways that I tried to convey my feelings."

"I am so excited about going to Fashion Week. Wait, are you sure you can afford this trip?" she teased.

"I've saved a few pennies for it."

"I can't believe we're leaving in five days. I have the best outfits planned. I know what I'm wearing each day for every event. I have my daytime, dinner, and nightlife outfits all picked out. I also have sexy little things for our time. You are going to love them! I've even styled a few looks for you."

"Looks?"

"That's fashion speak. I've put together several pieces for you, too."

"Didn't you just tell me that I'm an impeccable dresser? I think I can manage my *looks*, as you called it."

"Have you ever been to a Fashion Week show, Avery?"

"I think it's been on my to-do list for a few years, but I haven't—"

"Hold the jokes." She gave the stop sign with her hand. "My style is second to none and I know how you're supposed to dress at a Fashion Week show. Let me do what I do best and we will be the best dressed couple at every event."

"I can see you're really into this, so I'm at your mercy."

"I like the sound of that."

I drove us back from the winery. We had purchased a case of the white that we drank during lunch. I reached over and tugged on Indiya's dress until I could see her thighs. I stroked my hand back and forth across their smoothness. She squeezed them together, trapping my hand in between. She reached over and rubbed my crotch through my pants.

I turned into the curve of my driveway and up to the house. I put the car in park and Indiya climbed from her seat and straddled me. I leaned my head back as she kissed me, feverishly un-buttoning my shirt at the same time. I slid my hands up her thighs and palmed her ass. No underwear. It immediately turned me on knowing she hadn't been wearing any all day and I moaned. She reached for my belt and tugged on it until it gave. She undid the button on my pants and started to yank on the zipper.

I grabbed her hand. "Careful. My man is right against the zipper."

Indiya backed away from me and opened the door, springing from my lap. She grabbed me by the hand and lured me from the car. My shirt was flapping open, belt hanging through one loop, and my pants unbuttoned. She leaned against the car and pulled me by my collar to her. I pressed against her and peered at her as I lowered my face to hers. She sucked my tongue into her mouth and gave me hot, quick kisses. I went deep. When she tried to speed up, I slowed her down. Made her follow my flow. Nice and slow until what I did, she did. I snaked my tongue in and out of her mouth and she did the same. I licked her lips and she tasted mine.

I pulled her body to mine and held her to me. I slowly began walking us to the front door. I kept one eye on where we were walking, the other on the beautiful woman in my arms. I lifted her by the waist when we got to the steps and deposited her back down in front of the door. She leaned against it, kissing my chest as I fumbled with the keys.

I unlocked the door, placed the keys in her palm, and closed her hand around it. "I want you to have these."

Indiya beamed at me, then pulled me inside the house, closing the door behind us. She kicked off her sandals and pulled me into the living room. She unzipped my pants. I took that as my cue and stepped out of my loafers. I let my pants drop to the floor and took off my shirt. She kneeled in front of me, pulling my boxers off on her way down.

She gently wrapped her hand around my dick and kissed the tip, flicking her tongue around it. I shuddered. She sucked a little more of me into her mouth and rolled her tongue around the head. I immediately began to move along with her, trying to get more of me into the warmth of her mouth. She took her other hand and massaged my balls while licking down the length of my hardness. Deftly, she drew me into her mouth. The jolt doubled me over.

She backed away from me and grabbed my wrist. "Lie down here on the floor."

I sank down into the soft, shaggy white carpet and lay on my back. She straddled me, her dress flowing over my stomach and upper thighs.

"Take this off." I gathered the bottom of the dress and began to lift.

She grabbed it from the waist and pulled it over her head. No bra. No panties. Sheer nakedness. I touched a hand to her flat stomach. She placed her hand over mine, then raised it to her lips. She opened her mouth and sucked my pointer finger, tilting her head to the side with each gentle pull. My dick was flexing, tapping on her ass with each jump.

She raised up and crawled backward down my body until she was face to face with my hardness. She grabbed the shaft of my penis, put me inside her mouth, then slid down until her lips brushed her hand. She sucked on me with urgency, her moist tongue firmly caressing me. Her head bobbed up and down as she went faster and deeper with each dip. I held still and refrained from pumping along with her. It felt too good and moving with her was a guarantee I wouldn't last. I held on to the nape of her neck as she worked her magic. She flicked her tongue from tip to shaft and back again.

My panting grew as Indiya worked her hand and mouth firmer and faster. I lifted her head, grabbed her hand, and pulled her up to me. I wrapped my arms around her and, in a fluid motion, flipped us so she was beneath me. Her breath caught with the suddenness of the move. I kissed along the line of her neck to the shoulder. Light and lingering touches of my lips. I slid down her body, stopping at her breasts, trailing my tongue over the mounds of her flesh and tracing the outline of her nipples. I licked, then blew on them until they were erect. I sucked her hard nipples into my mouth, gently biting and then soothing with the tip of my tongue.

I traveled down further to Indiya's stomach and placed a kiss on her abdomen. I felt her hand on the top of my head pushing me lower. I looked up at her and she laughed. I spread her legs wide, flicked my tongue at her, then dove into her pussy. My tongue darted inside and stroked her kitty. I twirled deeper inside. She bent her legs at the knee and raised her ass off the carpet. I sucked her clit into my mouth, gently pulling on it with my tongue. I cupped her ass and held her steady as she began to quiver. I plunged my tongue back inside of her, taking long laps of her sweetness.

Her moaning escalated. "You know what to do to make me sing. Right there, that's my spot."

Indiya was on the edge. I plunged again and she went over. As she cried out, I climbed on top of her and slid my dick inside in one long stroke. She cried out again, even louder. She was so wet; I was on autopilot. With each thrust, I pushed deeper and deeper inside. I was drowning in her wetness, sinking into her depths. I tried to kiss her, but the sensation of her pussy grabbed my mind and told me to focus on it alone.

Our breathing, our sounds, our bodies moving, transported me to somewhere divine. Somewhere I never wanted to leave. Everything blurred into the background except her body wrapped around mine and the feel of her pussy covering me like a warm blanket. My cries joined hers and the rawness of my voice caught me off-guard. I sounded like a man in pain in need of consolation. She clutched me to her, arms wrapped around my shoulders, holding me close as we thrust in unison.

I nuzzled my face next to hers and whispered in her ear. "Your pussy is heaven."

I pushed deeper still. I slid my arms beneath her back and ass, pulled her tighter to my body, and pivoted to the side. Indiya threw her leg over my hip and I thrust upward, pulling out halfway before thrusting again.

I grunted with each motion. "Indiya, your pussy's too good. I can't hold back."

"Come for me, baby," she cooed in my ear. "Come into heaven."

I burst through the gates with a gruff, powerful shout. The force of my pumps died down along with my yells. I collapsed onto my back, still gripping her in my arms, my chest rising and falling as I caught my breath. She peered up at me with a tender visage.

I kissed her forehead, eyelids, and tip of her nose. "Did that tell you how much I missed you?"

"I think it told me told me much more than that."

"Oh, yeah?"

"Yes."

"You sound pretty sure of yourself."

"I know what I know."

"Did you enjoy it?"

"Do you really have to ask? You're amazing."

"We're amazing. I can't get enough of you."

"I noticed. I had you screaming."

"Damn, you're going to call a brother out on a moment of vulnerability?" I laughed.

She giggled. "My kitty had you going."

"That's messed up. Nothing's sacred."

"My heavenly pussy is close."

"Awww, come on, baby."

"I'm kidding." Indiya stroked my chest. "Am I embarrassing you?"

"Yes, dammit."

"All joking aside, Avery, what we just shared was incredible. I don't only mean the sex, but the emotions.... They were raw, real."

"I felt it." I kissed her again. "I haven't let anyone get close to me in a long time, Indiya. You're in there and it feels good. You reminded me what it feels like to be me."

"I don't understand."

"I just mean that I haven't been myself for a while. Most of the time, I didn't know who I was, sort of like having an identity crisis. You didn't know it, but you've helped me reconnect with Avery."

"And that's a good thing?"

I relaxed my hold on Indiya and sat up. "Actually, it's a great thing."

"You gave me your key on our way in."

"I know I did."

"You really want me to have it?"

"We were joking earlier about whether I missed you or how much I missed you. The fact is, I did. A hell of a lot this week. Maybe you'll consider spending a couple of nights during the week over here with me. You can leave some clothes here. You're already here every weekend..."

"I'll bring some of my things over when we get back from London."

"That's what I wanted to hear, baby. Why don't we take a shower, put on some music, and have a bottle of our new wine?"

"Sounds like you're trying to get back into heaven."

"It's beautiful there. I never want to leave."

CHAPTER 46

Avery

My passport, credit cards, and cash were laid out on my dresser. I checked the exchange rate and the U.S. dollar was lagging the British pound by more than the previous week. Our economy was in desperate need of a recovery. My suitcase was on the luggage rack and I had already started packing my clothes. I gathered the toiletries I was taking and put them in a separate carry-on with an extra pair of underwear and socks. I traveled enough to know that keeping clean underwear with you was essential in case your luggage got lost.

Slacks, shirts, and shoes—in their separate travel shoe bags— were in the suitcase. I still needed to pack pajamas, casual attire, and a couple of suits. Anything else I needed, I could buy in London. I abhorred over-packing. Indiya was insisting on bringing me a few *looks* for the shows. I was curious to see what she had put together.

I was actually excited about the trip. I still wasn't fazed by attending the fashion shows, but I was proud to sport Indiya on my arm. Her beauty, energy, and sense of style made her a triple threat. I was ready to gallivant with her around London, dining in fine restaurants, having drinks at trendy nightclubs and then going back to our hotel for steamy late nights. London wasn't ready for us—we'd take it by storm, much like Indiya did to me.

Indiya came on the scene and I had cut back all of the other women. I wasn't seeing any of them anymore. I wasn't placing calls, sending texts, or attempting to take anyone out.

Indiya came into my life and surprised the hell out of me. She made me want to be myself and want to be with her. When I gave her the key to my house, I hadn't planned it. At that moment, I was moved to do it and I went with the feeling. If I wanted her here with me more, I wanted to show her that I meant it. I gave her the alarm code and let her know she was welcome anytime.

We had an early flight in the morning and though I was relatively set, I knew I had better call to check in with Indiya.

"How's the packing coming along?"

"It's coming."

"What does that mean, Indiya?"

"I have clothes everywhere and nothing has physically made it into the bag."

"I should have known you would try to bring too much."

"I won't do that. I'm just having a slight issue deciding what I should take. But don't worry. Your clothes will be in there."

"That's the least of my worries. My concern, and the reason I'm calling, is to make sure you're going to be ready in the morning."

"I have plenty of time to get it together."

"Why don't I send a car for you tonight? That way we can leave for the airport together in the morning."

"It doesn't make sense for me to come out to Brookville when JFK Airport is fifteen minutes from my house."

"Then I'll have my car stop and pick you up on my way to JFK."

"Avery, I'm going to be on time. You don't have to pick me up. It's unnecessary. I have my own car service coming for me at five-thirty."

"Do you have your passport?"

"Yep."

"I emailed your boarding pass."

"I've already printed it. Is there anything else you need to tell me before I get back to packing?"

"Simply that I'm looking forward to our trip."

"Me too," she said, sounding distracted.

"All right. I'll let you go."

"Okay, see you bright and early in the morning."

"You'd better be early." I laughed. "I'm loving you, baby."

"What's not to love?"

I ended the call and sat on the edge of my bed, smiling to myself. I was loving Indiya. I was loving everything about her. From her crazy say-anything nature to the way she came into my home and told me to stop being so pretentious, making me call the rooms by their proper names. I loved relaxing in the yard with her and the way it made me want to go out and buy a grill for us. The cooking classes, the laughs over dinner and movies, the winery, even her forcing me to meet Kev, had made me realize that I was loving her. I was especially loving her because she was making me want to be a better me. The me I used to be, not the one I had become.

I never thought I would truly feel for someone again. The emotions crept up on me and demanded that I acknowledge their presence. At that very moment, I officially accepted that I was loving Indiya Spencer. I knew that meant I'd have to change some things in my life in order to be an open book, but I would take it one step at a time. I'd be the man I was before I got caught up with Courtney and her father. Law wasn't the only career in the world. I was an intelligent guy, at the top of my class in law school. I could do anything I wanted. I could return to school for another advanced degree. I could volunteer for a worthy cause, a foundation, or even an orphanage in need of assistance. I could start a business, perhaps I would look into owning a winery. The point was I could start anew.

I finished packing my bag and set it by the door. My clothes were laid out for the morning and the alarm clock set. All I needed to do was take a hot shower, lie down, and get some sleep. As I turned off the lamp on my nightstand and climbed beneath the blanket, I wondered how late Indiya would be up trying to get herself ready to leave.

CHAPTER 47

Avery

The Town Car pulled up the curb in front of the American Airlines terminal. I stepped from the car and took my bags from the driver. We confirmed my return date and time, then I went inside to check my bags.

I called Indiya on my way to the airport, but the call went straight to voicemail. I left a message for her to call when she was on her way. I waited on a short line to check my bags and instead of going through security, went to sit in the chairs next to the arrival and departure monitors. I glanced at my watch. It was a quarter after six.

Indiya should have made it to the airport by then. I called again. Voicemail. I looked up at the monitors. Our flight was on time. I got up and walked down toward the security line to check if Indiya was in it. I returned to my chair when I didn't see her. I hunched forward in my seat with my elbows resting on my legs. My foot tapped nonstop.

My phone vibrated. It was a text from Indiya. It said she was on her way; that she overslept and was running late. Her phone was turned off and charging when I had called. I texted back that I was waiting near the ticket counter and we had an hour and fifteen minutes before our flight. She responded for me to go through security and she'd meet me at the gate. I waited another five minutes for her, then got on the security line. I looked over my shoulder repeatedly as I inched closer to the front of the line. I handed the TSA agent my passport and boarding pass. She looked from me to my picture and then back to me. She returned my documents and I went through screening. Twenty minutes after getting on line, I passed through security and proceeded to the gate. I hoped Indiya would be able to skip to the front due to our departure time.

Nearly every seat in the waiting area at the gate was occupied. It was going to be a full flight. I leaned against a pillar and looked at my watch again. The gate agent announced that boarding would begin in twenty minutes. I dialed Indiya again to see if she was on the security line yet. Her phone just rang. That was a good sign. She may have been passing through as I called. After a few minutes, I called again. The phone rang out to her voice-mail. I looked at my watch and pushed away from the wall. I walked over to an empty seat and sat down. I reread Indiya's text. She should have been at the gate by now. I fired off a text.

"Where are you?" I said, out loud, as I typed the words.

The gate agent came over the P.A. system. "We're going to start the boarding process. Please listen for your section to be called and have your boarding passes ready to be scanned. We're now boarding first-class passengers."

That was my call to board. I looked over to the stream of people walking to their gates. None of them were Indiya. We still had time, so I waited. If anything, we could board last.

They called the next section and the next. I stood up and loitered near the gate agent's desk. I looked at my phone. No calls or texts from Indiya. I started to worry something may have happened on her way to the airport. They called the last section. The final passengers waited in line to have their boarding passes scanned. I got on the end of the line. As passenger after passenger walked into the jetway, I became more frustrated. I wondered what the hell had happened to Indiya.

The gate agent held out her hand for my boarding pass as I stepped up.

I held on to it. "I'm traveling on this flight with someone this morning and it doesn't seem that they've made it to the airport. I checked us in online last night. Is there any way to see if she checked her luggage yet?"

"Unfortunately, we can't give you that information."

"I purchased both of our tickets," I said, a wave of anger overcoming me. "You can't look in the system to check if Indiya Spencer checked her bags?"

"No, sir, I'm sorry I can't."

I grabbed the top of my head, my boarding pass clutched in my hand. "Shit!" I uttered, turning my back on the agent. "I can't believe this!"

"Sir, we need to close the plane door. If you're going to board, you need to do so now."

I stared into the crowd of people walking through the terminal.

"Sir?" she said a little louder. "Are you going to board?"

I turned around and looked at the gate agent. "No." I shook my head. "No, I'm not."

I walked over to the now empty waiting area and sat down. I tried Indiya again. The phone rang and rang. No answer. I slouched in the chair and stared at my phone. No word from Indiya since her text that she was on her way. Something had to have happened to her.

The gate agent came over and sat next to me. "Sir, if you return to the ticket counter, they may be able to provide you with additional information. You can also make arrangements to have your luggage returned to you."

"Thank you," I said, not bothering to look up.

I sat in the waiting area for an hour, just in case Indiya showed up. My emotions were mixed. I was confused, worried, and more than a little angry. I tried to keep my anger in check until I found out what exactly happened.

I finally pulled myself up from the chair and went out to the ticket counter. The representative at the counter also told me that it was against policy to provide me with passenger information. I was out of options. I gave her my information for the airline to return my bag, then called the car service to pick me up and take me back home.

CHAPTER 48

Avery

I climbed from the Town Car with my carry-on bag. I stood in the driveway staring at the trees trying to figure out what I was doing back home six hours after I had left. I should have been well on my way to London. Instead, I was wondering where the hell was Indiya.

I went into the house and dropped my bag by the front door. I pulled my phone out and dialed Indiya as I walked into the living room. The phone went straight to voicemail. My heart skipped. Could she have been trying to call me? I hung up and waited a minute. My phone didn't ring. I dialed her again. It went directly to her message for the second time. I hurled the phone at the couch. It bounced off the pillows and tumbled to the floor.

"Where the fuck is she?" I shouted to no one but myself. "Fuck!"

I bent over to pick up the phone, then sank down to the floor. I sat with my back against the couch and looked at her text again, as if somehow the message had changed. The minutes ticked away with me waiting for the phone to ring. I kept thinking that maybe she was hurt somewhere and I should be calling the hospitals. I decided to give it another hour. If in an hour there was no word, I'd call the police and any hospitals in the proximity of JFK Airport.

I couldn't just sit there waiting. I had to do something to keep my mind preoccupied until I heard from or found out Indiya's whereabouts. I got up and took my carry-on into the bedroom. I started to unpack the items I had just packed the night before. I took my passport from the bag. I wouldn't be adding another stamp today. I took the passport and slowly walked down the hall to the kitchen, then ambled up the stairs leading to my office.

I stopped short. The door to my office was wide open. I never left the door open and was one hundred percent positive that it had been closed and locked the night before. I barreled through the doorway and immediately paced the room. Snapshots of what I was seeing flooded my senses. Papers all over the desk and floor, desk drawers overturned onto the chair and couch, my computer monitor on and the safe dragged out from its alcove beneath the desk. I rushed over to the safe. It was locked. I entered the combination and rummaged through its contents. My jewelry, money, and documents were all in order.

"What the hell is going on?"

I spun in a circle, taking in the entire room, the mess of it all. Then, I remembered. I had set the surveillance camera the week before. I charged the closet and threw the door open. The camera was recording. I pressed rewind and watched the timer on the video go back. The door was open and the room ransacked in all of the frames. I needed to go back further and rewound the video some more. I paused it. Hunched over trying to push the safe around the desk was someone dressed in all black—a bulky jacket and baggy sweats—wearing a baseball cap and shades. I rewound even more. The video going backward showed the door creep open. I froze the frame, then pressed "play." The time on the video read six a.m. The figure came into the room, back turned to the camera. They went around the desk and turned on the computer, leaning over the keyboard while typing. The phone on the desk started to ring and I jumped. I ignored it and kept watching the video. The intruder opened the desk drawers and went through them before pulling them out and shaking the contents onto the chairs, inspecting them again. They returned to the computer and stared at the screen, clicking on the mouse from time to time. Next they squatted down and tugged with both arms to pull the safe from the recess under the desk. It was obvious from the video it was taking a great deal of effort. The intruder managed to drag it to the corner of the desk before abandoning it altogether.

My office phone rang again. I looked back at it, willing it to shut up. It stopped, then immediately started again. I turned back to the video. The perp went to my desk organizer and started to go through the documents in the slots, examining some, tossing others aside, on either the floor or desk. Eventually they snatched one document out and spent time reading it and then took another document out of an envelope and read it too. The individual looked at their watch, then grabbed the entire organizer. They turned and started to rush from the room, but tripped on the corner of the safe and then fell, sprawled out across the floor. The baseball cap toppled from the intruder's head.

My breath caught. Indiya. I paused the video. It was Indiya.

The phone rang again and again and again as I stared at the monitor. What the hell was going on? I kept rewinding the part where she fell and the hat fell off. I couldn't believe it. I continued to play the rest of the video and watched her scramble from the room with my organizer.

The damn phone kept ringing. I jumped up and snatched it from the cradle. "What is it?"

"Avery, it's Mr. Charles. I have some information for you. When can you meet me?"

"Now is not a good time, Mr. Charles. Can't you tell me over the phone?"

"No, I need to see you."

"All right, fine. I can be at your office at three, give or take an hour. I have an important stop to make first."

I slammed the phone down and walked over to the door. I felt around the doorframe. The key was missing. I stormed down the hall, bounded down the stairs, and grabbed my car keys. I jumped in my car and sped out the driveway. I didn't care if there were any cops on the road. If they wanted me to stop, they had to catch me first. Nothing could keep me from what I needed to do, not even the threat of arrest.

CHAPTER 49

My car shot out of the Midtown Tunnel. I maneuvered around a slow-moving car and ran the first light. I slowed briefly at the corner of Third Avenue, then gunned a right turn. Horns blared as I forced my way to the middle lane, cutting off taxis and delivery trucks in the process. I sped up Third, slamming on the brakes at each red light I caught. I turned on Fifty-First and came to a stop as a line of cars waited behind a police vehicle blocking the middle of the street. I jammed on my horn. I didn't care that no one could move, I was in a hurry. Two policemen strolled to their car carrying bags that apparently held their lunches. I rammed on my horn again. They pulled off and traffic started moving.

I went up to Fifth Avenue, made a left, then drove one more block. I screeched to a stop in front of Saks Fifth Avenue. I threw on my hazard lights and left my car illegally parked at the curb. If I got towed, so what. I dashed from the car and through the front door of the store.

Inside, I quickly scanned the layout. I moved while I searched, looking from face to face, trying to find someone that looked like they could point me in the right direction. I ran up to the women's fragrance counter.

"Miss," I called out. "Excuse me miss," I said even louder.

A petite older woman, wearing too much lipstick, turned around. She eyeballed me, focused on my hands, and then smiled. "Do you need help finding something for your girlfriend?"

"No, I'm trying to find my girlfriend."

"I'm sorry."

"I need help finding my girlfriend. She works here."

"Does she work in fragrances?"

"No, she's a buyer."

"Unfortunately, I probably wouldn't know her. Perhaps if you go over to customer service, they can help you."

She directed me to customer service and I hastily dodged the meandering shoppers on my way over there. Two people were in front of me in the line. The person at the counter was pointing to a receipt and asking question after question. I was about to walk to the front, push them aside, and ask my own question, but I didn't want to get led out of the store in handcuffs. Eventually, the customer must have been satisfied with assistance she received and she walked off, still staring at that receipt.

I waited while the next person was helped. I swore under my breath, cursing both the customer service rep and the customer for being so slow. I checked my watch. I had been waiting to talk to customer service for ten minutes. My arms were folded across my chest as I shifted from foot to foot.

Just as I was about to interrupt and ask if anyone else was working, the customer stepped away from the desk. I approached before I was even called. "Yes, I need to know if one of your employees is working today."

"Do you know what department they're in?"

"She's a senior buyer."

"That would be our corporate office. I'm not permitted to give you that information."

"What the hell! This is customer service, isn't it?"

"Yes, but we're not allowed to disclose that type of information."

"Then why did you ask me what department she worked in?"

"Because if you were looking for a sales associate that may have helped you with a transaction, that would be different."

"There's a family emergency and I really need to reach this person."

"Let me call human resources to see if they can help you."

The customer service rep dialed her phone. "Yes, hi. This is Caitlyn in customer service. I have a gentleman here that's trying to locate one of our employees. I know. Yes, but he said there's a family emergency. Okay." She moved the phone from her ear. "What is the employee's name?"

"Indiya Spencer."

She spoke in to the phone, "He said Indiya Spencer. Right." She covered the phone and spoke to me. "And in what department did you say she worked?"

"I don't know what department. All I know is that she's a buyer here at your store."

"He says she's a buyer. Yes." She looked at me. "How are you spelling that name?'

That's right. Indiya's name was spelled in a non-traditional way. I gave the rep the proper spelling and waited for what seemed like an eternity.

She spoke into the phone. "You can't? Oh, okay." She looked up at me. "Sir, there doesn't seem to be anyone that works at Saks with that name."

"That's impossible. I know she works here because she told me."

She spoke into the phone. "He said he's positive she's an employee." She paused. "All right, thank you." She hung up.

"What did they say?"

"Sir, they said they do not have, nor have they ever had, an employee by that name."

I stood there dumbfounded. How could they not know their employees? "Are you sure?"

"They were positive, sir. No Indiya Spencer works here."

I mumbled some sort of gratitude, then turned to walk away. I was stunned. How could Indiya not work at Saks. We'd had numerous conversations about her job and how fulfilled she was with what she did for a living. And now, according to human resources, they had no such person working there. I couldn't wrap my mind around it. There had to be some sort of mistake.

I walked to the front of the store, deep in thought and plagued by confusion. As soon as I walked through the door, I saw the flashing lights. An officer was next to my vehicle on his radio. I stepped up beside him.

"Is this your car?"

"Yes, officer."

"Do you realize you're illegally parked?"

"I'm sorry; I had an emergency."

"Inside a department store?" He didn't wait for an answer, he simply started writing out a ticket. "I was just calling for a tow truck. If you would have come out five minutes later, your car would have been gone."

I didn't have it in me to debate with him. "I understand."

He handed me a hefty ticket. "I would suggest you don't pull a stunt like this again. Next time, you might just get burned."

"Believe me, I just did."

CHAPTER 50

I crumpled up the ticket the police officer had given me, hurled it to the floor, and sped off. The officer shook his head as I peeled out. He was the least of my problems.

I couldn't believe what was happening. Where the hell was Indiya? Why would she break into my office and why lie about working at Saks? I should have called the police once I saw the surveillance tape, but the last thing I needed was to shine a light on myself. It wouldn't be wise to have the police poking around my situation; no, I had to handle this on my own.

I rode the elevator up to Mr. Charles's office willing it to go faster. I was squeezing through the doors before they had completely opened. I walked down the hall to the office on the end. I held the frosted glass door open for an elderly woman leaving the office, then proceeded to the desk.

"Avery Woodson to see Mr. Charles."

The receptionist looked up at me with a curious expression. "Go right in, Mr. Woodson. He's expecting you."

I went down to the corner office and rapped on the door. Mr. Charles was at his desk. He stood and escorted me inside, shaking my hand while he led me to the chair in front of his desk. He sat in the chair next to me, not behind his desk.

"How are you, Avery."

"I'm having a hell of a day, Mr. Charles, and it seems to be getting worse with every passing minute."

Mr. Charles patted my arm. "Well, I'm afraid what I'm going to tell you is not going to make it any better."

"Let me hear it," I said, steeling myself.

"When you met me at the diner, before you went to Detroit, you asked me to check into something for you."

"Yes, I asked you to find an address for my lady, Indiya."

"Yes, you did." He paused. "I found an address for her."

"You have perfect timing, Mr. Charles." I clapped my hands together excitedly. "You don't know how perfect."

"There's more you need to know, Avery."

"All right, well, what is it? I'm in the middle of something right now and in a hurry."

"We checked all possible resources for an Indiya Spencer and came up with nothing. No driver's license, home address, bank information, social media accounts, or any other identifiers we check. I had been waiting to receive the data from the license plate number you provided for your lady friend's car. It came in yesterday, but I needed to do a bit more digging before I called you."

"So you can give me an address for her."

"I will in a moment."

I looked at my watch. "Mr. Charles—"

"Avery, the car came back titled to someone else altogether, not Indiya."

"Well, then, who?"

"The car is titled to Kim Gross."

"Gross?" I frowned. "Kim Gross?"

"Yes, Avery."

"You can't mean Ruthie's sister-in-law?"

"That's exactly who I mean."

"Wait a minute. This doesn't make sense. Why would Indiya have Kim Gross's car?"

"Listen to what I'm telling you, Avery."

My hand was clenching the armrest on the chair. "I'm listening. I'm just trying to understand."

"When I received the license plate number from you, I had one of my investigators try to find out as much as he could. The car is titled to Kim Gross, but the registration is not. The car is registered to Indiya Gross."

"Indiya Gross? Indiya's last name is Spencer, not Gross."

"I know you're confused and I don't have all the answers for you, but I do know this—Indiya Gross is definitely Kim Gross's daughter."

I sat there in stunned silence trying to process what Mr. Charles had told me.

He continued. "Do you understand what that means?"

I stared at him shaking my head from side to side.

"Avery, that means Indiya is Ruthie's niece, Delroy's daughter. Do you understand, son?"

"My mother's dead husband's daughter?"

"The address associated with the registration is in Rockville Centre. It's a rented house and the lease is in Delroy's name."

"She's renting a house in her father's name?"

"I know this is a lot to swallow and I wish there was more I could tell you."

"I'm at a loss right now, Mr. Charles." I felt like I was in a fog. "I don't know what to say."

"Why don't you take a couple of days to process everything and we can talk again. I'm sure I can find out additional information for you by then."

"I don't have that kind of time. I need the address."

Mr. Charles eyed me apprehensively. "I don't think it's wise for you to have it right now."

"I need that address, Mr. Charles. Now."

He sighed. "You need to make me a promise first. You will not take this address and go over there and do something that you will regret."

I stared at Mr. Charles, my foot bouncing double time.

"Did you hear me, Avery? I'm not giving you this address until you promise to keep your cool."

"The only thing I can promise, Mr. Charles, is that I won't do anything I'll regret to Indiya Spencer, because she doesn't exist."

CHAPTER 51

M r. Charles talked to me for about ten minutes more before he handed over the address. He looked as if he thought he was going against his better judgment. I took the information from him and bolted from his office. I got to my car, plugged the address into my navigation system, and waited for the route to display. I knew my way to Rockville Centre, but I wasn't familiar with the streets.

When the map appeared on the screen, I just peered at it. I didn't start driving, I merely sat behind the wheel wondering how any of what Mr. Charles had shared was possible. Indiya was Ruthie's niece? Why in the world would Indiya or Ruthie want anything to do with me? My head was beginning to throb with the increasing anger I was feeling. Indiya was a damned liar. She wasn't who she said she was at all. Her damn last name was Gross, not Spencer. She was Delroy's daughter. Saks had never heard of her. She bailed on our trip. And she broke into my office, running off with my personal information. Indiya sucked me into her web of lies and left me with nothing but unanswered questions. I was going to Rockville Centre and if she was there, God help her.

I pulled out of the parking space and made my way back to the tunnel. A chorus of car horns blared at me. I looked up and the red light I was sitting at had changed to green. I was too busy thinking about getting answers to notice. Drivers sped around me, mouthing profanities as if I could hear them through a closed window.

I replayed what Mr. Charles had told me. What would be the chances of Mr. Charles unearthing Ruthie in his search for Diane and I just happened to be in a relationship with her niece? There was no way any of this was coincidental, that much I knew. I wanted there to be a plausible explanation for all of this, but that was stupid wishful thinking. My anger flared. I had been stupid. I let my guard down and let Indiya in. I let her into my home. I let her into my life. And worst of all, I let her into my heart. Now she had my desk organizer with documents she should not have access to—bank statements and credit card bills. And my power of attorney for Robert Hudson. I needed that document. I shook my head. Thank God she couldn't lift the safe and carry that out of the office.

My offshore account information was in that safe. Accounts that housed over thirty million dollars. All of my passports, driver's licenses, and social security numbers for Julian, Marcel, Camden, and Avery Hudson were in that safe. I had paid a lot of money, serious money, to an underground syndicate to get those documents. Documents that could pass scrutiny from any agency, federal or otherwise. When Greg Francis threatened that I had better watch my ass at all times, I knew I needed to be someone other than Avery Woodson. I slipped off the grid and into the shadows as Camden, Marcel, and Julian. I became them and lived their lives. A man scorned. No faith in others. No trust in women. Always alone in the world. I was better off that way.

Traffic on the L.I.E. slowed to a crawl approaching the Grand Central Parkway exit. I banged on the steering wheel, shouting for the cars to get moving. I had to get to Indiya. This woman had come into my life like a storm, demanding that I keep it real with her, and she did the complete opposite. I wanted answers. Mr. Charles was asking too much of me. I couldn't promise that I would refrain from wringing her neck when she opened the door. I was going to get an explanation and my shit back from her. Maybe not in that order, but I was definitely getting both.

I made it to the Grand Central and rocketed to the Cross Island Parkway. Within minutes, I was on the Southern State and getting closer to the exit for Rockville Centre. I cut two cars off, switching from the left lane to the right, and zipped off the parkway. I paid attention to the GPS because I didn't know where to go. I headed down Peninsula Boulevard, then made a left onto a wide street with tall arching trees that gave the impression of a green canopy overhead. I turned right onto a dead-end. The GPS told me that the house was ahead on the left. I parked near the corner and would walk the rest of the way.

I looked at the numbers on the Tudor-style homes and determined Indiya's was in the middle of the block. As I neared the house, I could see her car sitting in the driveway. I peeked in the windows to see if any of my belongings were inside. It was empty. I slowly went up the walkway, telling myself to stay cool like Mr. Charles had instructed. No good could come of me hemming her up as soon as the door opened.

I pressed the doorbell and hoped she wouldn't look out of the peephole. I thought about covering it, but changed my mind. I wanted her to know it was me and that I had found her. When she didn't come to the door, I rang the bell again. I looked along the side of the house to see if there was another entrance. There wasn't any. As I was peering off to the side, the sound of the door opening caused me to jump. I abruptly turned forward. I found myself gazing at a woman that wasn't Indiya. Middle-aged. Brown skin. Shoulder-length hair with hints of gray. Full lips and tired eyes. There was something in those eyes.

I cleared my throat. "Good afternoon." I tried to make my voice as neutral as possible to mask the anger that was brewing inside.

The woman stared at me.

"I'm looking for Indiya Spen—" I shook my head. "Indiya Gross."

She watched me as if trying to comprehend what I said.

"Excuse me, but does Indiya Gross live here?" I asked, impatience creeping into my voice.

"Avery?"

The way she said my name. A chill ran down my spine. I looked into her face again. I knew that face. Older, yes, but still the same. "Diane…Diane Woodson?"

Her bottom lip began to tremble and her eyes misted over. "You know who I am?"

My breathing had come to a halt. I could not believe my eyes. I nodded. Diane Woodson, my mother, was standing less than three feet in front of me.

She opened the storm door with trembling hands. "Come in." She stepped to the side for me to pass.

I just stared, feeling as if this couldn't be real, thinking if I moved or proceeded any further, I would wake up. My head was telling me this apparition of Diane Woodson would disappear at any second. I wanted to believe this was happening, but it all seemed too surreal.

"Avery, come inside," she said, snapping me out of my stupor.

I took a tentative step inside of the doorway.

She reached out, then pulled back her hand. "Please, come in."

I stepped all the way into the foyer, not taking my eyes off her as I passed. We stood face-to-face inside the foyer. "You live in Rockville Centre?"

"Yes," she answered, clasping her shaking hands together.

"All my life, I've been wondering where you were and here you are just a stone's throw away from me?"

"I've only been in Long Island for six months."

"Only?"

"I know you must have a lot of questions—"

"You live here with Indiya?"

"Yes," she looked perplexed, "but, how do you know Indiya?"

"If you don't mind, I'd like to ask the questions."

Diane nervously nodded her head. "Like I said, I know you must have plenty. At least come into the living room where we can talk." She started into the room and I slowly followed, my feet feeling like lead. She sat in a high-back chair and motioned for me to take the one across from her. "Can I get you something to drink?"

I gave no answer. I finally asked, "How did you know it was me when you opened the door?"

"I'd always know that face." She smiled weakly. "I moved here six months ago with the intention of introducing myself to you."

"And, yet, it never happened."

"I didn't want to impose on you."

"Impose on me? Are you serious?"

"I couldn't assume that you wanted your long-lost mother popping into your life."

"What child wouldn't want to know their mother?"

"There are many things that I don't expect you to understand, but I'm hoping you'll at least hear me out."

"How did you know where I was?"

"Through the years, I've kept tabs on you, Avery. From the day I had to leave you at the orphanage until this very moment, I did my best to know where you were. I lost track of you for a while when you left Washington, D.C., but eventually I found you again."

"I guess you had me at a disadvantage."

"I wanted to be a part of your life. I just didn't know if it was the right thing to do."

"And leaving me at an orphanage was?"

"Avery, I was forced to make tough decisions at a very early age. I felt leaving you, with a chance to have a good home, was better than anything I could have done for you as a seventeen-year-old single mother without a pot to piss in. It wasn't easy for me to leave you there and that's something I have regretted every day since. But I didn't have a choice. It was either leave you so that you could have a roof over your head, clothes on your back, and food in your stomach, or have you living on the streets."

"But I have your graduation picture. You looked as if your life was so full of promise."

"That was one picture that did not represent my life."

"Where were your parents?"

"They put me out when they found out I was pregnant with you. At first I stayed between a couple of my friends' homes, but never for long. Their parents didn't like having me around to be a bad influence on their own seventeen-year-old daughters."

"I get that you were seventeen, but why didn't you try to keep me with you?"

"It was impossible, Avery. I was virtually living on the streets. I didn't have a job, a roof over my head, a family to support me; I had nothing. How could I drag a baby into my dire situation? You deserved better."

"You think I had better?"

"If you had a roof over your head, then you had better than I could offer."

"I had a place to lay my head, yes, but no love. You can paint whatever picture you want, but I know my life would have been better with you."

She frowned. "You don't know. You have no idea what my life was like. You can't even imagine where I've been and the things that I've been through."

"Then why don't you tell me?" I said, leaning back in the chair. I was challenging Diane to tell me her story because I deserved to know exactly how I ended up here. Why my life had to be the way that it was.

"This is not easy for me, Avery. I never imagined my first meeting with you to be like this. I wanted to find you, not the other way around. Before I go any further, you have to know I always planned to come for you. Somehow the years just got by me."

"They tend to do that." I watched her intently. This was my mother, sitting in the same room with me. A vision of her former self. Still beautiful, but no longer looking like she could take on anything.

"I was sixteen years old and a senior in high school when I discovered I was pregnant. I had been seeing this boy that lived a few blocks from my family in Queens."

"I thought you were born in New York City."

"I was. Harlem Hospital. My father moved our family to St. Albans when I was five."

"Do you have any brothers or sisters?"

"No, I was an only child."

"Are your parents still living?"

"I wouldn't know."

"You don't know if your parents are alive or not?"

"When my parents put me out, pregnant with no money and nowhere to go, I never looked back."

"Is that why it was so easy for you to leave me and not look back?"

"That's not fair. Just listen to what I have to say before you form an opinion."

"I've had a hell of a lot of years to form an opinion about you."

"Well, hopefully, I can change what you think about me. I want you to understand why I made the decisions that I made. I only ask that you reserve judgment until I finish what I want to tell you."

"I'll try."

She exhaled a shaky breath. "I had very strict parents. From the moment I started dating this boy, they didn't like it. He lived a few blocks away, so they claimed they didn't know him. My parents didn't care that I told them he was smart and went to private school. He was my first boyfriend and he wasn't even allowed to call the house. They also forbade me from seeing him. Of course, I did the exact opposite. I would meet him after school when he got off the bus and we'd walk to the park or library to hang out. I'd tell my parents that I was at a friend's house or had an after school activity and I'd be home late. On the weekends, we'd go where there were always crowds and the entire time I was looking over my shoulder to make sure my parents weren't checking up on me. As young girls often do, I fell hard for this boy. We were making plans to go to the same college so we could be together without interference. For hours on end, we would talk about our future together and how great it was going to be. The dreams of the young and naïve…"

She stared at nothing for a moment, appearing to get lost in her thoughts. "One day, I met him at the bus stop and he had a strange expression on his face. I asked what was wrong and he told me his family was moving to Indiana. His father had gotten a new job and they were moving in two weeks. I was devastated. I didn't want him to go. We promised each other that we would still attend the same college so we could be together.

"The week before he was supposed to move, we talked about having sex. We loved each other and, until then, our relationship had been relatively innocent. We wanted to be together before he left for Indiana. One day after school, we went over to his house and fumbled our way through the act. I had told my parents that I was going to one of my girlfriends' to study, but I forgot to tell her. She called my house to speak with me and my parents found out that I lied regarding my whereabouts. My father got in his car and drove around the neighborhood looking for me. As my boyfriend and I were coming out of his house, my father was driving down the street. He threw his car into park, snatched me by the arm, and shoved me in the front seat. He asked my boyfriend if his parents were home and when he told him no, he said he would be back later to talk to them.

"When we got home my parents went crazy. My father was yelling at me, demanding to know if anything happened between me and the boy. I told him nothing happened, that we were just watching TV. My mother shouted that she didn't believe me. Ultimately, they grounded me for a month. I couldn't leave the house except for school, in which they started to drive me in the morning and pick me up in the afternoon. I wasn't allowed any phone calls or television. My father stormed out of the house, returning an hour later. He stood in my bedroom door and reported that he spoke to my boyfriend's parents. According to him, my boyfriend was getting the same treatment—dropped off and picked up at the bus stop and zero phone privileges. It was his last week before moving to Indiana and I couldn't see or speak to him. I was miserable.

"The day he was supposed to leave, I cried from the time I woke up until the time I went to bed. I couldn't believe he was gone and I didn't have an address or phone number for him in Indiana.

My parents told me to get over it and to focus on my studies. They were big on education. When it came to me, it was pretty much all they cared about. Neither of them had attended college and they were determined that I was going. I agreed. I was going—not because I valued education—but to get away from them.

"A month later, I threw up one morning at school. The school nurse, convinced I had a stomach bug, sent me home. I returned to school the next day and when I got sick again, I became scared. I realized my monthly hadn't come and I knew what that meant. I was pregnant. I didn't tell a soul. I figured if I could hide it until I graduated, then maybe until it was time to leave for college, I could raise my baby with the father. Well, I made it to graduation, but two weeks later, my mother caught a glimpse of me in my nightgown and saw my rounding stomach. I was four months pregnant and had a slight baby bump. She immediately started crying. My father came running into the room, wanting to know what was wrong. My mother told him I was pregnant. The names they called me…liar…whore…idiot. They called me everything but a child of God. When I tell you that my father beat me into unconsciousness, I'm not exaggerating. When I regained consciousness, my parents had packed a suitcase and told me to leave their house. They said they didn't want me or my bastard child under their roof."

She paused, holding back the tears the memory had obviously stirred up. "I need a minute, Avery. Excuse me."

She left the room. I sat in silence wondering what kind of people would do that to their only child. They had to be extremely cold to send her off with nothing and no regard for the grandchild she was carrying.

After a few minutes, Diane returned with two glasses filled to the brim. "I hope you like sweet tea. I made it myself."

I smiled at her as I accepted the glass. "I love sweet tea, especially when it's homemade. Thank you."

Diane sipped her drink, then set it down on the end table next to her chair. "I'm sorry about that. I have only told this story a couple of times in my life. As you can imagine, it's really painful and releases emotions that I bottled up many years ago."

"Take your time."

"As I mentioned earlier, after my parents put me out, I stayed with a few friends. Unfortunately, yet understandably, their parents didn't want me around. They wanted their daughters focused on getting ready to leave for college and not ending up in my predicament. When I had worn out my welcome at my last friend's house, I started to sleep at a Catholic church not far from my high school. I knew that the doors were unlocked during the day because all through high school I had seen people entering on my way to and fro. So, I started to sneak in late in the afternoon and hide in the bathroom until nightfall. Once I was sure that church had been locked for the night and no one was around, I would come out. Downstairs in the church, there was a kitchen with a refrigerator and pantry. On most days, I could find something to snack on.

"I had been going around during the day trying to find a job. I inquired at supermarkets, beauty parlors, convenience stores, even gas stations, but there wasn't much available for a pregnant teen with no skills. After a few weeks with no success, I started to sit outside of a diner on Linden Boulevard asking people if they had any change they could spare. Things had gotten that bad for me. One day, I was sitting outside of the diner and ran into one of my girlfriends from high school. I was seven months by then and had been struggling on my own for three.

"When she saw me, she burst into tears. We hugged for what

seemed like an eternity. She told me she decided not to go away for college, opting to stay local instead. She was attending Hofstra and lived on campus. She suggested that we sneak me into her dorm and I could stay in her room with her. She didn't have a roommate, though she was supposed to, and there was an extra bed. She said it would be no problem to bring me food from the dining hall and I could shower late at night when it was quiet on the floor. I was hesitant because I didn't want to get her into any trouble, but she insisted that she wasn't going to let me say no. That evening, as she distracted the attendant in the lobby, I slipped by and met her at the elevators. She took me up to her room and there I stayed until I went into labor. As the paramedics rushed me out, she was being bombarded with questions from the resident advisor as to who I was and what I was doing in her room." Diane shook her head. "I was so grateful to her for what she had done for me."

"Did you stay in touch with her?"

"No, I didn't. After they rushed me to the hospital, I gave birth to you a few hours later. A social worker came to see me and asked all sorts of questions about my family, where I lived, did I have a job, how was I going to support my baby. Things that I couldn't answer. I didn't have any insurance and they wanted to know how I planned to pay my hospital bills as well. I was scared that they were going to take my baby from me and I wasn't going to let that happen. When the nurse brought you in for your feeding, I bundled you up real tight, got dressed, and snuck out of the hospital. It was the late seventies and security wasn't like it is today." She snickered.

"I was tired and sore, but I walked to the Long Island Rail Road station and got on a train to Manhattan. When the conductor passed through the car for tickets, I pretended I was asleep. I guess he saw me with a newborn in my arms and decided to leave me alone.

"When I arrived at Penn Station, I saw a police officer and asked if he could tell me where to find the closest shelter. I walked through the crowds of New York City, holding you close to my chest, to get there. When I did, I broke down in tears. It was a rundown hole-in-the-wall with thugs loitering out front doing Lord knows what. I was given a bed and an old crib for you, on the women's floor. Thinking about that place makes me cringe to this day. I was a sheltered teen and wasn't accustomed to any of what I was experiencing. It didn't take long for me to fall into a depressed state. I would feed and change you, but not much else. By the second week at the shelter, I knew that was no life for either of us. I couldn't provide for you. I needed for you to have a home and a better life than I could give you. I convinced myself that if I took you to an orphanage, I could always come back for you before someone adopted you. I just needed time to get myself together and then I'd bring you home with me. Of course you know things didn't work out that way. You were three weeks old when I left you there."

Diane choked up, her voice strained. "That was the hardest thing I ever had to do in my life. Leave my baby behind for someone else to care for because I wasn't able. I met with a social worker, gave her my graduation picture from my wallet, and prayed that you would have a good life as I walked out the door."

"I was there until I was *fourteen*. You never came back."

The tears flowed down her face. "I know."

"You didn't care."

"That's not true. I knew you were better off."

"I was better off in an orphanage than with you? You didn't even come for me after you married Delroy Gross."

Surprise registered on her face.

"Yeah, I know about Delroy. When you married him, I had to be about eight or nine years old. Why didn't you come for me then?"

"My life with Delroy was complicated."

"Ruthie told me where you and Delroy used to live. I saw your house. There was lots of room for a little boy to live there with his mother."

"I have to ask, how do you know about Delroy, Ruthie, and even Indiya?"

"I've been looking for you for years. The gentleman I hired to help me found your marriage license to Delroy which eventually led him to Ruthie. She insisted on meeting me in person and I went to Detroit."

"You met Ruthie?"

"A few weeks ago."

"And Indiya?"

"Almost four months ago."

"That's around the time Indiya came to New York."

"What I want to know is why?"

"I'd like to know the same thing."

"You said she lives here with you. Shouldn't you know?"

"When Indiya showed up on my doorstep, I was completely surprised. Indiya is my deceased husband's daughter and we've never really had a relationship."

"Ruthie told me Delroy had one child from his first wife. Never in my wildest dreams would I have thought it was Indiya. Why did she come here if you two weren't close?"

"She showed up at my door, with her luggage, telling me that she accepted a new job in Manhattan and the apartment she was supposed to rent fell through. She cried that she had nowhere else to go. I was apprehensive, but I agreed to let her stay with me temporarily until she could find her own place."

Confusion registered on my face. "How did she know where to find you?"

"She said that Ruthie told her I was in New York."

"Ruthie? But I thought you hadn't spoken to her in twenty years?"

"Who told you that?"

"Ruthie."

"I speak to Ruthie every few months." She leaned forward in her seat. "What else did she tell you?"

"That she had no idea where you were and the last time she saw you was at her brother's funeral, before you ran off with all of his money."

Anger flashed across her face. "That lying hussy!"

"Which part is a lie?"

"All of it!"

"She knew you were in Rockville Centre?"

"Yes, she sent Indiya here. Which makes me question whether Indiya really lost her apartment or even had a new job in the city."

"Where did she tell you that she was working?"

"At Saks Fifth Avenue."

"When was the last time you've seen her?"

"About five this morning. She was leaving on a business trip."

"I can answer one of your questions. Indiya does not work at Saks."

"How do you know that?"

"I was there looking for her today. Human resources never heard of her. Well, they had never heard of Indiya Spencer."

"Spencer?"

"That's the name she gave me when we met—Indiya Spencer."

"Indiya's last name is Gross, like her father."

If this conversation began with me having a million questions, now I had two million.

"Why would Ruthie lie to me?"

"For as long as I've known Ruthie, she has been a self-centered, greedy, selfish person. When Delroy and I first got together, she used to accuse me of having broken up his marriage. It didn't matter to her that I had not started working at Ford until they had already been separated for a month. I had nothing to do with the demise of his marriage to Kim. I think somewhere in Ruthie's mind, she was convinced they would reconcile. Delroy was not interested in continuing their marriage. Kim knew that, and that's why she moved to Chicago with Indiya."

I made a mental note that Indiya had at least told the truth about where she was from. Not that it meant much in light of everything else.

"Delroy," she continued, "was taking care of our household, Kim's household, and even Ruthie's. He had a lot of weight on his shoulders. His blood pressure was high and he was constantly stressed. He and I had a serious discussion where he told me he could not do everything for everybody. Yes, he had to do for Indiya—that was his child—but Ruthie was more than capable of getting a job to take care of her family. She seemed to think that he was rolling in the dough, which he wasn't. I guess compared to what she had, it looked like Delroy was well off.

"The truth of the matter was that he was buried in debt and always in fear of losing his job in middle management. It took some time for him to make a change, but when he realized that he was worn out, he cut Ruthie back. Naturally, I got the blame. According to her, I had turned her own brother against her. It was a recurring theme for years. Delroy would tell her to stop the nonsense until, finally, he ceased going to see her and didn't call like he used to. He was tired of hearing her sing the same sad song. He wanted his sister to stand on her own two feet. No matter how many years had passed, she still complained about her husband leaving her and not taking care of his kids. If you talk to her today, she's still crying about that and those kids are all grown."

She laughed. "I know I sound hard on her, but I do care about Ruthie. She is my sister-in-law, after all. Many times, when I had no one to talk to, she was there. I used to pour my heart out about you. How much I missed you and wished you were with me. When you went to college and then law school, I would brag on you all the time. Although I didn't know the exact details of your life, I was proud just the same. I knew you owned a home in Long Island and had a couple of places in the city. I thought perhaps I had made the right decision for you."

"How do you know all of this?"

"I kept my eye on you over the years. When I was younger, I would call the orphanage every month to find out if you were still there. It broke my heart to know that you were never adopted. When that nice woman and her husband eventually took you in, I was elated. I knew there would be better days ahead for you."

"Oh, you knew that?"

"It was what I hoped for."

"Well, it wasn't all candy and roses for me."

She froze and her eyes went wide. "I'm sorry. I just assumed…"

"Don't assume, Diane. I had a tough life."

"I'm sorry," she whispered.

"So, after I went to live with the Hudsons, how did you know where I was?"

"By that time, I had a steady job and was married to Delroy. I hired someone to keep track of you and let me know where you were. I made sure they weren't intrusive or invading your privacy,

I just wanted to know where you were physically so, one day, I could come find you."

"And you told Ruthie whatever information you found out?"

"I bragged on you a lot. She was my sounding board."

"Why would Ruthie think you ran off with Delroy's money?"

"First off, if Delroy had any money, as his wife, it would have been mine. Second, he didn't have any money. He had a small insurance policy that couldn't provide for a soul after his funeral expenses were paid. I sold the house and the bulk of that money went to pay off his debt. Somewhere in Ruthie's twisted mind, her brother was rich. Her brother didn't have a dime to his name when he passed."

"If you're telling me the truth, then I'm led to believe that she asked to see me to specifically tell me lies about you."

"Obviously, you aren't the only one being lied to. Indiya showed up here lying to me."

"Did she tell you where she was going on this bogus business trip?"

"No, she didn't."

"And you had no idea that Ruthie or Indiya had been in contact with me."

"Honestly, no. You told me how you got connected to Ruthie, but what about Indiya?"

"Until today," I took a deep breath, "I believed she was my girlfriend."

"What?" She didn't conceal her shock.

"I've been in a relationship with Indiya."

Diane stood up and paced the room. "She never mentioned to you that she knew me or that my husband was her father?"

"She lied about her last name. Do you really think she shared that with me?"

"No, no, of course not." She stopped moving and looked at me. "Was it serious?"

I hesitated. "I guess. I love her. At least I think I did."

Diane sank back down into her chair. "Avery, I don't know what's going on, but it can't be good. Ruthie and Indiya both connecting with you…telling you lies… I don't see anything good coming from it."

"That's how I ended up here today. Indiya and I were supposed to leave for London this morning. She never showed up at the airport and then she stole some important information from my home office."

"Oh, no, Avery. Have you contacted the police?"

"I'm going to handle this by myself."

"No you won't; because now you have me."

CHAPTER 52

I left Diane's house with a promise to return the next afternoon. There was still so much to discuss, but I needed to get home to see exactly what was missing from my office. I had run out so fast to meet Mr. Charles that I had not gone through the mess that she had made. As pissed off as I was, there was still a lightness inside of me. I had met my mother. She was the last person I had ever supposed I would encounter when beginning my day from hell. I thought I would be in London by now, having a romantic dinner with the woman I love. A woman I now realize I didn't even know.

I walked into my house and listened to the silence. I turned on lights in every room to make sure I was alone. When I went up to my office, I watched the surveillance tape again. What was Indiya looking for and why? If she needed something, she damn sure should have asked me. Instead, she chose to violate my space, my home, and my privacy.

I reflected on the elaborate lie she had told me about her home being full of the crap that she purchased. Of course I couldn't come to her house, she was living with my mother. She intentionally had deceived me. This had to be what they called karma. How many women had I deceived in the past three years? I couldn't begin to count the number of untruths I had told. I had misled many and it finally came back on me.

I went over to my desk and sifted through what was on it. Mail with the names of all my identities was thrown askew. I knew the power of attorney was missing, along with my bank statement for Avery Hudson. My cell phone rang and I pulled it from my pocket. It was a private number.

I answered thinking it was my mother. "This is Avery."

"I know you want to kill me right now."

I paused a moment. "Can you blame me, Indiya?"

"I suppose not."

"Where are you?"

"I've done some traveling today."

I went over to the couch, knocked the papers to the floor, and sat down. "That doesn't tell me anything."

"It tells you enough."

"Now you're going to hold your tongue?"

"I'm not good at it, however, I'm trying damn hard today."

"So you're playing games?"

"Believe me, I'm not trying to."

"How am I supposed to believe that with what transpired today?"

"It's hard to explain."

"Try."

"You had something I wanted."

"Obviously, it wasn't me since you left me stranded at the airport."

"I wish that were true, but it isn't. Not meeting you today killed me."

"You sound alive and well to me."

"I should go. You're not ready to talk to me."

"Indiya, don't hang up this phone."

"Are you asking or telling me?"

"Please, don't hang up."

"I guess I owe you that much."

"What did I have that you wanted?"

"Let me ask you something first."

"Go ahead."

"Are you Avery, Julian, and—someone I'm already familiar with—Marcel? The truth, please."

"I used to be."

"You're not anymore?"

"I don't need to be. They no longer serve any purpose."

"Are more women like Roxi out there?"

"There were, but they're not in my life anymore."

"What about Avery Hudson?"

"He's a bit more complicated."

"That's what I thought."

"And why do you think that?"

"Because Avery Hudson is rich."

"Since we're making introductions, who are you? The truth."

"Why would you ask me that?"

"Because today I met someone who knows you."

"And who might that be?"

"Who might you be?"

"I feel you already know."

"Then tell me."

"My name is Indiya Gross."

"Would you happen to be related to Ruthie Gross from Detroit?"

"Now who's playing games?"

"All I want to know is why, Indiya?"

"Could you be a bit more specific with your question?"

She was right, at that moment, I did want to kill her. "Why did you come in to my life?"

"I already told you. You had something I wanted."

"So, did you get it?"

"I got more than I bargained for. I got to know you, which I didn't expect, and love you."

"How can you say you love me?"

"I think you, more than anyone, know that nothing is black and white. I do love you, Avery."

"Then be honest and tell me what you wanted from me."

"A better life."

"I wanted to give you that."

"Maybe you did and that surprised me."

"But you still decided to take it."

"I did. Life is about tough choices and I made one."

"Let me guess, Ruthie sent you."

"Yes, she did."

"Why would you target me? I never did anything to your family."

"My Aunt Ruthie said Diane had a debt to pay."

"I'm not Diane."

"No, you're not. But you had the means to settle up."

"Had?"

"The thing about the name Avery is that it's gender neutral. A man or a woman can be an Avery."

"So instead of Indiya, you've become Avery?"

"According to my ID, and just for today. Long enough for me to transfer money from Avery Hudson's account to…well…to someone else's."

"You took my money?"

"Not all of it. I left you with a hundred thousand."

"You stole five million dollars from me, Indiya?"

"It wasn't my intention to take that much. In fact, I really didn't know how much you had. Before I met you, I thought I could walk away with a couple hundred thousand, maybe. When I saw your bank statement and told Aunt Ruthie how much was there, she told me to take it all."

"I think I'll go pay Ruthie a little visit. Perhaps she can be convinced to give it all back."

"She's already gone, Avery, so don't bother looking for her."

"What fun would it be if I didn't try?"

"About as much fun as my mentioning your multiple identities to the authorities."

"And yet you love me…"

"I know it's hard to believe under these circumstances, but I do. And I know you still love me."

"That's not saying much. I'm not the best judge of character when it comes to love."

"I know that's the hurt talking, or maybe it's pride. Regardless, you love me, Avery."

"I shared things with you that I hadn't told anyone else—about my mother and my life. How could you not tell me that she was in Rockville Centre? How could you keep any of this from me? Who you are? That you knew Ruthie? You let me go on a wild goose chase when the entire time you could have reunited a mother and son."

"I wrestled with keeping Diane from you because you got inside of me, in my heart and my head. I know you could tell what we shared was real. Your anger can't convince you that it wasn't. I'm not proud of what I had to do."

"You had to do this?"

"My family had nothing. My father was our only lifeline and Diane ripped him away from us."

"Are you serious? Diane did not take your father away from your mother or his sister. You need to talk to Kim and get the truth."

"Does it really matter at this point?"

"You're walking off with millions of my dollars and have the nerve to ask if it matters."

"I'm sorry it had to come to this, Avery."

"You have five million reasons as to why you're not sorry."

"I have to go, Avery. My next flight is boarding."

"Do you plan on living your life on the run?"

"It worked for you. I thought I'd give it a try."

"It was all about the money and that's too bad. We could have had so much more."

"It's not all bad. You have your mother. Isn't that what you've always wanted?"

Indiya disconnected our call, but not before I heard the announcement that flight 102 to Brazil was boarding.

CHAPTER 53

Avery

Diane had made dinner and we were sitting at her dining room table about to eat. I smiled in spite of myself. A whole baked chicken, macaroni and cheese, collard greens, candied yams, yellow rice, gravy and biscuits were spread out in front of us. She said grace and then fixed my plate. The moment was surreal. How many times had I imagined this exact scene? I thanked her as she handed my plate to me.

"Everything looks delicious."

"I hope you enjoy it."

I didn't care what it tasted like, my mother had made it. I took a bite of everything on my plate and put my fork down. A tear rolled down my cheek.

"Are you okay?"

I tried to answer but I couldn't. Tears flooded my eyes. The more I attempted to hold them back, the more they sprang forth. My mother came over to me and knelt by my side as my body shook as I cried.

"I'm sorry, Avery." She gently took my hand in hers. "I know saying sorry isn't enough, but I mean it with every ounce of my being."

I looked over at her and tears were also streaming down her face. I grabbed my napkin and wiped my eyes. "I haven't cried since I was six years old." Now she cried harder. "I have dreamt of you all my life and we're finally here together. My first dinner that my mother prepared for me." My voice caught again. "No matter what happens between us moving forward, I'll never forget this moment."

Diane stood up and hugged me from the side, resting her head on top of mine. "I've been wanting to do this since you were three weeks old." I placed my arm over hers and let her hug me. She pulled away after about a minute. "Your dinner's getting cold."

I smiled and continued to eat. "This is the best meal I've ever had."

Diane nodded, fighting back her tears. We managed to get through the rest of dinner without any more emotional melt-downs. She had made strawberry shortcake for dessert and I was doing my best to squeeze it in with everything else I had already eaten.

There was so much I wanted to know about her and kept firing off question after question. "Where did you go after you sold your house in Detroit?"

"I moved to Miami. I felt that I needed a change and wanted to get away from everything and everyone in Detroit."

"You mean Ruthie."

She laughed. "That's exactly who I mean. I got a job, went to college to get my degree, and opened a small boutique in Miami Beach."

"You went to college?"

"I sure did. I may have been years late, but I did it."

"Is your boutique still open?"

"I sold it for a nice profit before I moved here. I didn't know how long I would be in New York and I didn't want anything tying me to Miami. What about you? I know you went to law school and were with a large firm when you were in D.C., but what about now? Where are you working?"

"I'm actually in the midst of a career change."

"You're not practicing law anymore?"

"Not since I've been in New York."

"If you don't mind my asking, what do you do to get by?"

"You're better off not knowing."

She eyed me pensively and then nodded. "I have some money saved up if you ever need anything."

I couldn't help but to smile again. Indiya may have wiped out Avery Hudson's account, but I had millions more offshore that I could easily access.

"I appreciate that, Diane, but I think I'm all right. I invest wisely and I'm going to be looking into a couple of new ventures very soon."

She looked a bit more at ease once I said I invest, but the question still lingered in her eyes.

"As long as you're okay."

"I am and one day I'll explain why I'm not practicing law. Today is not the day."

"I understand. I'm looking forward to getting to know you better."

"I am, too, because I'm still trying to get to know myself."

My mother cleaned the kitchen while I sat on a stool at the island, drinking a glass of her homemade sweet tea. I knew it was about time for me to be heading home, but I wanted a little while longer with her. We had only scratched the surface of where she had been and what she'd been through over the years. As we got to know each other, I intended to ask whatever I wanted to know.

I hadn't shared much about my experiences and I could tell that she was curious yet fearful. I would open up in due time.

She had to be afraid that her decision made my life worse, rather than better. Ultimately, I wouldn't know the answer until I heard all of her story. Through the years, I had assumed that my life would have been better with my mother and that may not be the case. Indiya was right about one thing; I had my mother and it was what I always wanted. Even if I decided that she should and could have come for me when I was a child, I would not let that hinder getting to know her now. She was here now and exactly what I needed.

She dried her hands on a dishtowel and joined me at the island. "So, you think Indiya hopped on a plane to Brazil."

"She said her next flight was boarding, then I heard the announcement. It's my best guess."

"Are you going to look for her?"

"I'm thinking about hiring someone to do that."

"I can't believe Ruthie and Indiya. I never would have expected them to do something like this. I feel responsible."

"I don't blame you."

"I blame me. Ruthie's obsession over my taking Delroy's money led them to do this. She couldn't get it through her head that Delroy had nothing. It's because of me that they knew about your success. Indiya came here to carry out Ruthie's twisted scheme to defraud you. I came into your life and brought trouble to your doorstep."

"They defrauded you, too. You didn't know Indiya was coming to New York and you didn't introduce her to me. She orchestrated that on her own. Don't worry; I'll take care of Ruthie and Indiya."

"I called Ruthie's number and it had been disconnected. I even reached out to Kim and she told me she had a falling-out with

Indiya a few months ago and hasn't spoken to her since. I hope you can find them. It makes me physically sick to know they stole from you. I'm not going to ask again how much, but at least tell me if it will cause you hardship."

"I'll be all right, Diane. What Indiya and Ruthie got away with won't hurt me."

"You promise that's the truth?"

"I promise."

"What about your heart? You told me you think you love Indiya."

"That's another story." I was having trouble reconciling that the woman I fell for, and thought fell for me, was only in my life for money. "I'll get over it."

"I probably don't have the right to give you advice, but don't let what happened with Indiya close your heart to love."

"I'll have to think about that."

"Since I was seventeen, I've lived my life that way and it's not healthy. My heart was broken when your father moved away. It was crushed when my parents threw me out. And it was completely destroyed when I had to leave you behind. It's time for me to start to repair it."

"Have you ever searched for your parents or my father?"

"When it came to your grandparents, I never looked back."

"Will you ever?"

She smiled sadly. "I just might if it's not already too late."

"What about my father?"

"Our paths did cross again in Indiana and ended with our arrests for a domestic altercation. We were young, he was drinking heavily, and when I told him about you, things got physical. I'll save that story for another day, but, if you want it, I can give you the last known address I have for him."

I nodded. One parent at a time.

CHAPTER 54

Julian

When I saw her walk in, I knew I had to switch it up. She was alone. She stood in the back against the wall, staring straight ahead. She didn't survey the room for anyone and didn't see me off to the side. I cruised to the stage and took the mic.

"Good evening." The crowd responded in kind. "It feels good to be up here. I've been away too long." The audience hooted their agreement. "Tonight I want to do a piece I've done before, but means as much now as it did then. This one is for Miko." I bowed my head for a beat, then gazed out into the audience.

"Your ebony skin reminds me of home.
Sacred. Abundant. Lush.
Land waiting to be explored.
Sun in the sky golden like honey waiting to be poured.
Niles that overflow with the waters of life waiting to be tasted.
Exotic and rare species waiting to be wild.
Breezeless deserts as hot as fire waiting to be quenched.
Your ebony skin I'm ready to explore,
with warm honey I'm going to pour,
your flowing waters I'm willing to taste,
rare and exotic I want to see you wild,

your hot fire I promise to quench.

Wait no more.

Take me home to lush lands, golden sun, overflowing Niles, exotic species and breezeless deserts and I'll take your sacred ebony to abundant paradise."

I waited for the cheers to die down, then repeated, "For Miko."

I walked off the stage and sat at my favorite spot in the back. A few people at the tables next to me nodded or reached over for dap. I loved that energy. There was nothing like it. I would go up to do another piece later. Something new that I was still working out in my mind.

I wasn't sure if she would, but she finally did.

Miko slipped into the seat beside mine. There was no need for me to look over, I knew the scent of her oils.

"Thank you for the personal shout-out. That was a first."

I turned my head toward her and she was smiling. "I've done that piece for you before."

"Yes, you have, but you didn't specifically dedicate it to me."

"I didn't? Well, I should have. You look beautiful tonight, Nubian queen." Her hair sat atop her head in a bushy ponytail. Instead of her usual stud, there was a tiny hoop in her nose. Glittery eye shadow complemented her perfectly sculpted brows.

"I missed you, Julian."

"I haven't gone anywhere."

She twisted her lips. "Come on now, Julian."

"Well, if I did, I'm back now."

She regarded me with inquiring eyes. "Do you have another piece or are you done for the night?"

"I could be…"

"Why don't you come over to my place for a nightcap?"

I slowly moved close to Miko and placed a soft kiss on her lips. "Do you have any honey?"

"Lots."

"I'm ready when you are."

CHAPTER 55

Marcel

The elevator stopped again and an elderly man exited. I pushed the close door button and rode up two more floors. I stepped off and headed down the hallway, rearranging the bouquet while I walked.

I kneeled down to place the vase of roses in the corner of the door and it opened.

"Marcel?"

"Hey, Quinn." I stood up and smoothed my shirt. "I was just leaving these for you."

"You weren't going to ring the bell?"

"I didn't want to bother you...in case you had company."

She put her hand on her hip. "Get on in here."

We went into the living room and sat down. "Where's Tony?"

"I'm not seeing him anymore."

"Little man bit the dust already?"

Quinn laughed. "Why do you have to call him 'little man'?"

"He was a little petite," I said with a smirk.

"He was not, Marcel. Granted, he wasn't as tall as you, but he was not petite."

"My bad. I don't want to insult your man."

"He's not my man."

"Does that mean you're single?"

"It depends on who's asking."

"The man sitting in front of you is asking."

"The man in front of me likes to disappear a bit too much for my tastes."

"That was the old Marcel."

"And who are you?"

"New and improved Marcel."

"Is that right? And why should I believe that?"

"I can show you better than I can tell you."

Quinn's doubt was stamped across her face. "Why am I even considering what you're saying?"

"Because you know I'm telling the truth."

"I don't know any such thing."

"But you *want* to know if I am."

She smiled and it was sweet and sexy at the same time. "You are incorrigible."

"I've been called worse."

"Pick me up at seven."

"Who said I wanted to take you out tonight?"

"I did and you will. You're not the only one who's new and improved."

I growled at her. "I like it."

"You better not be late."

"Now, would I do that?"

"Yes, old Marcel would."

"I told you, I'm new and improved."

CHAPTER 56

Camden

I slid the gift box across the table. Natalia refused to look down at it. I filled our glasses with champagne and held mine up for a toast. She crossed her arms and rested them on the table. I shrugged and sipped from my glass.

"You took the time to make yourself pretty. Are you going to spend the entire night grimacing at me?"

"That's the kind of mood you put me in, Camden."

"How did I put you in a mood when I haven't seen you?"

"Doesn't that answer your own question?"

"Why did you agree to have dinner with me, Natalia, if you're not going to talk to me?"

"I'll talk, but you're not going to want to hear what I have to say."

"Maybe not, but start talking and I'll let you know whether I want to hear it." Her frown lines deepened. "That was a joke. Go ahead, I'm listening."

"People make time for what's important. Even the most powerful men in the world make time for family and fun."

"In this scenario, you're implying I should make time for fun?"

"Camden."

"I just want to be clear since we're not family."

"If you're not going to take me seriously, then I'm not going to bother."

I threw my hands up in submission. "Continue, please."

"If rich and powerful men like Warren Buffett and Bill Gates can make time, then why can't you?"

"First off, I'm no Buffett or Gates. I'd like to be, but I'm not. That's why I work so hard, so that maybe one day I'll be on their level."

"In the meantime, you plan to ignore your personal life."

"I don't ignore my personal life. Everything has its place. You and I are together now, aren't we? This moment wouldn't be occurring if my personal life received no attention."

"There's no winning with you."

"This isn't a competition, but you're right. I win all the time. Now, why can't we enjoy our dinner, go back to your place, and give our personal lives some much needed attention?"

"I guess that means you're done with this discussion."

"Absolutely. Open your gift."

She stared at me.

"I'm asking."

Natalia removed the gift wrap and opened the small, red velvet box. She smiled at the charm bracelet inside. "You do have great taste, Camden."

"In all things, but especially when it comes to you."

That earned me a real smile. "I can't wait for you to add more charms to it."

I knew what it took to thaw her out. "We'll see."

She gazed at her new bauble as she spoke to me. "I really missed you, Camden."

"I can see that," I said with a laugh.

CHAPTER 57
Julian

I zipped up my jeans and raised my seat. Romel moved back over to the passenger side of the car. She pulled down the visor mirror and checked her face and hair. Her shirt was unbuttoned, bra showing. Romel was brazen and, even though she was a loose cannon, I liked her that way.

She let her window down. "I need some air in here."

"The AC is on."

"I'm overheating…since you had me doing all the work."

"You took the lead; so, I sat back and enjoyed the ride. Literally."

"It would be nice if you treated me like a lady."

"Because you sexed me in the car, I'm not treating you like a lady?"

"Don't be a bastard, Julian."

I had to laugh. "You need to work on whatever issues you have. I was into what just happened in here."

"I bet you don't have sex with Miko in the car. You take her out to restaurants and write poems about her."

Again I laughed. "If you want this to continue, then don't speak on Miko again. You're not her and she's isn't you. If I wanted to be with Miko right now, then I would be."

"Are you going to see her tonight?"

"Romel."

"I want to know."

"It's obvious you can't handle this and I should have known, considering you blabbed to Miko."

"I did not tell her anything. She was getting on my nerves with her nonstop pining over you and I alluded that you had been flirting with me. I never told her we slept together. She was testing you to see what you'd say. I promise you that."

I nodded. "Either you can handle this or you can't. The decision is yours."

"And you couldn't care less either way?"

"We're here, aren't we? I need you to do one thing for me. Accept what our situation is and stop trying to change it. I'm feeling you and that's what matters."

Romel exited the car, leaning into the window as she buttoned her shirt. "I can handle it."

"One more thing, this stays between us."

CHAPTER 58

Marcel

My iPod was on repeat in the docking station. Roxi's song blasted through my apartment. She was snuggled against me on the couch, moving subtly to the rhythm. I tapped my hand against her hip to the beat. I started to sing along to the lyrics.

Roxi sprang up. "Not you trying to sing!"

"What are you talking about? I can sing. I have a smooth, mellow voice."

"Let me hear you," she said, cheesing.

I stood up and lured her into my arms. Slow dancing her through the living room while I crooned in her ear. She joined in and harmonized with my bass.

At the end of the song, she stepped back. "All right, you do have some pipes."

"I told you I did." I took the song off repeat and let the next track play. "But I'll let you do the singing."

Roxi did a sexy stroll over, until her body touched mine, and danced for me. She was dropping it and bending over with her ass in the air like she had done it for a living. I coaxed her to the couch and back into the circle of my arms.

"This feels nice, doesn't it?" she said.

"Mmm-hmm."

"I'll be back on the road in three days."

"So soon?"

"Yeah, but after this trip, I'm home for two months."

"Oh, good."

"Will you be able to see me?"

"Why wouldn't I?"

"I would think your girlfriend would be occupying your time?"

"She's gone."

There must have been something in my voice because Roxi looked up at me. "Are you okay?"

I kissed her forehead. "I'm here with you; I couldn't be better."

She leaned back against me. "She's a fool."

"You're sweet, Roxi."

"I can be sweeter…"

"That's why you're my favorite artist. Now let's go make some music together."

CHAPTER 59

Camden

The art gallery was filled to capacity. I walked the perimeter of the room, checking out the various paintings and sculptures. The featured artists were extremely talented. I hadn't been to an exhibition in some time. I did a double-take and spotted Hazelle across the room, elegantly dressed and engaged in a lively discussion with a man and a woman.

I stayed out of her line of sight, but observed everything she looked at and commented on. Her friends wandered away and left her in front of a large painting. It was a jazz club scene with a pianist predominantly featured in muted colors. Her friends returned and she exaggeratedly smiled and gestured toward the painting.

I found the curator of the show. "I'm interested in the painting that beautiful woman over there is looking at."

"You mean Hazelle Mason?"

"You know her?"

"She attends quite a few of our art exhibitions."

"I want to buy that painting for her."

"That painting is fifteen thousand dollars."

I handed her my credit card. She swiped it using her Square Register on her iPad. "Please let her know that anything that can make her smile in that manner, she should look at every day."

I turned to leave the room. I took a final glance at Hazelle and caught her eye. She started to follow me, but was intercepted by the curator. I got to the lobby and heard her call my name.

"Camden."

I stopped before I reached the door. "Hazelle."

"Surely you can't buy a lady such an expensive gift and not give her an opportunity to thank you."

"You're welcome."

"I didn't thank you yet."

"I thought that was it."

"Most definitely not. I'm inviting you to dinner tomorrow night where I will thank you properly." She smiled and gave me a little wink.

"With such a beautiful smile to go with the invitation, how can I say no?"

CHAPTER 60

The locksmith was almost done changing all the locks on my house in Brookville, including the one to my office. I didn't anticipate that Indiya would return, but it was better to be safe than sorry. She taught me a valuable lesson: never let your guard down unless you want to get burned.

I chatted with my mother while he worked. She agreed that I needed to change the locks and even suggested additional surveillance on the outside of the house. I didn't know if I needed to go to that extreme, but I'd consider it.

I closed the front door behind the locksmith and went into my bedroom. I laid my cell phones out on the dresser and checked the voicemails on them, one by one. I had received six messages—Miko, Quinn, Natalia, Romel, Roxi, and Hazelle.

I took a deep breath and sighed. It seemed old habits die hard.

ACKNOWLEDGMENTS

There's nothing like the love and support of your family and friends! I would like to thank each and every person that has supported me through the journey of writing this novel. I appreciate those that encouraged me, prodded me and even those that distracted me—because the distractions are always a lot of fun.

As I typed the final words of *You Might Just Get Burned*, I smiled and thanked God out loud. I thanked Him for allowing creativity to touch me once again. I have been making a concerted effort to acknowledge all of my blessings large, small and everything in between. I'm appreciative that you took the time to read this novel and I hope that you enjoyed it.

I'm thankful for family and friends, old and new, who have been supporting me in abundance—I can't express how appreciative I am. Every opportunity I get to show my family love, I'm going to do it. Mom and Dad, not all parents get it right, but you two exemplify parenthood. Nothing compares to the two of you. Selena and Chris, we'll always be kids at heart, full of jokes and constant teasing. Nieces, I especially thank you for keeping me on my toes. You ladies help me to channel my silly side.

Zane, you have been a blessing to many and though I've told you before, thank you for helping me to live my passion. Charmaine, your positive energy makes working with Strebor a joy.

Sara Camilli, thanking you immensely for helping me to remember to take it one word at a time. It worked!

KelStar, your limitless reassurances help me to believe that I can accomplish anything. Kimber, Veronica, Carleen, Jamila and Nik, you're the cogs in my wheel. I love you guys!

Kappa Lambda, Happy 40th! Delta's love is the sweetest love!

To everyone reading these words, thank you. You inspire me to put pen to page. There's more to come. Until then, see you on Facebook, Twitter and all that jazz.

Stay tuned…

www.ShamaraRay.com
www.facebook.com/pages/Shamara-Ray
Twitter: @ShamaraRay

ABOUT THE AUTHOR

Shamara Ray is a graduate of Syracuse University. She first enticed readers with her debut novel, *Recipe for Love*, and followed it up with *Close Quarters*. Shamara has a penchant for the culinary arts and enjoys entertaining friends and family in her Long Island home. She is currently working on her next novel.